ONE MAY SMILE

ONE MAY SMILE

For Rosemary
Happy reading!
from Penny

05-12-13

PENNY FREEDMAN

Matador
9 Priory Business Park
Kibworth Beauchamp
Leicestershire LE8 0RX, UK
Tel: (+44) 116 279 2299
Fax: (+44) 116 279 2277
Email: books@troubador.co.uk
Web: www.troubador.co.uk/matador

ISBN 978 1783061 662

British Library Cataloguing in Publication Data.
A catalogue record for this book is available from the British Library.

Typeset in Book Antiqua by Troubador Publishing Ltd
Printed and bound in the UK by TJ International, Padstow, Cornwall

Matador is an imprint of Troubador Publishing Ltd

For my sister, Ros, and my sister-in-law, Naomi –
great ambassadors both.

Penny Freedman studied Classics at Oxford before teaching English in schools and universities. She is also an actress and director. She has a PhD in Shakespeare Studies and lives with her husband in Stratford-upon-Avon. She has two grown-up daughters.

Her previous books featuring Gina Gray and DCI Scott are *This is a Dreadful Sentence* (2010) and *All the Daughters* (2012).

FOREWORD

Three years ago I took part in a wonderful British Shakespeare Association conference, held at Kronborg Castle in Elsinore – the setting for Shakespeare's *Hamlet*. The conference was the brainchild of my niece, Abigail Rokison, and a group of her Cambridge students performed the play, promenade-style, in and around the castle, to great effect. My sister designed and made the costumes. In sending Gina to Elsinore to do costumes for a student production, I have, to some extent, stolen this scenario but Ros's costumes had far more flair than Gina's grudging efforts can produce and the Cambridge students were charming, grown-up and quite unlike the neurotic bunch I depict here. And no-one got killed.

Having ventured away from familiar Marlbury, I must thank my Denmark consultant, Katrine Wallis, who read my manuscript with an eagle eye and put me right on all matters Danish. Any remaining errors are all mine.

My tables, meet it is I set it down
That one may smile, and smile, and be a villain
(*Hamlet,* Act 1, Scene 5)

OXFORD UNIVERSITY DRAMATIC SOCIETY

presents

HAMLET PRINCE OF DENMARK

by

WILLIAM SHAKESPEARE

14th – 17th July 2011
Kronborg Castle Helsingør

CAST

James Asquith	Hamlet. Prince of Denmark, son of Old Hamlet
Jonathan McIntyre	The ghost of Old Hamlet, King of Denmark Claudius, brother to Old Hamlet, now King
Zada Petrosian	Gertrude, Hamlet's mother, now wife to Claudius
David Underwood	A gravedigger Osric, a courtier Polonius, the Lord Chamberlain
Stefan Pienkowsky	Laertes, son of Polonius Francisco, a castle guard
Sophie Forrester	Ophelia, daughter of Polonius
Tom Yeoman	Horatio, a student, friend to Hamlet
Conrad Wagner	Rosencrantz, a fellow student of Hamlet
Marianne Gray	Guildenstern, a fellow student of Hamlet

Alan Peters	Barnardo, a castle guard
	A travelling actor, playing the king
	Fortinbras, Prince of Norway
Kelly Mahon	Cornelia, an ambassador
	A travelling actor, playing the queen
Emma Dalton	A travelling actor
Clare Dartmouth	A travelling actor
Adam Barrie	Director
Marianne Gray	Assistant Director
Ray Porter	Technical Director
Tom Yeoman	Music
Gina Gray	Costumes
Kelly Mahon	Stage Manager

1

DAY ZERO

A truant disposition, good my lord. 1.2

Aestivation biologists call it – a sort of summer hibernation. Reptiles and amphibians do it a lot, apparently, and I'm heading there myself in my unlit lair, hardly in touch with the outer world on this slumberous July afternoon. I am already in vacation mode, slow-moving, vacant-minded and humming gently and untunefully to myself as I contemplate my time off for good behaviour. Three weeks! I have never taken three weeks' holiday all in one go before, and the urge to compensate for this indulgence is probably the reason why I am, at present, kneeling on the floor in my windowless inner office (in truth hardly more than a large cupboard) surrounded by heaps of files, newly organised and labelled, the outcome of a year's work in the English Language Unit of Marlbury University College, the evidence that proves I deserve a holiday.

I feel smug down here on the floor as I contemplate my shiny files, and disinclined to move on to the next stage of what will, in truth, be a busy and fractious day, the last before going away; a day of lists and last-minute phone calls, hasty emails and unwise last-minute purchases. I sit leaning against a filing cabinet and close my eyes. *Five minutes,* I think. *Five minutes of doing nothing.* And suddenly I am under attack. A thunderous knocking at the door of my outer office penetrates my shell of quiet. It is followed by the rapid tramping of male feet, and suddenly the air around me darkens and I look up, bewildered to find that I am sharing my cupboard with enough Greeks to block the pass at Thermopylae. My dormant brain tells me that they are very cross about something but as they are all talking at once I have no idea what it is. My Greek students tend to go for high-volume, uninflected streams of words that the English brain finds hard to disentangle at the best of times – which this isn't. I look round them for enlightenment and spot among my surprise guests a face I recognise. Then I understand, with a nasty plunge of the stomach, what – or rather, who – this is about.

You will appreciate that I'm not in a strong position for conflict resolution, crouched here on my knees. I have been down here for so long that at least one of my legs has gone to sleep so there is no chance of my leaping lithely to my feet and establishing my authority. And, frankly, even if that were possible, I would hardly impress in my washed-out T-shirt, old jeans and bare feet. Well, I wasn't expecting students to call, was I? It's vacation, isn't it? I'm aestivating. Still, I can't just go on sitting here while they all talk over my head as though I were a toddler.

'Costas,' I call through the din to the hirsute young man I remember as a cherubic lad in my foundation year class a couple of years ago, 'play the gentleman and help me up. Then we'll go through to where there is light and air and you can tell me – quietly – what the problem is.'

As a young teacher I was advised to deal with aggression by speaking quietly and slowly, leeching the heat out of the situation, and this does generally work. Not this afternoon, however. Costas does reach out a sheepish arm to help me up, but once I'm on my feet his companions don't retreat. I know southern cultures expect less personal space than northern ones so it is possible that my Greek visitors don't think that they're invading mine. I certainly feel invaded, however, and there's an overpowering smell of angry male sweat that makes me feel that an open window is desirable. What's more, they are still all talking at once and I still can't understand what they're saying. Since the low and slow approach doesn't seem to be working, I ditch it and take a deep breath.

'SHUT UP!' I yell, and in the brief moment of surprise I elbow my way from among them and make it out of the cupboard to stand by the open door of my office, take in a few breaths of air and to ask, as they stream out after me, 'Now, what's the matter?'

As they all take breath to answer, I command, in my best schoolteacher voice, 'I want Costas to answer. I want to hear just from him. The rest of you can be quiet.'

There is a mutinous mutter – it really doesn't do to speak like this to Greek men – but Costas is given the floor. 'You have a student, Anastasia Christodoulou,' he declares, as though defying me to deny it.

'I do,' I agree, and then correct myself. 'I did.'

'I am the cousin of Anastasia.'

'I know you are.' I look round. 'And are you all the cousins of Anastasia too?'

'Friends!' they cry.

'Friends of Anastasia or of Costas?'

They are friends of both, it seems, as they fill my office with expansive gestures to demonstrate the extent of their friendships, the warmth of their hearts. They are all – all – friends and they must all speak to me. But I'm having none of it.

'Do you know the expression *mob-handed*?' I ask. 'No? Going *mob-handed* means going around in a large group threatening people, and that's what you're doing and I don't like it. I'll talk to Costas, as he's Anastasia's cousin, but I'd like the rest of you to leave. You can wait outside if you like, and if there's anything more to be said after Costas has had his say, you can say it then.'

There follows a rapid, angry discussion in Greek and I remain at my post by the door. I'm not sure how this will turn out but if they won't leave, then I shall have to. I'm not staying here to be bullied; I shall simply make a dignified exit. Except that my shoes are lying in the other room, where I kicked them off, and there is a phalanx of Greeks positioned between me and them. The teacher in me registers an excellent example of zeugma here, to be stored up for classroom use: *she departed with dignity but without her shoes.* I'm not sure I can carry that off.

As it turns out, I don't have to. The swirling vigour of their discussion finally quietens; they turn to Costas to issue battle orders; they march out, scowling. I close the door and seat myself behind my desk in the feeble hope that Costas will forget about my jeans and my bare feet. I offer him a chair but he prefers to pace about, stoking his outrage. He is a nice lad really and I haven't been kind in picking him out from the troops for single combat, but that's too bad.

'Your decision about Anastasia,' he says, 'is unacceptable, completely unacceptable, and it must be reversed.' He emphasises his last words by driving a fist into the palm of his other hand. I suspect that he has seen his father do that. 'You are the chief examiner. You can do this.'

I lean back in my chair. 'Wrong on all counts, I'm afraid, Costas,' I say. 'The decision to disqualify Anastasia's literature paper was the only acceptable decision in the circumstances, it certainly shouldn't be reversed and I absolutely don't have the power to do it anyway. Even the Vice-Chancellor can't do that. We have to abide by the regulations.'

His sneer tells me what he thinks of the regulations but I'm not prepared to have them shrugged off as bureaucratic flim-flam. I take a breath and I cut to the chase.

4

'Anastasia cheated,' I say, and as he starts to protest I ride over him. 'She went into her English Literature exam wearing a baseball cap full of post-it notes with quotations on them. There is no ambiguity about this. It was cheating at its most blatant.'

'It was a misunderstanding.'

'A misunderstanding?' I can hear my voice starting to get screechy.

'She had them for revision before the examination. It was just a mistake.'

'Oh come on. The invigilator saw her. She took the cap off and looked at the notes three or four times before he approached her. There was no misunderstanding. She was simply cheating and the rules are clear: anyone caught cheating is disqualified, and that's that.'

'You don't understand. It has been hard for Anastasia.'

I don't understand? What I understand and would like him to understand, but can't say, because it would be unprofessional, is filling my head to exploding point. I would like Costas to understand that ever since Anastasia Christodoulou arrived to take the foundation course for overseas students at Marlbury University College, in order to qualify for a degree course in Law, she has been the bane, not of my life, because that has several other banes in it, but certainly of my work life. In her single person she succeeded in doubling my workload as director of the English Language Unit; I have a substantial box file packed solid with paperwork to prove it. Delve into it and you will find that she managed to piss off more or less everyone on the campus, from the Professor of Jurisprudence to Nigel in the Accommodation Office (to whom she offered a brown envelope full of cash if he would turn another student out of a room which she preferred to her own). You will find endless memos from academic staff about seminars unattended and coursework undone; three separate paper trails necessitated by suspicions about plagiarised essays; print-offs of e-mail correspondence with the warden of her hall of residence over smoking in a non-smoking room and repeated complaints from her neighbours about noise, and a copy of an official police caution issued following abusive behaviour to a traffic warden. You will also find several medical certificates, almost certainly forged, and a snappy note from the Student Counselling Service asking me to make it clear to Miss Christodoulou that there is heavy demand for counselling and that sessions cannot be fitted in around her social life.

'Would you say,' I ask mildly, 'that Anastasia had been happy here this year?'

'No!' He is outraged at the suggestion. 'It has been a terrible time for her.'

'Exactly. So isn't it best all round that she won't be coming back for another three years of misery?'

'But my uncle,' Costas protests, as though it is only my amazing stupidity that has stopped me from thinking of this. 'My uncle will arrive here tomorrow. She cannot tell him. It is impossible. She would rather die.'

'You mean he doesn't know she failed?' Costas says nothing. 'So why is he coming here tomorrow?'

He gazes at me miserably then flops into the chair he rejected earlier. 'Anastasia could not tell her parents that she failed so she told them she doesn't want to carry on – she wants to take another course somewhere else.'

'And her father's visit?' I ask.

'My uncle's mind is not easy to change. He has come to make sure that Anastasia is enrolled for her Law degree. And so, of course, he will learn the truth.'

'And you thought that between now and tomorrow morning I could snap my fingers and make the cheating – not to mention the fails in her other papers – disappear?'

For the first time he actually looks embarrassed. 'No. I don't think so, but you can speak to him – persuade him that it would be better for Anastasia to take a different course.'

'And I wouldn't mention the fact that Anastasia can't actually take a course here?'

'No.'

'And what sort of course would Anastasia like to take, may I ask?'

'She would like to work in a kindergarten.'

A kindergarten? I try to picture it and it's like Cruella De Vil working as a veterinary nurse. I conjure up the milky, sticky, poster paint world of my granddaughter Freda's nursery as it was when I dropped her off there this morning, and into it I transplant the Junoesque form of Anastasia, stomping in her killer heels among the floor-based toddlers, sending them scuttling for cover, or scowling and pouting her way through a reading of *Mr Gumpy's Outing* in her sullen monotone, or leaning over to supervise pasta-shape-picture production and mesmerising her little charges with a view of the flower tattoo low on her left breast.

'Does Anastasia actually like children?' I ask, dazed.

'Of course.' Costas sounds shocked that I should doubt it, but I suspect that he is young enough to believe that liking children goes automatically with the XX-chromosome pair.

'Well she doesn't seem to like anyone else,' I say.

He looks reproachful. 'Anastasia is a quite normal girl. She has had troubles here.'

I don't say *And she's certainly spread them around*. Instead, I allow a beat and then I get to my feet. 'Well, Costas.' I say, 'I'm sure I'd enjoy the challenge of telling Mr Christodoulou that his daughter should give up the prospect of life as a high-flying lawyer for a career in potty-training, but unfortunately I can't do it – literally can't do it. I go on holiday tomorrow morning. I shall be out of the country when he arrives.'

And that more or less deals with the matter. The troops outside glower at me and one of them slams a fist into my office door and tells me I haven't heard the last of this, but they take themselves off. No longer in the mood for housekeeping, I bundle my files any old how into the filing cabinet and head out for some therapeutic holiday shopping before I pick up Freda.

I was stretching a point when I told Costas that I was going on holiday. I am off to Denmark, to Helsingør, better known to us Brits as Elsinore. It is where *Hamlet* happens, and I'm sure it's a charming place but the reason why this isn't exactly a holiday is that I'm going with my daughter, Annie, and some of her Oxford chums to organise the costumes for a militaristic, police-state-style production of *Hamlet*, which they are putting on in the castle. You might wonder 1) why no student could be found in the whole of Oxford University to take on costuming and 2) why, in any case, it should fall to the assistant director's overworked mother to take it on. The answer to 1) seems to be that everyone wants to be a star and no-one learns to sew at school any more; the answer to 2) is that, at nineteen, Annie carries in her head an exact credit and debit account of how much maternal cash, effort and proof of love has been expended on her, as compared with her sister. The fact that I helped out my elder daughter, Ellie, by doing the costumes for a school play she directed last year has apparently been looming large in Ellie's credit column and Annie has made it clear that it's balancing up time. I make it sound as though I've been bullied into this, but that's only half true. Actually, I quite fancy it: I like young people, I like *Hamlet*, I have a predilection in favour of Denmark as a rational, civilised not-too-hot country and I haven't been on a holiday anywhere for a long time. The holiday aspect is marred somewhat by the fact that I have to take three-year-old Freda with me, though. With unfortunate timing, her mother, Ellie, married a fellow-teacher last week and has gone off on honeymoon. Her new husband, Ben Biaggi, is taking her to Italy to meet his extended family and it didn't seem appropriate for them to be accompanied by Freda. Ben, you understand, is not Freda's father; the latter has always been a shadowy figure about whom Ellie has resolutely refused to speak.

So I whiz round M&S, picking up a few garments that I hope will lend some freshness and bounce to my tired summer wardrobe and adding a couple of pairs of embroidered dungarees for Freda. In Boots I splurge on special sun cream for Freda, insect bite cream, travel sickness pills, paracetamols, Calpol, Germolene and a mammoth box of plasters. Travel hopefully, that's what I say. I pick Freda up from the nursery and find that far from being excited about our adventure she is wisely apprehensive. She has never been abroad before (we only remembered very late in the day that she would need a passport) and she's not sure whether she's going to like it. For all I know she may have doubts about my ability to negotiate the perils ahead. If so, that makes two of us.

I get her fed, bathed and bedded on an early schedule, clearing the decks for an evening of packing and fretting, and it's when I'm standing contemplating piles of clothes and assessing quantity versus manageability that the phone rings. It is the duty porter at the college.

'Sorry to bother you, Mrs Gray,' he says, 'but I can't get hold of anyone from the International Office. We've had a call from the hospital about one of your students, a Miss Christodoulou. No details but can you get up there? They need to talk to someone, apparently.'

And so it comes about that instead of packing, washing my hair and having an early night I run down the road to persuade a neighbouring teenager to leave her nice, flat screen television and come and watch our inferior box while keeping an ear open for Freda, and then I get on my bike and pedal up to the hospital. It takes an age to find out where Anastasia is, of course, and when I get there I discover that the harassed houseman wants me to sign a consent form in case they need to operate. He is tight-lipped about what happened to Anastasia but it seems to have involved an overdose of barbiturates.

'Barbiturates as in sleeping pills?' I ask, and he shrugs noncommittally.

When I ask if she'll be all right, he says, 'Oh yes,' as though that was never in any doubt.

'So why did I have to sign for her having an operation?'

'Oh it's just procedure,' he says, closing his file, off to the next case.

I ask the ward sister if I can see Anastasia and she takes me into a stuffy little six-bed ward, where I find Anastasia yellowish-pale and unresponsive, hooked up to a drip.

'Are you sure she'll be all right?' I ask the sister.

She rolls her eyes dismissively. 'These girls,' she says.

I cycle round to the college, where I go to my office, log on to the system, find Costas's e-mail address and send him a message telling him what has happened (though maybe he knows already?) and asking him to contact his uncle and warn him. I can only hope that Costas is an obsessive e-mail checker. Then I leave messages on the office phones of Monica in the International Office, Gillian in our office and Janet, the Vice-Chancellor's secretary, warning them of a likely visit from Mr Christodoulou and, with a heavy heart, I give my mobile number in each case and say that I shall be happy to talk to Mr Christdoulou at any time.

Back at home, I pay off my babysitter, drink two glasses of wine, stuff our clothes into a suitcase, don't wash my hair and retire to bed, where I spend an almost completely sleepless night assailed by visions of Anastasia as I last saw her, minus her make-up and her scowl, with her expensively streaked and tousled hair scraped back into an elastic band, shrunk to infancy in her hospital bed. *She's just a child, for God's sake!* the voice in my head screams at me. *How the hell did you come to forget that?*

2

DAY ONE

You are welcome to Elsinore 2.2

This was a mistake. Of course it was a mistake. How could I have thought otherwise? When I told you so chirpily that I liked young people and was therefore keen to come on this trip, I was thinking of the bounce and energy of the young, their whole-heartedness and optimism, but there's not much of any of that to be seen in this rattly little van as we cover the grey miles of Sjælland between Copenhagen and Elsinore. I myself was feeling remarkably chipper considering my sleepless night, early start and plane journey with Freda. I even felt ready for a call from Mr Christodoulou when I switched on my phone as we landed. But that was before we were met by a man with a van and it turned out that Denmark is experiencing a British summer – rain, winds and temperatures in single figures. The van man is called Ray; he is the company techie, i/c sound and lighting, and he has heroically brought this minivan across on the car ferry, carrying my hampers of costumes with him, and has picked Freda and me up from Copenhagen airport, along with a couple more company members who were on our flight. Annie wanted me to travel on the ferry too, to take responsibility for the costumes, but I refused to undertake a twenty-hour boat journey with Freda.

12

I know Annie suggested it only because she dreaded the possible embarrassment of being on the same flight as an obstreperous three-year-old niece, but she got round this by flying out two days earlier than us. Rehearsals start tomorrow and we are the last contingent.

Anyway, it would all be all right – my cramped position, jammed behind a costume hamper with Freda asleep on my lap, the minute-by-minute possibility of a call from a raging Greek father, the relentless rain – if only my companions would cheer up. Really, they could hardly look more miserable if we were in a tumbrel on our way to the guillotine. I have met them before, when I went and took measurements for their costumes some weeks ago (I've learnt from experience that it's no good asking people to provide their own measurements: men guess wildly and women lie), and I've got these three at least sorted out. Annie gave me some homework to do, sending me a draft programme with photos and mini-biographies, and some of them have stuck in my mind, but others remain vague. One thing I noticed is that they've mostly just graduated. Annie, at the end of her first year, is an anomaly in the group, and I have my own theory about that, which I shall discuss with you later. Their imminent ejection from the dreaming spires may, of course, explain why they're looking so miserable. It's a hard old world out here these days and even an Oxford degree doesn't guarantee you much in the way of a lucrative job and a desirable lifestyle.

They are conveniently arranged for me as the seating in this van, as configured at the moment, consists of long bench seats down either side and a short one across, behind the driver's seat, to form a horseshoe effect, with the costume hamper and luggage piled in the centre. Seated on one side, I can survey everyone. I take a look round them to see if I can match them to their potted histories. The pale, smudgy-eyed girl with the limp, white-blonde hair who is stretched out along the bench seat opposite is Sophie Forrester. She's air phobic, so took the ferry and threw up all the way we gathered when we met her and Ray at the airport. I caught him exchanging looks with some of the others and there was a lot of eye-rolling in Sophie's direction, so I imagine she didn't suffer in silence. She seems a mousey young woman but maybe she's a bit passive aggressive. She's asleep now in the aftermath of sea-sickness and Dramamines. *Drowned Ophelia*, I think, and it occurs to me at this point that since this production of *Hamlet* is at the centre of my saga, I should sketch in a bit about the play for those of you who have other things to carry round in your heads than the plots of 400-year-old plays. Just because they're my special subject, I realise, they don't have to be yours. And those of you who don't need this information can, of course, look away now.

So here it is. At the start of the play, Prince Hamlet's father, Old Hamlet, King of Denmark, has died and has been succeeded by his brother, Claudius, who slipped onto the throne before young Hamlet had time to get back from university in Wittenberg, and has now married his brother's widow, young Hamlet's mother, Gertrude. A bad enough situation for Hamlet, you would think, and he is already having suicidal thoughts when his friend, Horatio, takes him up onto the castle battlements and introduces him to old King Hamlet's ghost, who tells him that he was murdered by Claudius and enjoins Hamlet to avenge his death.

Revenge tragedies were very popular in the 1600s, when *Hamlet* was written, and the expectation would be that Hamlet would set about plotting a terrible revenge. He can't do it, though. Instead he adopts a variety of diversionary tactics. He pretends to be mad, he abuses his girlfriend, Ophelia, and he gets a group of travelling actors to put on a play about the murder of a king, in the hope that Claudius will reveal his guilt. To find out what is the matter with Hamlet (apart from the fact that Claudius has pinched both his throne and his mother) Claudius summons two of his student friends, Rosencrantz and Guildenstern, to spy on him and enlists the help of his Lord Chamberlain, Polonius, Ophelia's father, to use Ophelia to trap Hamlet into self-revelation while Claudius and Polonius eavesdrop. Polonius, unfortunately, takes the eavesdropping habit too far and hides behind a tapestry in Queen Gertrude's sitting room to listen to her private conversation with Hamlet. Hearing a noise, Hamlet assumes that the eavesdropper is Claudius and stabs Polonius through the tapestry, killing him.

At this point, Claudius packs Hamlet off to the King of England, accompanied by Rosencrantz and Guildenstern, who have a letter for the king, ordering Hamlet's death. Hamlet, however, gets seized by pirates on the voyage and is returned to Denmark, not before altering Claudius's letter so that it commands that Rosencrantz and Guildenstern be killed. While he is away, Laertes, Polonius's son, returns from university in Paris, demanding vengeance for his father's death, and Ophelia goes spectacularly mad and dies by drowning. Hamlet returns in time to meet the men who are digging her grave and disrupt her funeral by fighting with Laertes. Claudius and Laertes join forces; Laertes challenges Hamlet to a fencing match in which he uses a poisoned foil. The final scene is one of utter carnage, in which almost everyone ends up dead. Claudius, Hamlet and Laertes are all stabbed, while Gertrude is poisoned by the drink Claudius has prepared, as a fail-safe, for Hamlet. This scene has the potential to be comic unless handled well. The rudderless state of Denmark is saved by the timely arrival of Fortinbras, heir to the Norwegian throne, who claims Denmark as his.

Reduce any piece of literature to the bare bones of its plot and it is difficult to see wherein its greatness lies, but I hope you can see that it's an arresting tale, and that Hamlet embodies the human condition in his struggle to play the role that has been handed to him. For me, the particular pleasure of the play is the way we see the effects of Claudius's crime of fratricide spread out to pollute almost every character in the play – Polonius, Gertrude, Laertes, Ophelia, Rosencrantz, Guidenstern and Hamlet himself are all tainted, all behave dishonourably, led into dissimulation, spying, disloyalty, cruelty and murder. You could produce a pictorial representation of the play as a petrie dish under a microscope, in which deadly spores fan out to invade and destroy healthy cells.

So, that's the play we're doing and along from me, beyond the hamper, where he has room for his long legs, is the man I thought would be playing Hamlet when I went to take their measurements. He's looking very much the gloomy Dane now: blonded hair, heavy eyebrows, an air of moody detachment and a suit of woe – specifically a black jacket with the collar turned up that must have been murderously hot to wear at sweltering Gatwick. He's achieved his air of detachment largely by not taking his eyes from his iPhone, to which he has been riveted ever since we were allowed to switch them back on when we landed. Is he dealing with an avalanche of e-mails, updating his facebook page or – and I suspect this is the case – playing some addictive game? Whatever it is, it seems to be designed to remove him from the messy world of human interaction. He's Conrad Wagner, son of J.C. Wagner of Wagner Pictures by his first and least glamorous wife. He's good-looking, probably unhappy, presumably rich, and a hopeless actor – which is a pity, since his programme biography tells us that he intends to make acting his career. It was Annie who told me he was hopeless (*a startling lack of talent* was *The Oxford Mail*'s verdict on his last stage appearance, apparently). She has an axe to grind because, as well as being assistant director, she's playing

Guildenstern to his Rosencrantz. This has caused me some problems on the costume front since I can't get a clear answer either from Annie or from Adam, the director, about whether Guildenstern is to become Ms Guildenstern or Annie is going transgender. When I've pressed the point, they've looked at me as though they can't believe that anyone – even a woman of my advanced age and retarded understanding – could be that literal-minded. *Think androgynous, Gina*, Annie drawled, running a hand over her new Emma Watson-style cropped hair. (She has decided to call me *Gina* for the duration of the trip, since her usual *Ma* is too juvenile, she feels, and I am to address her as *Marianne* – her Oxford name. Remembering not to call her *Annie* is at the top of a long list of prohibitions I have been given, including asking her where she is going or where she has been, commenting on her clothes, offering her food, expecting her to look after Freda and mentioning anything at all about her childhood years.) My problem with *androgynous* is that I could dress her and Conrad in unisex jeans and sweatshirts but in the autocratic, police-state world they're going for I think Rosencrantz and Guildenstern would scrub up a bit for the royal court and not drift along in their denims. So I've resorted to a sharp trouser suit for Annie, and she can customise it as she chooses. Whether she wears a tie or not will probably be the clincher.

But I'm wandering – blame the sleepless night. Meet the third member of my cheerful trio of travelling companions. James Asquith is playing Hamlet and looks quite the student prince of Wittenberg at the moment, making notes on a book he's reading, which I'm pretty sure is in Arabic, though it might be Hebrew – it's a language you read from back to front, anyway. Annie tells me he's *awesomely clever*, has just got a First, and is about to start a doctoral thesis on something, though she's vague about what. I'm amused to see that he has managed to ease Sophie's head off his lap, where it was nestling earlier. They've been an item for some time, Annie says, and Sophie's made no plans for the future because she's expecting to stay around and eventually become a wife, when James gets the fellowship that must surely come his way. Tears before bedtime, I would say, judging by the body language I'm getting from him. And isn't it a touch posey to be reading Arabic when everyone else in the company will be reading Scandinavian *noir*; Stieg Larsson, Henning Mankel, Peter Høeg, Jo Nesbø?

We passengers have been silent for most of the journey. I tried a few early conversational sallies about the domestic architecture we could see outside but was met by the most minimal of non-verbal utterances. The question is, are they silent because of me? Is it like having the teacher sitting next to you on the school outing? Would they be chatting merrily if I weren't here? Or does Freda frighten them? Do they fear that if they speak she will climb all over them and make them uncool? I have no idea, and I must admit that I have myself been blanking out the one occupant of the van who has been speaking. Ray, our driver, has given us a running review of place names as we passed them, all in a heavy parody of a Scandinavian accent that was mildly amusing for five minutes and is now distinctly annoying.

'Hel-sing-ør,' penetrates my willed deafness, though, and I look out to see that we are indeed on the outskirts of a town and that the rain has stopped. With impressive confidence, Ray takes us away from the town centre and out along Strandvejen (which I translate to myself as *Beach Road*), where our *villa* is situated. The others are evincing a mild interest by now and we look out to see a rain-washed sky above the Sound and the misty roofs of the Swedish coast on the other side. We slow down, looking for numbers, and pass a cluster of small shops – a general store, a *konditori* (which turns out to be an appealing-looking tea shop), a *butik* with a lot of underwear in the window and a *damfrisør*, which may indeed frizz dames but also, to judge from the pictures in the window, gives them shiny asymmetric haircuts in glossy colours.

When we stop finally outside number 161, we stare silently. I haven't given any conscious thought to what this place might be like but I realise now that my subconscious has put *seaside* and *villa* together to produce an expectation of a forbidding Victorian house with a yellowing *Bed and Breakfast* sign nestling discreetly in its net-shrouded window. *Alma Villa, Scutari Villa, Balaclava Villa*, to be found in any English seaside town that has known better days. But this! This is something else: a villa of the Romantic period, rambling, whitewashed, ivy-covered, with a shrub-lined gravel drive sweeping up to a huge oak front door.

Children suddenly, my companions jump up, scramble out of the van and dash off round the side of the house towards the beach. I follow more slowly, carrying Freda, who has woken up to find herself in a strange place and is, inevitably, crying. I dig in my bag and find three Smarties, prudently saved for such an emergency, hand them over and proceed up the drive and round the house.

There is a garden at the back, screened from the beach by a bank of huge rosa rugosa bushes sporting enormous hips, and beyond are steps leading down to the beach. Drawn reluctantly by the hubbub coming from that direction, I cross the grass and stand at the top of the steps surveying the scene. A game of beach cricket has been interrupted for greetings and there is a great deal of hugging and kissing going on. Fragments of conversation float up to me. *Stopped counting when she got into double figures*, I hear Ray say – which I take to be a reference to Sophie's seasickness, though I may be wrong. *House is unbelievable*, I hear. *Owner's an art dealer. Terrible paintings everywhere but a great house*. And then, quite close, just at the bottom of the steps, more quietly, somebody speaking to James, *Going to be a bit tricky if Claudius and Gertrude aren't speaking to each other. And Adam's spending a lot of time with Zada – 'cos she's feeling SO insecure about playing Gertrude.* Right. So, if I've got this correct then, Zada Petrosian, who's playing Gertrude, has broken up with the chap who is playing Claudius (Jonathan someone, I think) and Zada is now having a thing with Adam, the director, and I wonder how Annie feels about this because my assumption was that Adam only gave Annie the job of assistant director because he fancied her, and she clearly hero-worships him. I was all prepared for my feminist hackles to rise if it turned out that what he really wanted was for her to dogsbody and comfort his bed when he felt like it, but it seems that he may be finding the comfort with the exotic Zada, and I would feel sorry for Annie except that in recent years I was the one who had teenage boys pouring out their hearts to me over my kitchen table when Annie had pitilessly dumped them, so I feel that a bit of her own medicine will do her no harm. I look around from my vantage point and spot her sitting on a rock talking to Sophie. She is obviously not looking for me and I decide to take the opportunity to go into the house and reconnoitre the sleeping arrangements. We're a company of seventeen and the villa has ten bedrooms, with a couple of tents in the garden for any overspill. I worry that Annie won't have thought to bag a room for Freda and me.

Entry to the back of the house is up some steps and through a long, covered verandah. Then we're in a breath-taking central room, which even the praise overheard on the beach hasn't prepared me for. In the villa's palmy days, this was obviously a great *salon* for entertaining; now the wall on the sea side is all glass and the height of the room is exaggerated by the whitewashing of the other walls, which reflect dazzlingly the light off the sea. In contrast with the spareness of this décor, there are high double doors in one wall still bearing their empire-style moulding picked out in gold. I'm sure I've seen a film in which Garbo sweeps through doors like this. Or perhaps it's Vivien Leigh in *Gone with the Wind*. I put Freda down and go over to try them, but the squeak of bedsprings warns me off and I set off in search of a bed of my own.

We find a large kitchen in what I think of as classic Scandinavian style, as yet still in a reasonably hygienic state, apart from an oozing carrier bag in a corner, apparently acting as an auxiliary rubbish bin. Near the kitchen door there is a narrow flight of stairs – too humble to be the only staircase in this house – and we make our way up to find a longish corridor of closed doors. I knock on each and look in. The first three are multiply occupied by the look of them but down at the end is a small room with a high window which has obviously been no-one's choice. Too much like the college rooms they are leaving behind, I imagine. It suits us well, though: the bed is a generous single – three feet at a guess – and there's a narrower one underneath that rolls out. I trundle it out and push it against the wall.

'There!' I say brightly. 'A big bed for Granny and a little bed for Freda.'

Freda hauls herself up onto the bigger bed and sits there, swinging her legs and patting the coverlet, inviting me to join her. 'We can share this bed,' she says, 'because you might feel lonely.'

Now one of the benefits of my divorced state is that I don't have to share a bed with anyone. I've no objection to going to bed with someone, and have done several times in the past few months with my occasional partner, David Scott, and the sex is fine – really very nice – but then I rather wish that he'd go home and leave me to sleep in peace. And I heard a discussion on *Woman's Hour* a few months ago about whether dogs should be allowed to sleep on their owners' beds. A doctor, whose dogs sleep not just on but in her bed on occasions, claimed that in terms of hygiene it's far more dangerous to sleep with another person than with a pet. You catch all kinds of horrible things from other people, she argued, and that, presumably, is even before you get to exchange of bodily fluids. Well, I don't expect to catch anything from Freda, who is sweetness itself, but she could catch something from me, couldn't she?

'Sweetheart,' I say, sitting down beside her, 'wouldn't you like to have a nice bed all to yourself, like you do at home?'

'No,' she says. Her face starts to crumple. Tears threaten.

'OK,' I say hastily. 'That's fine. We'll see how we feel at bedtime, shall we?'

She snuggles up to me and leans her head on my arm. 'We shall be cosy,' she says.

I'm unpacking our bags when there's a tap on the door, which opens to reveal Sophie's peaky little face. 'Oh, hello,' she says.

'Hello. How are you feeling?'

'Oh, you know – OK.' She's looking round the room. 'This is nice,' she says.

'Yes.'

He eyes linger on the truckle bed. 'Actually,' she says, 'I was wondering – I've been looking around and most of the beds seem to be taken. You haven't got a spare bed in here, have you?'

It seems rude to ask where James is sleeping and why she's not sleeping with him but she seems to intuit my question. 'James has found a room over on the other side of the house,' she says, flushing a faint pink, 'but to tell you the truth, I'm still feeling pretty ropey and I could do with a night on my own.'

Already feeling put-upon, I am ungracious. 'Well, as you see,' I say, indicating Freda, 'there are two of us in here already.'

'Yes,' she says, and her face looks as though it's about to

crumple just as Freda's did.

I harden my heart, though, and am preparing to tough it out when Freda, still sitting on my bed, points to the truckle bed and says, 'We don't need that bed there. Granny's going to share my bed with me.'

I lock eyes with Sophie and smile weakly. 'Well, problem solved,' I say.

I have to tell you that this is not at all how this trip was meant to be. When I told David about it originally, he was all for coming with me – booked two weeks' leave and everything. We were going to stay at the Marienlyst, a delightful four-star hotel just along the Sound, where we would spend the long, romantic summer evenings drinking and dining and all the rest of it. It would have been particularly good because David is in Brighton at the moment, seconded to a review of the West Sussex police force, and our weekend relationship has been fractious at best. Two weeks together looked like a chance to relax and breathe a bit. Then Ellie asked me to have Freda and I could hardly ruin her honeymoon by refusing. David got furious, as though I had sabotaged our romantic idyll on purpose, and I've ended up here, an old mother hen, not just with Freda to look after but no doubt all these other chicks as well, and I shall spend the fortnight metaphorically wiping noses, bathing grazes and kissing bruises better. Not to mention some quite unmetaphorical work keeping the kitchen disease-free. If I were the weeping type, I could weep with frustration.

We find duvet covers and pillow slips in a cupboard and we're in the middle of making up the beds when my phone rings and my heart lurches, expecting Mr Christodoulou.

'Gina? Where are you?'

Definitely not Mr Christodoulou, but it takes me a moment to realise who it is; *Gina* confuses me. 'Annie?'

'*Marianne*. Where are you?'

'I'm making up beds. I found us a room. I assumed you hadn't bagged one for us.'

'This isn't school,' she says tetchily. 'People don't go bagging things.'

'Fine. But I do have Freda to think about.'

A sigh. 'James and Conrad want to see the castle so Ray's taking the van into town. Do you want to go?'

'When are they going?'

'Now.'

'Five minutes to go to the loo.' I hear her sigh again. 'Freda –' I say.

'ALL RIGHT.'

Conversation is a good deal more animated on this drive. Even Sophie seems to be feeling better as we speed along the white road under a glittering sky, with windows open to the brisk breeze. Zada has come with us – *some shopping to do* – and Adam, who wants to show us around, and they are both in high spirits. I have met him only briefly once before; all our costume discussions have been by e-mail. He is skinny and wiry in a hyperactive way, and he has at least a three-day stubble so I assume there is a beard coming on. We newcomers get a bit less bouncy as we approach the castle. It's very fine and it stands majestically above the Sound, but it also adjoins the docks and has a lot of building going on around it – they are creating a *kulturhavn*, I read. A culture haven? What would that be, exactly? Whatever, it is certainly a major tourist attraction. The sun after the rain has brought the visitors out in force and Ray parks the van beside a line of Swedish cars, presumably fresh off the ferry from Helsingborg, across the Sound, whose owners are now queuing for ice creams at the gaudy stall opposite the castle gates.

'Fucking tourists,' Conrad mutters, but when I join the queue to get an ice cream for Freda the others tag along quite willingly.

'It's just like this at the Tower of London,' I point out, 'and it may feel better inside.'

As indeed it does. As we turn through the gates and cross the bridge over the moat, the vista changes before us. Massive red brick walls fall straight down to the reed-fringed water below. No willows grow aslant the brook but other trees droop their branches to the water and, high above, the castle, disdaining us ice-cream-lickers below, raises its shining green copper roofs to the sun. The tourist chatter outside is muffled and we stand for a moment, gazing up in silence till the boys run up the high, grassy rampart to our left, where a row of heavy cannons are lined up to point across the Sound.

As Sophie and I reach the top, hauling Freda between us, she says, 'It's difficult to imagine a ghost walking up here, isn't it?'

'I don't know,' Adam says. 'It'd be all right at night with the wind wailing and the sounds of the sea below.' Ray, who seems to feel it's his duty to entertain, wraps himself in an imaginary cloak of vast proportions and stomps up and down. '*For this relief much thanks,*' he says. 'It can't have been much fun being on watch up here.'

Sophie suddenly gives an odd, shrill laugh and goes running down the slope, whooping, brandishing her ice cream cone. A quiet group below who are, according to their leader's sign, on a church outing from Smidstrup, look up in alarm and the rest of us follow more sedately. We troop through the gatehouse, and look into the shop, where we're back in tourist world again: furry trolls, little mermaids, Elsinore tea towels and Shakespeare fridge magnets. But turning our backs on these delights we break out to find ourselves in *Hamlet* country once again, on our stage, in fact.

We are in an enormous square central courtyard with a fountain in the middle of it and doors opening on one side to the state apartments, on another to the dungeons and on a third to the chapel. While Adam is pointing out to the actors where the entrances and the dressing room will be (in the King's wine cellar, apparently), I try to visualise how my costumes will look in this space. Adam's modern military dictatorship setting has posed a problem about colour. Black leather and jackboots, as well as being old hat, won't do if Hamlet's black garb is supposed to be a contrast; khaki is dull and I'm very glad I wasn't tempted to go for Third Reich grey because that would have disappeared against all this grey stone. As it is, I've gone for a dark maroon. The place I hired the costumes from in Brighton had an assortment of uniforms in this colour, which I like to think of as a congealed blood tint, and I'm pleased with my choice, I think, though I'll have to see them under the lights to be sure. I hope Adam's going to set the farewell scene between Laertes and Ophelia round the fountain. I can imagine it there, but my job is only to make sure they've got some clothes on. We stand around for a bit while Adam and Ray have a technical discussion about power supplies, cables and lamp angles, and then Conrad proposes a visit to the dungeons. I'm quite a fan of dungeons but I don't want to give Freda nightmares so I arrange to meet them at the van at five thirty and go off to find somewhere for her to run around.

She's tired by now but we find a downhill slope, which she toddles down happily and my eye is drawn to a collection of artists' studios crouching in the shelter of the castle's outer walls. Evidence of the *kulturhavn* perhaps? In the window of one is a display of bowls in blue and white, which I have to look at. What is it about blue and white? Summer skies and puffy white clouds, I suppose. I stand for a while translating the krøner price tags on them. The prices come out so high that I think I've got my decimal point in the wrong place and do it again. But I was right the first time and this stuff is phenomenally expensive. I lower my sights to a little white salt dish with a swirl of blue in it and a tiny blue glass spoon: simple, elegant and a snip at £60.00. I don't intend to go inside anyway since three-year-olds mix with glass no better than bulls do with china, but as we walk past the open door I am arrested by a remarkable sight. Zada Petrosian is standing by a till surrounded by a buzz of activity. Two assistants are wrapping items of glass from a collection laid out on the counter and packing them into boxes while a third is entering prices at the till.

The force of my astonished gaze seems to reach as far as Zada because she looks up from something she is writing and calls out, 'Don't worry, I'm not taking this lot back in the van with me. It's being sent direct. I'm shopping early for Christmas. Isn't it irresistible?'

'Gorgeous. Have fun,' I say and start to move away.

'Don't go,' she calls. 'Come in and see.'

'Well, I don't think Freda –'

'OK. I won't be a minute. I'm just writing this address label. Wait for me and we can go and have a coffee.'

I remember this about her from before, when I took her measurements, this ease and immediate familiarity as though she's known me for years. The others were a bit awkward, embarrassed about being measured and not sure how to treat me. She chatted away easily, bemoaning her figure faults (non-existent apart from more bust than is strictly fashionable) and entertaining me with accounts of sartorial disasters she had known. It occurred to me afterwards that she may be used to being fitted for clothes – even for designer clothes. Her father is phenomenally rich, I know that. He's an oligarch of some kind – Armenian, not Russian – living in the UK. He's the kind of man who entertains cabinet ministers on his yacht. Zada's stepmother is English – an Honourable, I think. Zada herself is a wonderful conundrum at first meeting: she looks so exotic, with deep, dark eyes and fantastic cheekbones, but she sounds pure Sloane – all drawled vowels and swallowed consonants, courtesy of seven years at Cheltenham Ladies' College. She looks made for Greek tragedy and sounds as if she should be at a point-to-point. I imagine she will play Queen Gertrude as a sort of tragic airhead – a bit like Princess Diana.

She emerges now, not looking at all tragic, glowing with shopping pleasure. 'Hello Beautiful,' she purrs to Freda, then looks at her watch. 'Actually,' she says, 'let's get something to eat. I'm starving and meals are a bit random back at the villa. Last night we ended up going out for hot dogs.'

There turns out to be a tiny but delightful café down near the gatehouse and over prawn smørrebrød, luscious with dill-flecked mayonnaise, she says cheerfully, 'It's *so* embarrassing getting caught on a shopping binge, isn't it? My worst was when I was first going out with Jon. I'd had a start of term test – *collections*, they're called at Oxford.'

'As they were in my day,' I say.

'Of course. I'd forgotten you were there. Well, I couldn't do it at all. It was the start of the summer term of my first year and I was sitting there in the college library, knowing the wretched thing was impossible, and the sun was simply streaming in through the window and I just thought, *sod this*, and I handed in my pathetic effort and walked out, straight down the High and off on a retail mission. I met Jon later as I was coming back literally staggering with bags and he was appalled.'

'I've only met him once,' I say. 'He seems quite a serious person.'

'Well he can be really funny actually, but he's not frivolous. Whereas I,' she gives a sigh, 'I am deeply frivolous.' She gives a throaty laugh and I wonder if she's a smoker.

'You and he were together a long time, weren't you – since your first year?'

'I thought he was the love of my life, and we were fine in

the Oxford bubble but then I realised it was absolutely not going to work out in the real world.'

'Why?'

'Oh, money – and the strings that go with it. Ironically, it was actually this play that knocked it on the head. It was such a fun idea to be doing a last Oxford thing and for us to be acting together, doing Claudius and Gertrude, and then Daddy announced that we were taking the yacht on a big family cruise. Jon was invited along – I think Daddy had decided it was time for him to propose or get lost – but the dates he'd arranged clashed with the play. I assumed we'd drop out of the play. I was really sick about it but I knew you don't say no to Daddy. Jon said he wasn't dropping out for anything and we had a row. It was trivial really but we both said things we'd been bottling up and that was that.'

'But you decided to do the play?'

'Oh Daddy rearranged the dates, but it was too late then. We'd looked into the future and seen that it was bloody.'

'Have you got job plans?'

'Zilch. If I was interested in politics Daddy's got the contacts to get me something with the EU, using my languages, but I'm absolutely not interested.' She looks across at Freda, who is carefully dismantling a ham sandwich, and says, 'What I really want is to have babies.'

'Really?'

'Really. I think I'm one of those women who can't settle down to life until they've had their children. I'm permanently broody.' She rummages in her bag. 'I need a ciggie. Do you mind?'

She goes outside and I clear up some of the mess around Freda's plate. Listening to Zada talking about her father has made me think about the Christodoulous again and I check my phone to make sure I haven't missed a call. I don't want to talk to him but it worries me that he hasn't rung. Who has he been shouting at if not me? It's too late to ring anyone at the college now so there's nothing to be done – except worry, of course. Freda has finished her demolition job and is getting droopy and fretful with tiredness. I make a *look at the time* signal to Zada out of the window and she grinds her cigarette underfoot – to the evident displeasure of several passers-by – breezes in, summons the bill and says, as we're waiting for it, 'I do feel bad about Marianne. I feel it was a rotten trick to snaffle Adam like I did.'

'I'm sure she'll survive.'

'I suppose. It's just I know I'm not really serious about him. Actually, I've got a theory about Gertrude. Adam wants her to be very sensual and the relationship with Claudius to be loaded with sex. Well that's pretty awkward as things stand and anyway I don't see why it has to be about sex at all. Hamlet thinks it is, but then she's his mother and he doesn't like to think about her having sex at all. I think Claudius has good political reasons for marrying his brother's widow – it strengthens his claim to the throne if he marries the Queen Mum – she's the *'imperial jointress of this warlike state'* – and maybe she just needs someone to look after her. I mean, she's been a queen and Hamlet tells us that his father was so protective that he wouldn't even let the wind blow on her et cetera, so she wants to go on being looked after. And I think that's my problem. I'm used to being looked after and I've hitched up with Adam because he's the king around here.'

She snatches the bill as it arrives and says, 'I'm getting this – apology for being *so* boring. Last heart to heart, I promise. It's all going to be fun from now on.'

We're not the last back to the van; they're waiting for James as well as us, sitting in a row on a low wall, looking out at the harbour. Freda, who has reached the frenetic stage of tiredness, refuses to sit, however, or to be held by me. She starts to rush around and I am forced to hare after her, knowing that any moment she will trip and fall. As I'm pursuing her I spot James some distance away, talking to a young woman. I don't have time to look at them for long, needing as I do to keep an eye on Freda, but when I picture them afterwards I remember that she was wearing a pair of denim dungarees and a pink t-shirt, and that their body language was oddly neutral: not intimate, not friendly, not hostile, just *businesslike* is the word that comes to mind. I don't know if she was Danish or English and I didn't get the chance to see if there was a parting handshake, which would have been the clincher. And anyway, as Annie no doubt would tell me, it's none of my business.

3

DAY TWO

Come, give me a taste of your quality.
Come, a passionate speech. 2.2

As I should have predicted, Freda panicked at the idea of being put to bed and left alone in a strange room in an unknown house. She has had a pretty communal upbringing up till now: first in a chaotic house shared by Ellie with an ever-shifting group of fellow lodgers, and then in my house where, for various reasons, there were more of us than felt quite comfortable. When she and Ellie moved in with Ben a few months ago, I warned Ellie sternly against letting her sleep with them. I was ignored, however, and the chickens, as they so often do, have ended up in my roost, if you take my meaning, because there I was yesterday evening with her sitting up in bed refusing point blank to sleep *by my own*. Thus it came about that at 8.30 I put myself to bed; not long afterwards Sophie appeared saying an early night was just what she needed and we were soon all tucked up like babes in the nursery while the grown-ups let their hair down downstairs.

As a consequence, this morning we all wake early, Freda distinctly lark-like, I rather less so, and Sophie like the waking dead. I urge her downstairs with the lure of coffee and find in the kitchen cupboards several packs of expensive-looking coffee and a positive charivari of cereals, but no milk in the fridge. Sophie and I are sipping black coffee and Freda is picking unenthusiastically at a bowl of dry cocopops when the back door bursts open and Ray appears, panting slightly and glowing with exercise and virtue. He stands there looking at us as I remember my once-upon-a-time husband used to do whenever he had been out doing something energetic, apparently expecting praise and admiration for his efforts. We look back at him and I say merely, 'Well, you are the early bird.'

I'm glad I'm not more cutting because he says, 'And I have juicy worms', yanks off the backpack he's wearing and produces a fat bag of rolls, still warm from the baker's, and two litres of milk. I give him my nicest smile.

'Brilliant!' I say. 'What a marvellous necessary man you are, Ray.' As soon as I've said it I am horrified. It's a quote from *The Changeling* and it's about De Flores, who is a repulsive murderer and seducer. I watch for his reaction, ready with apologies, but he looks unruffled. Not an Eng Lit student then. I take a look at him as he's pouring himself some coffee: he's a big chap – beefy – with freckles and thick sandy hair and he looks a bit older than the others do. Mature student or taking eight years to finish a DPhil? There's the hint of an Australian accent in his speech, which I had discounted as affectation since quite a lot of students acquire these on gap years spent in the laid-back Antipodes, but now I think he may be a genuine colonial on a second degree. He takes a couple of rolls, says he's going to grab a shower, and leaves us to our breakfast, which Freda and I both enjoy, though I can't persuade Sophie to eat anything.

An hour or so later we're ready to depart for the first day's rehearsal in the castle. Some pile into the van, including Freda and me, while others head for the bus stop. In the van are Emma and Clare, who have taken on the job of catering. They are cheery, apparently unflappable girls who warm to Freda and offer to take her with them in the van to the supermarket and deliver her to me at the castle before taking the food home. Freda loves shopping and I could do with an unfettered morning to sort the costumes, so I agree gratefully although I know that as soon as they've gone I shall be assailed by fears for her safety: will they crash the van? Or let her fall out of the supermarket trolley? Or turn their backs while someone abducts her? And then how will I face Ellie, on her honeymoon, happily unaware of my neglect? And so on, and so on. Freda, happily doubt-free, waves to me out of the van window as they drive away. I text Ellie, as I promised to do every morning, and tell her that everything is just fine.

We are, of course, a considerable tourist attraction, here in the heart of the castle. Our stage area has been cordoned off, but once rehearsal gets under way there is a permanent audience standing round the perimeter, watching. Most of the cast blossom under the attention, and even I feel a little frisson of importance as I supervise the transport of my costume hampers through the crowd, with a castle official going before me opening doors labelled ADGANG FORBUDT. Only James seems ill at ease. From rehearsals in Oxford Annie said he wasn't going to be a brilliant Hamlet, but he's intelligent and has a good voice and Adam thought he would be all right. Today, though, he seems completely non-plussed, stiff and awkward, more Coriolanus than Hamlet under the gaze of the vulgar throng. But it's not the throng that is the real problem – it's Conrad. He manages to be always in James's sight line and I believe he is actually mouthing the lines ahead of James.

They struggle through as far as the latter part of Act 1 scene 2, but when James gets to *'O that this too, too solid flesh would melt'* it becomes clear that soliloquizing is going to be a stretch too far for him. He is groping for lines and twice Conrad ostentatiously prompts him from memory. The second time,

Adam calls out quite sharply, 'Thanks, Conrad, but leave the prompting to Kelly, will you?' but the damage is done and he can only attempt limitation. 'Soliloquies we can work on later,' he says and, with an eye perhaps to pleasing the crowd, switches us deftly to the final scene of the play, on the grounds that it requires the same personnel as 1.2 – apart from those who have died on the way, of course.

The change of scene doesn't help. James, who is wearing long shorts and what looks like an old-fashioned aertex tennis shirt, looks – and obviously feels – foolish with a rapier strapped on over these togs. He gets increasingly tetchy, stopping constantly to nit-pick over details and sapping any energy the others can muster. It is bewilderingly self-destructive of him because every time he starts this textual nit-picking, Conrad is there, chipping in with his views, staking a claim. The schoolteacher in me wants to send him outside to stand in the corridor – I know all about silly attention-seeking boys like this – but Adam, for all his confidence, doesn't know how to deal with him. He's used to managing people by charming them, I think, and he doesn't know how to slap someone down.

When they get to the duel, James and Stefan, who is playing Laertes, are all over the place. They have rehearsed it in Oxford with a fight trainer, but you wouldn't think so this morning. They are awkward, tentative, half-hearted and completely unconvincing. Conrad has gone silent, but he sits hunched forward, watching with exaggerated intentness, following every move. Bored and embarrassed, those who aren't needed slip away to the quiet of the battlements; even Annie deserts her post at Adam's side. Only Conrad, Sophie and I stay to watch, he with narrowed, unblinking eyes, she blank-faced and vacant, I awaiting the return of Freda

I'm starting to fret about what has happened to Freda. Even allowing for the fact that they are feeding a multitude, shopping in a foreign language and young enough not to be bored with shopping, Emma and Clare seem to me to have been an unconscionably long time and I'm already beginning to frame the terrible conversation I may have to have with Ellie before I spot them ambling through the archway on the far side of the courtyard, toting shopping bags. Freda is hurtling ahead of them and I go speeding to meet her. The bags, it turns out, contain our lunch, and the girls are proposing that we picnic up on the battlements, so Freda and I go with them to help to carry and organise the food. As a result, I miss a drama the origins of which I shall never get to discover. All I can say is that when I return to the courtyard to see if the actors are ready for a lunch break, I find our impromptu audience dispersed, Adam, tight-lipped, making adjustments to the rehearsal schedule, James impassively smoking a cigarette and Conrad with his arm round a weeping Sophie. 'Lunch, anyone?' I ask brightly, and am largely ignored, though Adam hauls himself wearily to his feet.

'*Stay me with flagons, comfort me with apples,*' he says.

'*For I am sick with love*?' I ask. 'Is that the problem?'

'Not with me,' he says, 'I can assure you. Where are we eating?'

'Up on the battlements.'

'Lead the way.'

As we leave the courtyard, he fishes a cigarette out of a crushed packet in the pocket of his skinny jeans and lights it with a less than steady hand.

'To mangle Romeo,' he says, '*Here's much to do with love but more with hate.*'

'Hate?'

'You haven't noticed the hate whirling around this production?'

'You think Conrad hates James?'

'Undoubtedly. And Sophie hates James, and everyone

hates Conrad, and I hate myself for letting him anywhere near this thing. I was soft enough to give him Rosencrantz because I felt sorry for him. Well that's a lesson learnt for the future.' He takes a deep drag on his cigarette and then says, 'If I've got a future. If I can't pull this show round, my directing career is over before it's begun. There's no established route to being a director – you have to make and take your chances as you can. This is my chance to make a splash and it's going tits up.'

'And you blame Conrad?'

'He's set out to destroy James and James is letting him do it.'

'Have you tried talking to him?'

'Of course. He's actually mad, I think. Certifiable. Says James cracking up is just proof that he's not up to the part. Doesn't say *take it away from him and give it to me*, but that's what he's waiting for.'

We've been walking fast. He's a skinny bundle of nervous energy at the best of times and his legs are a lot longer than mine so I'm having to do undignified little skips and runs to keep up with him. Suddenly he stops and turns to look at me.

'I'm not the only one,' he says. 'Other people have got a lot riding on this as well. Tom Yeoman – the work he's put into writing the music – composing is even more random than directing as a career, I imagine. And Stefan. He's a good actor but he's applied for PG acting courses and had no luck yet. This on his CV could just swing it if we get some decent reviews. I've got a promise from a couple of the nationals to review it – they'll send some green junior but they'll still be national reviews.' He drops his cigarette and grinds it hard under his foot. 'And if they're crap then we're all blown to buggery.'

We eat sprawled on the rough, springy grass that grows up on the battlements, and the sunshine and dappled shade, the gulls' cries and glitter of the sea below, the salamis, sweet cheeses, rye bread and cans of Carlsberg do something to cheer us all up, but the prospect of a stressful afternoon keeps us lingering long over our comforting apples and even Adam is in no hurry to chivvy anyone back to work. He sits talking quietly to Stefan long after his apple has been reduced to nothing more than pips and stalk. Emma makes a start on clearing up but Clare is deep in talk with Tom Yeoman. He is mechanically pulling up tufts of grass and she has a consoling hand on his arm, stroking and smoothing. I gathered only just now, as I was helping to carry the lunch up here, that Clare and Emma volunteered for this job only because their boyfriends are here – Tom in Clare's case and David Underwood in Emma's. He's a serious lad who looks old beyond his years and is playing Polonius and the gravedigger. I realise that I've been in danger of regarding the two girls – and presenting them to you – as a pair, Siamese twins with no individual characteristics. Much like Rosencratz and Guildenstern, in fact. Actually, they are quite different in appearance and, I think, in temperament. Clare is tall and broad-shouldered with a substantial bust and a calm, unflappable air. She has a degree in Music, plays the cello and seems destined to mother people. Emma is small and red-headed, energetic and practical. She's a farmer's daughter from North Wales and I can quite believe that she has delivered calves single-handed. Thank heavens they're here is all I can say. Whatever artistic disasters lie ahead, we shall, at least, be fed – and I shan't have to do the feeding.

Eventually, we get up and straggle back to find James pacing the courtyard with Ray, going over lines. Ray must, I suppose, have slipped away to find James when he didn't turn up for lunch. I'm beginning to think he's really a rather nice chap. There is no sign of Conrad or Sophie but just as we get started on the second half of 1.2, they appear, breathless, at the entrance from the gatehouse. Sophie is looking more animated than I've seen her in the last twenty-four hours and Conrad is looking smug. He starts talking from the other side of the courtyard, his voice ringing round the stone walls.

'Sorry if we've kept you waiting,' he roars. 'Thought you'd have plenty to be getting on with the rate things were going, so we just popped out to hire ourselves a car. Thought we might fit in a trip to Copenhagen tomorrow while James is wrestling with a couple of soliloquies.'

No-one looks at James, though I shall wish later that I had, and Ray barges in to fill the buzzing silence that follows. 'What've you got, Conrad?'

It is Sophie who answers, hanging on Conrad's arm, almost squealing with delight. 'It's a convertible – pale blue and beautiful – but don't ask me what make – I've no idea.' She squeezes Conrad's arm and looks up at him as he towers above her. 'I do like a man with a good credit card,' she giggles.

'I got it from Karin's brother,' Conrad says, looking at James. 'He gave me a good deal.'

James colours but says nothing and after a bit of awkward shuffling they limp back into rehearsal. I watch for a while but it's unbearable really, like bear-baiting. I can't believe that James can be so easy to rattle but Hamlet is a part that undoes even the best of actors – Daniel Day Lewis had a breakdown when he played it. James is only a student amateur, after all, and Conrad is intent on undoing him. Conrad will have to be dealt with somehow, and I could do it – I have reduced big boys to tears in my time – but it's not up to me and I'm too scared of Annie to go barging in. There's really nothing for me to do at all, in fact, until my costume rails are delivered tomorrow and I can unpack, so I take Freda off into the town with me for the glamorous purchase of a second kitchen bin and some liners, and we spend the rest of the afternoon sitting on the grass near the gatehouse, making daisy chains. Ray has now got permission to park the van here and beside it is a handsome blue convertible – a Mustang, I think. (I'm not at all interested in cars – I don't even drive one – but ten years of being married to an auto fanatic have left me with a lot of irritating information in my head which I can't get rid of.) It must be Conrad's new acquisition and I can see how, if she likes that kind of thing, it might turn Sophie on. I wonder whether Freda and I might have our room to ourselves tonight.

When the others return to the van later they are subdued but not, at least, at one another's throats. Conrad and Sophie rev away, while those of us who can fit in pile into the van and others go off to catch the bus. I'm thinking about hiring my own transport too, so I can come and go as I like, and avoid travelling in the van with Annie, who watches me for misdemeanours with such eagle-eyed scrutiny that I feel that I might develop Tourette's syndrome out of reflex perversity. A bike with a child seat would do the trick.

Emma and Clare feed us well on pasta and meatballs and Freda is so exhausted by her day that she allows herself to be put to bed with the promise that I'll be joining her *soon*, so I am allowed downstairs this evening. We sit companionably on the veranda drinking beer and watching the ships on the Sound become mere points of light as the sky and the sea darken. The conversation drifts and hovers, settling finally, inevitably, on the play. I'm saying nothing; it hardly needs Annie's warning scowls to alert me to the danger of turning into the seminar leader if I let myself get started. Besides, they don't need my opinions – they have more than enough of their own.

So I sit on the edge of the circle and I can't see faces in the deepening dusk. I'm only half-listening as voices I mostly don't recognise float out towards me.

'That's just the point,' someone is saying. 'He's not a tragic hero at all, not in the proper sense. It's his situation that makes him tragic.'

'*O cursèd spite*
That ever I was born to set it right?'
'Exactly.'

'Of course, it's very much a playwright's idea – I suppose that's why it fascinated Stoppard – take an artificial, formal convention like the revenge tragedy and put a real person in the middle of it – a thinking, feeling, civilised renaissance man – and see what you get. Chaos of course.'

'You could imagine Feydeau doing the same thing.'

This jolts me out of my little reverie. Hamlet and Feydeau? That's a bit of a stretch, isn't it? Apparently not. The ball is caught without a fumble.

'Well yes. If you take Bakhtin's ideas about laughter – *laughing truth degrades power.*'

I wasn't much good at this sort of thing when I was a student, these free-flowing discussions where half-formed ideas are sent skimming around, nothing gets scrutinised and everything has its own validity. I wanted to shout that the emperor had no clothes on. Not tonight though. Someone has put the lights on in the room behind us so I can see faces now in the light that filters through, casting curious and revealing shadows. I look round at them, clever, confident, animated, and unhappy every one of them, I would say. I watch Adam, who is lounging back in his seat, an arm slung carelessly, possessively, round Zada's shoulders, and I notice again how thin his face is, how sharp the jaw line, the youthful flesh melted away by the heat of energy and will. Zada isn't listening to the conversation; her face is a blank and has fallen, as those strong-boned faces so easily do, into a tragic mask. I would hardly recognise the laughing shopaholic I had tea with: the glow of animation is all gone, her eyes are deep-shadowed above those high cheekbones and her mouth, drained of colour, droops. I'm not the only one looking at her; as I look away I see that Jon McIntyre is watching her intently.

41

I thought he was the love of my life, Zada said to me yesterday. And what does he feel about her, I wonder? I was impressed by him at the rehearsal this morning. He's a public school Scot, I guess. In real life he has one of those crisp, witty Scottish accents, but playing Claudius he does Standard English with no trouble. He was focussed and on the ball this morning, word-perfect and quick on cues. He's doing Medicine and he has a reassuring air of competence which should take him far. I'm not surprised that Zada's parents were happy to have him for their daughter; I'd have taken him for one of my girls like a shot. He looks tired, though: his blue eyes are bright enough as they watch Zada, but they're red-rimmed and his Scottish-pale skin is as white as paper.

Some of the others look all right: Ray looks happy enough, drinking lager out of a can, and David Underwood, Polonius and Gravedigger, looks relaxed, his funny, clever-boy, old-young face no beakier than usual as he sits with Emma, looking on, smiling. Clare and Tom aren't here, I notice.

James is talking. He has picked up the introduction of Bakhtin into the conversation and now he has taken the floor and everyone else has gone silent. He's fluent and authoritative but there's a hard, ironic edge to what he says, and a contemptuousness in his tone that has warned everyone else off. We all sense, I suppose, that this display is compensation for today's humiliations. When he stops talking, there is silence. No-one, not even Adam, is going to risk being embarrassed by James in this mood. They are creatures of two worlds, I think: bright, confident children of the day with jokes and laughter, summer tans, loves and friendships, and shadowy creatures of the dark, timid, suspicious and alone.

There's a noise from inside the house, the glass doors from the sitting room burst open and Conrad and Sophie appear, laughing into the gloom. The silence breaks, people stir and pour more drinks, scattered conversations start up, someone lights some candles, the mood lifts with the light. Conrad, happy and expansive, starts to describe eating reindeer at a restaurant they have found along the coast, while Sophie mouths in mock-horror, 'I kept thinking of Rudolph!' When the beep of an incoming text message breaks through the general laughter, Conrad fishes his phone out of his pocket, glances casually at his message, flushes crimson and throws the phone down on the coffee table. Sophie, watching his reaction, goes to pick the phone up, but he snatches it from her. hurls it out into the garden and barges through the group, back into the house. Sophie looks round helplessly for a moment, then turns and follows him.

Much later, when everyone else has gone to bed but I feel it my duty to check that the candles are all snuffed out on the verandah and the doors are locked, I hear the sound of the phone trilling out in the darkness and I look out and spot it glowing and vibrating on the grass. I retrieve it and cut off the call because I'm not about to start answering students' phones for them but, shamefully nosy as I am, I sneak a quick look at the message that had such a dramatic effect on Conrad. Text messages, I argue speciously to myself, are like postcards: they're just there in plain view, so they can't be private. So I read it. The message is surprising and mildly unsettling, but why it caused Conrad such fury remains a mystery. 'So what was that about?' I ask the looming shadows.

4

INTERLUDE

They say they have letters for you. 4.6

Marianne Gray

From "Marianne Gray"   m.gray@ox.ac.uk
To "Eleanor Gray Biaggi"   elliegraybiaggi@mailnet.co.uk
Sent 13th July 2011 23. 28
Subject Be glad you're not here

Ciao Signora Biaggi!

Hope you're having an ace time and soz for pouring out troubles to you but have to unload and figure you'll be having a good enough time to cope with my moans.

El, I feel a total idiot. I knew it wasn't going to be a long-term thing with me and Adam – he's off to a traineeship at one of the Glasgow theatres after this – but when he asked me to be AD on this thing I thought at least we'd have some time together here and end on a high but now bloody Zada, who's playing Gertrude, has got her claws into him and she's rich and exotic and wears gorgeous clothes and I don't stand a chance. And I don't think I'm really going to be AD-ing at all – Adam just treats me like the office girl – just i/c rehearsal schedules. And it's not as if the acting bit is any fun. Conrad is

44

complete crap to act with – gives me absolutely nothing and spends all his time needling James (Hamlet). He started that during rehearsals in Oxford but he's really stepped it up now and James is cracking under the strain. I can see Adam's worried but he's not talking to me about it.

And it makes it worse having Ma here cos you know how she is. She'll see exactly what's going on and I can't bear to have her being sympathetic and patronising to me. And I feel a fool having her here anyway. I thought she'd be cool but she's been lugging Freda around with her ever since she got here, looking all grannyish and I'm sure everyone is thinking it's really weird her being here. El, I love Freda, you know I do, but I wish you'd timed your grand tour better. And Ma keeps calling me Annie even though everyone else has called me Marianne for the past year. It's so typical of her to give me a decent name and then change it to something you'd call an Edwardian scullery maid.

Well, I'm not the only one who's miserable so that's something. Actually, we're all pretty stressed, which is weird when this is supposed to be fun. There's a lot of relationship stuff going on which I won't bore you with since you don't know who anyone is and it'd be like those people who try to tell you about what's happening in a soap you never watch. BUT all is not lost. I have my eye on the very nice boyfriend that Zada dropped for Adam. He's called Jon and he's a bit freckly and Scottish-looking but sweet, I think, and doing medicine, which Granny would approve of. We've chatted a bit and I think he's interested, though how we go on from here with Ma's eagle eye on me God knows. Anyway, watch this space.

Hope the Biaggis are loving you.

xxxxxxxxxxxxx

MARIANNE

Gina Gray

From "Gina Gray"   gina.gray@freenet.com
To "David Scott"   D.S.Scott@mailcon.co.uk
Sent 14th July 2011 08.15
Subject Wish you were here?

Hi David

This extraordinary villa we're living in has WiFi so I'm writing this on my laptop at the kitchen table while Freda is eating cocopops and I am hoping that a nice man is going to appear with pastries from the baker's as he did yesterday. Otherwise I shall have to eat cereal too, but there are no what you might call grown-up cereals in the cupboard.

Anyway, we're all right – journey, house, costumes all fine. Sleeping arrangements are less than ideal, but I've no doubt you'll think I've only myself to blame for that. We shared a room the last two nights with a funny, victimy girl. She seems to have found herself a man to look after her now, but I have the feeling that my shoulder is going to be permanently damp with tears for the next two weeks – and not Freda's. Not Annie's either. Things have gone tits up for her but she's giving me a very wide berth.

So there we are. The sun is shining, the villa is delightful, the play is a masterpiece, the costumes are perfectly chosen, the tourists are fascinated and the actors, I fear, are flaky at best. Too many hormones, too much angst. And to think that you could have been part of all this...

Talking of which, I hope you're doing something with your leave. I'm sorry, sorry, sorry that I had to bring Freda with me and we couldn't spend these two weeks romancing at the Marienlyst, but deciding to have a crap time just to show me how much I have messed up your life isn't a very mature way to behave is it? *Autorhinectomy* a classicist friend of mine labelled that sort of behaviour – the Greek for cutting off one's nose to spite one's face. Go out and enjoy yourself. You are in Brighton, after all. Lie on the beach.

Love and all the rest

Gina

Eleanor Gray Biaggi

From "Eleanor Gray Biaggi"   elliegraybiaggi@mailnet.co.uk
To "Marianne Gray"   m.gray@oxford.ac.uk
Sent 14th July 2011 10.04
Subject re: Be glad you're not here

Ciao Sis! Do I really have to call you Marianne? After all these years?

All hugs, kisses, smiles and food here. Huge quantities of the last. I shall be vast by the time I leave.

Sorry about your troubles. Go for the nice guy if you can. And don't blame Ma for everything. She's doing you a favour. And she's not the worst person to talk to if you've got problems. Mind you, her hourly updates on Freda are a bit over the top, loving mother though I am!

Chill, Babe. You're supposed to be having fun.

Arrivederci, El

David Scott

From "David Scott"   D.S.Scott@mailcon.co.uk
To "Gina Gray"   gina.gray@freenet.com
Sent 14th July 2011 11.28
Subject re Wish you were here?

Well thanks for your care and concern so sensitively expressed. And you wonder why Annie doesn't come to you for sympathy?

Thank you particularly for reminding me that we have a beach in Brighton because I really hadn't thought of that.

Actually, the one thing I have promised myself for the next two weeks is not to open, read or reply to any emails. So if you have any other helpful advice I'm afraid you'll have to keep it to yourself.

David.

5

DAY THREE

Thou wretched, rash, intruding fool, farewell! 3.4

Freda and I are first down to breakfast again. We're without Sophie this morning, though she did spend the night with us. I had thought that she might be in the arms of Conrad, the man with the attractive credit card, but there she was again in her truckle bed when I went upstairs last night, and this morning she has her head under the duvet and refuses – quite rudely, actually – to be stirred. I make a large pot of coffee, fairly confident that this will rouse the sleepers of the house, and I sit with Freda as she eats her cocopops in the hopeful expectation that the efficient Ray will again come trotting in with buns.

I've picked a sunny corner of the kitchen table, under the window, where I can look out onto the shrub-strewn drive and appreciate the promising warmth of the morning. I get my phone out and text a message to Ellie with a rider from Freda to the effect that she is eating coco pops. Then I gaze out idly and I'm alerted by an improbable scene almost under the window. I crane forward to get a better look. Conrad and James are standing by the pale blue Mustang, apparently in amiable discussion. I can't hear what they're saying – a conservation-conscious Dane has double glazed this window

– but it definitely looks amiable. Conrad even laughs at one point. Then they stroll away, round the side of the house in the direction of the beach. Well, here's a turn up. Neither of them seemed to me to be the breach-healing type and yet here they are, apparently healed. It occurs to me, as I watch them go, that they were at school together – and not just any school, as they say in the adverts, but Eton no less. I read that Conrad was there in his programme entry: *Conrad Wagner was born in Beverley Hills, California. He attended Emanuel Academy of Beverley Hills, Eton College, Berkshire, UK and Christ Church, Oxford. He plans to make a career as an actor and is currently looking to engage an agent.* James didn't mention his schooling in his entry but I'm sure Annie told me he'd been at Eton. She's impressed by such things but I expect she'll grow out of it. In fact I expect they'll all grow out of a lot of things, including the nerve-end emotions that make them such jangling company. The truth is, I find it difficult to take them seriously. I find it all quite interesting because I have an almost insatiable appetite for human interactions but I can't help feeling that they're just trying out relationships – the way puppies and kittens try out fighting and hunting. Of course, I took my own relationships desperately seriously when I was their age and I'm not so old that I can't remember the agony, so I guess I should make an effort to be more empathetic with these fraught young things.

And, as if on cue, I see another fraught young thing approach the Mustang. Zada has come out of the house and is strolling towards the car. She stops a short way from it and appraises it, head on one side, then moves closer, circling it and running a hand appreciatively over it as I imagine she would a horse. She tries the door on the driver's side, finds it open, takes a quick look around and then slips into the driving seat. I am riveted. Is she about to drive off in it? But no. She simply sits there for a minute, then gets out, closes the door and comes in with a gaggle of others in pursuit of breakfast. There follows a clamouring for coffee, the making of piles of toast and jam, and a general hubbub of jostling, laughing, yawning, eating, drinking and smoking. So intensely engaged are they in all this that they hardly notice the arrival of James and Conrad in dripping swimming trunks, standing in the doorway, towelling vigorously. What is it with these boys that they need to present themselves to be admired after any untoward physical activity? And while I'm on the subject, where is Ray this morning?

When someone does notice them, a silence descends like the Monty Python boot as all heads swivel round and we watch Conrad, all casual unconcern, pad across the kitchen to the cork board where Annie has efficiently pinned up the schedule for the day. He consults it and then, in the hush, calls across to James, 'We're neither of us needed this morning – they're doing Ophelia's mad scenes. D'you feel like helping me with the car? Points and plugs need cleaning, I think. It nearly died on us last night.'

I stifle a snort of laughter because James, for once, is taken completely off balance. He recovers well, though. His mouth does drop open in astonishment for a moment but he is quick to cover it with a laugh. 'Conrad,' he drawls, 'I have to tell you I know absolutely nothing about the insides of a car.'

'No problem. You can hold the spanners for me.'

I don't hear James's reply as he picks up his towel and turns to go. Later, though, when Ray appears and we're straggling out to the minivan to set off for rehearsal, we see Conrad and James speeding out of the gates. Like several others, I take a quick look at Sophie to see how she's feeling about being displaced from her seat in the lovely Mustang but she is meekly climbing into the minivan, outwardly unperturbed.

I've been worried about how to amuse Freda this morning,

but I find, when I descend into the wine cellar where my costumes are waiting, that the rails have been delivered. *O joy, O rapture unforeseen!* They were promised for today but I find that it saves disappointment never to expect deliveries when promised and then, as this morning, it's such a lovely surprise when they turn up on time. There's nothing Freda likes more than unpacking things so she sets to with a will. She's a bit random about where she puts things and she can't hang things up, of course, but we get on pretty well. And they seem to be doing pretty well outside too, every time we emerge into the light of day because Freda needs a drink or the loo or something to eat or another drink. We find the sun shining, people mostly on top of their lines and Sophie surprisingly good as a rather scarily bonkers Ophelia. Her mad scene dress – a Miss Havishamesque tattered bridal gown – was one of the first out of the trunks, so I've given it to her to wear and it certainly seems to have brought her to life. At lunch time there's a decision to go and eat on the beach and we call in at the harbour car park to let Conrad and James know. All, it seems, is tranquil here too. We pass Ray, who has been off on an errand of his own this morning and is sitting on a bench eating an ice cream, and we find Conrad, with his head under the car, wriggling out to say they're nearly finished and they will find us on the beach. He takes another spanner from James, who is sitting with his back against the boot, reading, and he works his way back under the car.

Everyone departs for the beach except Freda and me. We are detained by Freda's need to take my hand and to walk precariously along the shallow wall that runs round the perimeter of the car park. Thus it is that I am the only one of our company to see what happens a minute or two later. What I see is this – though I don't understand it till much, much later: I see Conrad emerge from under the car and say something to James, who puts down his book and stands up, laughing. Words are exchanged. Then there is an alarming moment: Conrad savagely winds down the jack and raises his arm in a histrionic gesture, jack in hand, so it looks as though he is going to attack James with it. Instead, though, he flings the jack to the ground and storms off in the direction of the town. James watches him go, then he packs up the tool box, stows it in the boot, takes the keys out of the car's ignition, locks the car, stands looking at it for a moment, pockets the keys and walks away towards the castle.

Neither of them arrives to join us for lunch on the beach, but when we get back to rehearsal in the afternoon, James is there, tight-lipped and non-committal, running through his lines with Ray. Nobody – except Annie, who can't do Guildenstern without Rosencrantz – seems much bothered that Conrad is missing. Freda and I return to our labours and any danger that she might be getting bored with this game is forestalled by the delivery, in our absence, of a full-length mirror. She tries on every piece of headgear – military caps, crowns, coronets and the gravedigger's beanie – and sends herself into fits of laughter as she disappears into the hats, and the crowns end up round her neck. I am not required; she is star and audience of her own show.

It's as we're packing up at the end of the afternoon that Conrad finally appears. Even at a distance he is evidently so drunk that at first people think he is clowning and there's some half-hearted laughter as he weaves his way across the courtyard. Close to, though, he is red-faced, sweaty and pumping aggression. He turns on James.

'What the hell do you think you're doing?' he slurs venomously. 'What have you done with my car?'

James's face and voice are tight with disdain. 'What I think I'm doing, Conrad, is rehearsing this play. And it would have helped us all if you'd been doing the same. And the car is just where you left it.'

He turns his back on Conrad and starts to move away. Conrad shouts, 'Cunt,' and makes to follow him but Ray steps in to block his way. Conrad executes an odd little sideways dance step and then, abruptly, slides to the ground. James keeps on walking without looking back. The rest of us stand stupidly, looking at Conrad's prone figure until Adam moves in and nudges him fairly roughly with his foot.

'Christ,' he says, and contempt and disgust are surprisingly strong in his voice, 'he's passed out.' He looks round at us all. 'What the hell are we going to do with him now?'

I have a feeling that I should be taking charge, as the only real grown-up present, but I'm forestalled by Jon McIntyre, who pushes his way through from the back of our circle of onlookers and kneels down beside Conrad. He slaps his face lightly and lifts one of his eyelids. I'm not sure where he is in his medical degree – has he seen any actual patients yet? – but he manages to look quite professional about it.

'He's completely out,' he says. 'We'll just have to carry him to the van so we can get him home and put him to bed.'

'I'm not having him in the van in that state,' Ray says. 'If he throws up in it I'm the mug who'll be cleaning it up.'

'And what about the car?' Sophie puts in. 'We can't leave it in the car park all night, can we?'

'OK.' Jon is still kneeling beside Conrad. 'If someone will help me to get him into his car, I'll drive him back. Then if he vomits he'll be the one to clean it up. I assume he's got the keys on him.'

He starts to pat Conrad's pockets for the clink of keys, but I know they're not there so I yell across the courtyard to James, who is about to disappear through the archway to the outside world, 'Hang on, James. We need the car keys.'

James turns and looks at me, and of course he's wondering how the hell I know that he's got the keys. He says nothing, though – just puts a hand in his pocket, pulls out the keys and stands there, dangling them from one finger. I'm about to trot off and fetch them but Jon raises a hand. 'It's OK, Gina,' he says, and there's some steel in his voice, 'no need to trouble yourself. James can bring them.' He raises his voice. 'I'll have those keys then, James,' he calls. 'I'm going to drive the car back to the house.'

There is a moment when I think James is going to refuse. The two men stand, facing each other across the space and it's like the prelude to a gun fight without the Stetsons, but then James starts to sprint towards us, and when he is maybe twenty feet away, he swings his arm up and bowls the keys at Jon, who catches them one-handed and calls, 'Thanks very much,' to James's retreating back.

It turns out that Ray can manage Conrad all by himself. He heaves him up in a fireman's lift and sets off at a steady pace across the courtyard with everyone else falling in as a rather self-conscious escort behind him. I nip back to lock up the costume store and Freda and I catch up with them as he stops for a breather before starting the descent to the car park. Then he's off again, steady as you like. I'm impressed and intrigued – not just by the physical strength but by the practised way he hauls him up onto his back. No-one else seems much impressed but I'm pretty sure he didn't learn to do that on one of those one-day First Aid courses. I don't know what he did before Oxford – only the actors got their CVs in the programme – but I don't think he spent all his time in a lecture theatre.

As they are manoeuvring Conrad into the passenger seat, he comes to a bit and starts struggling, but they strap him in and Jon gets into the driving seat, then lowers the window and calls to Ray, 'I think I'd better follow you. I'm not sure of the route on this first bit – getting out onto the coast road.'

Ray walks over. 'In fact, I was going to try the dual carriageway today. It was such a scrum getting out of the town onto the coast road yesterday. Follow signs to the E47, then take the turn off to Humlebæk. It should be pretty straightforward. We'll follow you in case you have any trouble with him. He might just come round and turn nasty.'

'More likely just to puke all over me. OK. Thanks.'

Things get raucous in the minivan as the group launches into a thoroughly merciless character assassination of Conrad. They start with the drinking but quickly move on to a more general attack which has at its essence, it seems to me, a shared outrage that after five years at Eton and three years at Oxford he has the effrontery to remain so *American* – so unembarrassed about being rich, so openly ambitious, so lacking in the British essentials of self-deprecation and irony. 'All of which wouldn't matter,' says Zada, who knows something about being a foreigner and fitting in, 'if he had a smidgeon of talent. Do you remember that review in *The Oxford Mail* that said he seemed to have taken Roger Moore as his acting model?'

'Have you seen what he wrote about himself for the programme?' Adam asks. 'I'm sure it's bad form to broadcast the fact that you were at Eton, isn't it, James?'

'Quite so. And as for explaining that the school's in Berkshire, well –'

'Well, that's for the benefit of any passing American, I assume.'

'Who will pronounce it *Birkshayre* anyway.'

'I love the way he says he's looking for an agent. If your father owns Wagner Pictures and you haven't managed to get an agent, you might think you'd get the message, wouldn't you?'

'Has anyone ever seen him in any of these walk-ons he talks about?

'I think they're more like carry-ons – when he was a baby – no lines to screw up.'

I feel a teacher's urge to intervene and make them ashamed of themselves but I can't face Annie's wrath so I shut up and after a while the bitching runs out of steam and they move on to competitive reminiscences of drunkenness they have known. They're young enough still to find falling over drunk funny. Except for Adam and James, who exchange looks as the stories get under way, and then direct their gazes at the outside world. As do I, with Freda lolling sleepily beside me. For a while, we follow the Mustang. Then, at the turn onto the dual carriageway, Jon nips into a break in the traffic, leaving us behind, and Ray announces that he'll need to stop for petrol at the service station just coming up.

As soon as we stop, everyone in the van decides to dash off into the shop like a party of kids on a school trip. I stay firmly in place. Freda is at the fractious end of the day when a retail opportunity is likely to have her demanding all sorts of things and getting histrionic if denied. So we read *The Very Hungry Caterpillar*, which travels in my bag and which she knows off by heart anyway, and eventually the others come running back with wine, cigarettes, crisps, bottles of water, chewing gum, postcards, sun cream and, in Zada's case, a large bunch of lilies. 'An end-of-the-day service station bunch is the saddest thing in the world,' she says mournfully, 'but if you buy it yourself it's not quite as bad as being given one.' Ray, who has been for a pee, gets back into the van and we head for the exit, only to find that there is no escape. Traffic is backed up along the road in a static queue and there is nothing for us to do but to sit and wait for it to start moving.

A game of *Botticelli* gets under way as we wait. If you don't know it, it goes like this: someone chooses a famous person and tells the others the initial letter of his/her name; they then ask yes/no questions to try to guess the name. The first person to guess then chooses another famous person, and so it goes on. It's called *Botticelli* because people you choose are supposed to be at least as famous as Botticelli, but fame isn't a universal – it depends on the circles you move in – so there are usually arguments and, in my experience, the game frequently ends in recriminations and disarray. I've got a feeling that somebody suggests playing it in the second act of *Hay Fever*. I opt out today, anyway, and as Zada is entertaining Freda with an unfathomable Armenian counting game, my mind is empty enough for the contents of David's email, which I read this morning and which I've been suppressing ever since, to force themselves to my attention. Well, I refuse to accept that there was anything the matter with my email to him. He's still cross about missing out on a holiday, obviously, but I'm done with saying sorry. There's only so much apologising a woman can do and I reach my limit pretty quickly. So, he's sulking and going out of radio contact. Well, let him. It keeps things simple. And it looks like Mr Christodoulou isn't going to phone me either, so that's fine. Live in the moment. Freda and me, and a dozen screwed-up semi-adults. Lovely.

I suppose it's my preoccupation with these thoughts that explains how I come to have no premonition of what is about to happen. I would like to be able to tell you that when, eventually, the traffic starts to move, someone kindly lets us in and we crawl on towards home, this is the moment when a spine-tingling knowledge comes to me of what we shall find to be the cause of this queue, but in all honesty I can't. In honesty I have to admit that I am fully absorbed in self-reflection, and it is only when we draw level with the accident itself that, like everyone else, I see what has happened. A car transporter is slewed across the road and behind it, its front wedged cruelly beneath the transporter's back axle, its rear only exposed to view, is a pale blue car.

Without a word, Ray pulls over onto the verge and stops behind the police cars drawn up there. Two policemen walk over to us and Adam gets out of the van and goes round to talk to them. Zada has started to cry; Sophie mumbles, 'Sick!'

and stumbles out to throw up. The rest of us watch in silence the actions of officialdom. We see one of the policemen produce a notebook and Adam produce his passport; we see but can't hear dialogue – three-way and then two-way, between the policemen only; we watch as the three of them move to where something lies stiffly on the verge under a red blanket; we see a corner lifted, see Adam nod his head; see the corner dropped.

When Adam gets back into the van his mouth seems to be working too hard for the words that come out of it. 'An ambulance has taken Jon to hospital. He was conscious. Conrad –' he gestures in the direction of the blanket on the verge, '– is dead.' Nobody, I notice, looks at anyone else, and I guess they are all thinking more or less the same thing – that while they were engaged in the enjoyable business of tearing Conrad apart, the impact of steel on bone had finished the job off for them.

If we've all thought it then someone, I suppose, has to say it. Sophie screams into the silence, 'Don't you dare! Don't you bloody dare sit there pretending after all the things you were saying about him. You don't give a fuck about him, any of you, so don't pretend – just don't pretend.' She breaks off, thrusts her fist into her mouth and gives a great howl of grief. Zada goes and sits beside her, takes her in her arms and cradles her in her lap, weeping herself so that mascaraed tears drop onto Sophie's blonde head.

Adam climbs down from the van then calls back to Ray. 'They want me to stay for a bit,' he says. 'Give more details. You'd better go home. I'll make my own way back.' He speaks coolly enough and he has his usual air of easy authority but anyone who looks properly at him can see how hard he is working at staying composed. We can't leave him on his own, can we, on this foreign roadside, with the blue car protruding so obscenely from under the enormous transporter and the blanket-covered shape on the verge? I wonder if Annie might offer to stay with him but she does something else instead, and the last thing I'm expecting.

'Give Freda to me,' she tells me, 'and you stay with Adam. He can't stay here on his own and he needs someone with him who won't crack up.'

So here I am, standing on the verge, waving to Freda as the van draws away. I've no idea if Adam is glad to have me here but he says, 'Thanks,' which is polite of him, and in the interminable time that follows, as the police and recovery crew go about the routine business of violent death and seem to have forgotten about us, we even manage quite an interesting chat about *Hamlet*. In the end, it turns out that we're not really needed. The police take the address where we are staying and ask a few questions about when and why Conrad hired the car, then ask me to give a second identification. I don't know what to expect but I feel very little, actually, as one of them lifts the corner of the blanket. It is Conrad, of course, but the dead, I learn, don't look quite themselves.

One of the police cars drops us off at the villa, where we find some supper left for us but hardly anyone around. I find Annie in my room upstairs. She has put Freda to bed and is sitting with her iPad. 'Just emailing Ellie,' she whispers.

'Make sure you tell her Freda's fine,' I say. 'Where's everyone else?'

'Emailing, texting, updating their facebook pages.' She gets up and I follow her to the door. 'This is a drama,' she says dryly outside in the corridor. 'It has to be communicated to the world.'

'Thank you for looking after Freda.'

'Thank you for looking after Adam.'

'I think you must actually be fond of him.'

She shrugs. 'I dunno,' she says, and leaves.

Sophie isn't in our room. I glimpsed her curled up in a

corner of the *salon* with something Danish on the television. I look at my laptop sitting on the dressing table. I would quite like to do some communicating, to off-load some of today's drama, but David has put himself off limits and I can't think of anyone else to tell. I could almost work myself into a fury about David's dereliction and I'm almost tempted to ring him up and shout at him but I'm too tired. I'm so tired, in fact, that although it's not yet nine o'clock, I undress, get into bed with Freda and fall into a tangled sleep.

6

DAY FOUR

Of deaths put on by cunning and forced cause. 5.2

'Never mind *a comfortable night* – that doesn't mean anything. I expect you're quite comfortable if you're in a coma, aren't you? If you can't feel?'

There is a pause. Zada is pacing the verandah, phone in hand, and the pause suggests that a nurse at the Helsingør Sygehus is trying, patiently, to explain to her the niceties of patient confidentiality, but Zada is soon back in action. 'Well, good,' she says. 'I'm delighted that you've given full information to his parents – who, by the way, only knew about his accident because I told them – but it is ridiculous – ridiculous – if I've got to ring Scotland to find out myself about his injuries. So I really – what? Who am I? Well. My name is Zada Petrosian, and I happen to be Jon McIntyre's fiancée.' She has spotted me watching her from the *salon* doorway so she grimaces and turns round to waggle two crossed fingers behind her back. 'Well, I would have told you before if you'd given me half a chance. Right. Thank you. OK. A fractured femur – that's a broken leg, isn't it? OK. Well, he wasn't planning to be a ballet dancer. Yes. Yes. OK. And can he have visitors. OK. Well, thank you. That's all I needed to know.'

'Broken leg?' I ask, going onto the verandah. 'Anything else?'

'Torn back muscles. Cuts and bruises.'

'And he can have visitors?'

'Two till eight.'

'Sorry I listened in, but you were quite public.'

'I know. I can't get a signal up in my room.'

'So you rang Jon's parents?'

'I did.' She puts her phone in her pocket, flops onto one of the cane sofas that furnish the verandah and lights a cigarette. 'It was quite heroic of me, actually.'

'How did they take it?'

'Oh, Scottishly. You know – brisk and practical. No hysterics. Even though I couldn't reassure them much. Jon's father's a doctor so no doubt he got the full story out of them at the hospital.'

'Don't you love the way the Danes call a hospital a *sygehus*?' I ask her. 'A sick house. Just what it is. While we dress things up with words designed to disguise. A hospital originally means a guesthouse; a cemetery means a sleeping place – a dormitory. There's no Danish equivalent to 'pass away' – you just die in Danish – *dø*. It's refreshing.'

'They never liked me,' Zada says, in a nicely Pinteresque non seqitur. 'They thought I was a flibbertigibbet. They didn't want me to marry Jon but now that I'm not going to they like me even less because I've made their puir wee laddie sad.'

'Well, he's got something else to be sad about now.'

'Actually, his mother is quite a duck. She at least said thank you to me for ringing. "Thank you for telephoning, my dear. I expect it wasn't easy for you." Oh. Sorry. I'm going to blub again. The world's worst blubber, me. There's not a mascara to be had that can cope with the spurting fountains of my tear ducts.' She wipes a careful finger under each eye and looks at me. 'Do you suppose it was his fault?'

'The accident? Technically, it's always the fault of the vehicle behind, isn't it? Because it didn't stop in time.'

'So what the hell was he doing? It's so out of character for Jon to drive recklessly.'

'I assume it was Conrad's fault – that he came round and started trying to grab the wheel or something.'

'But how could anyone prove that? It would just be Jon's word.'

'I suppose the post mortem will show how much alcohol Conrad had inside him. And there must have been witnesses to the accident. There were some other drivers being questioned at the roadside yesterday. Someone may have seen what went on inside the car.'

'We shouldn't have let Jon take him. It was bloody Ray's fault – not wanting him to puke in his precious van.'

'Well, Jon volunteered. Come and have some breakfast. There's coffee made.'

'I will in a minute. I'll just finish this ciggie.'

Round the table in the kitchen a desultory discussion is going on about the way forward. Adam is proposing to replace Jon by playing Claudius himself and he suggests that Stefan Pienkowsky, who is playing Laertes, doubles as Rosencrantz. Annie is juggling the rehearsal schedule to give Adam some time to learn the lines. They are subdued, mildly ill-tempered, vaguely resentful. This game isn't fun any more.

As Annie is reading out the new rehearsal arrangements, Zada comes in. She stands in the doorway listening for a moment and then asks, 'Have you definitely decided to go ahead? I mean, have you talked about packing it in?'

The effect is extraordinary. Suddenly, they are all talking at once. The sluggish ill-humour of a moment ago is gone; everyone is animated, urgent. Suggestions, proposals, questions fly round the table. There is a way out of this adventure gone scary, and they're heading for the exit. Only

Sophie is still. I look across at her, expecting to share a shrug or a smile, but I encounter instead a face of blank, white panic.

Adam thumps the table to put up some resistance, pointing out that we have a contract with the castle authorities and there may be financial penalties for cancelling. When pushed, though, he admits that there are some get-out clauses and the death of a cast member might well be one of them. 'I've got the contract upstairs somewhere,' he says, 'I'll root it out.' Getting up to leave, he adds, 'We've paid for this place for three weeks, though. We won't get that money back. I'll need to talk to Alex.' He goes, and Sophie slips out after him, like a shadow.

'Alex?' I mouth at Annie.

'OUDS treasurer,' she mouths back.

With Adam gone, talk turns swiftly to the practicalities of getting home. Could ferry and plane tickets be exchanged? Who was going to make the phone calls? How soon could they get packed up? I sit watching them in mild amazement, waiting for someone to ask the question that's buzzing in my head. In the end, it's Annie who asks it.

'What about Jon?'

I can tell that it has been an effort to ask it, to break in on their happy relief. Her voice has come out too loud and people are startled. They stare at her and then eyes swivel to Zada, who is sitting at the table now, buttering a piece of bread. She looks up, the ready tears filling her dark, tragic eyes. 'What are you looking at me for?' she protests. 'I'm not responsible for him. I rang his parents and they'll probably be here in a day or two. What more do you want?'

'Well,' says Annie, eyeing her with the expression of cold dislike which I know only too well, 'don't you think someone ought to be here when they arrive?'

'And does anyone know,' I ask in the silence that follows, 'if Conrad's parents have been told? Do we think they'll be coming over? Who's going to make arrangements about – I don't know – flying the body home, I suppose?'

This time it's Adam we all turn to look at. He has returned with a document in his hand and is standing in the doorway. 'Jesus!' he says. 'Don't all look at me. The police are dealing with it. I don't know how to contact them. They're in LA, aren't they? And certainly ex-directory. I can't – look, I'm just the director of this thing – just the fucking director. I'm not responsible for everything. What did you think? That you could all sod off home and leave me to clear up the mess?' He looks angry and baffled as he did yesterday evening, puzzled at how scared this makes him when he has always carried responsibility so easily up till now.

Of course I'm the person who is going to have to stay, because I'm the grown-up here, but even as I think this I also think what an appealing idea it is. The villa is paid for, after all. Freda and I could have a wonderful time here. Maybe it's not too late for David to come and join us. And if Annie is so concerned about Jon, perhaps she will stay too, and she can help look after Freda. With rapid brush strokes my mind paints in the picture – Annie and Freda frisking in the sea while David and I walk hand in hand along the beach. Even wining and dining at the Marienlyst is not out of the question if Annie is here to babysit. It's all nonsense, of course. Even if David could be persuaded out of his sulk, the four of us together here would produce every kind of social dysfunction from tight lips and wounded silences on David's part to slammed doors and violent expletives on Annie's, not forgetting tears and tantrums from Freda and me. It is in the full knowledge of this that I hear myself say, 'I'm quite happy to stay and tie up the loose ends. I'm in no hurry to get back.' And then because I don't want to have to look Annie in the eye, I seize Freda, who has been eating Nutella, and bear her away to wash her face and hands.

What happens now? I wonder this as I'm fighting with Freda, who takes being washed as an assault on her human rights. I can hear movement below and feet on the stairs. The gathering has broken up, but to do what? Are they reading the small print on their plane tickets? Looking on line for the next flight out? Retrieving stray pieces of clothing with a view to packing their bags? What does Annie plan to do?

Going downstairs into the hall in search of her, I see two figures through the glass panels of the front door, darkly outlined against the sun. One raises an arm and bangs on the door; I open it and find myself confronted by two uniformed police officers, one male, one female. Freda immediately hides herself in my skirt and I don't blame her; they do look intimidating, not least because of their bulging gun holsters. How can it be that the police go around wearing guns in a nice, civilised place like Denmark? The man says something in Danish – probably nothing more alarming than 'good morning' – but the guns seem to have sent my brain into panic mode and all I can do is to shake my head in a vigorous mime of incomprehension. He looks me up and down and his eyes seem to linger for a moment on my breasts, which is something that hasn't happened to me for at least ten years, I would say. When I glance down at them myself, though, I see that my t-shirt is attractively adorned with tiny brown hand prints, just like they do at Nursery. Impassively he asks in English, 'Conrad Wagner was living here?' He pronounces the name like the composer rather than American-style and I'm almost about to correct him before I think better of it and simply say, meekly, 'Yes. Yes, he was.' They sweep past me into the hall, and over his shoulder, as he glances into the kitchen, the policeman asks, 'Is there someone who is in charge here?'

'Well, there's the director.'

'Director?'

'Of the play. We are – were – putting on a play here, at the castle. Shakespeare. Hamlet Prince of Denmark. It's a group from Oxford University.' I stop, and then add lamely, 'In England.'

'So you are students?'

'Well, I'm not, obviously. I'm just – I'm in charge of the costumes.'

'But the others are all students?'

'Yes. Well, most of them have just graduated, actually, so they – look, we told the police all this last night.'

The woman chips in for the first time. 'Those were traffic police only. Now we need to speak to you all. But first to your director. Is he here?'

'Did someone mention me?' To my relief, Adam emerges from the *salon*, coffee mug in hand. He takes in the two officers and sighs. 'More questions? I told your chaps every –'

The policeman cuts him off, barging past him into the room beyond. 'We first need to speak to you alone. In here, please.' The three of them disappear into the *salon* and close the door on me, but I recognise a drama in the making so I slip upstairs to change my t-shirt and come straight down again, in time to see the man leaving and the woman stationing herself inside the front door. Adam turns from the door and I see that his face is shiny with sweat. Then he starts shouting. He races first up the main staircase and bangs on bedroom doors, then thunders down and hares up the back stairs to the landing where our room is. Then he dashes out onto the verandah and calls out to the garden and the seashore below. He shouts names, apparently at random: 'James… Zada… Ray… James, where are you? … Zada … Down here. Everyone. Come down here. Now!'

It's just like Macduff rousing the household after he has found the king murdered in his bed. *'Banquo and Donalbain… Malcolm… Malcolm and Banquo…'* All we need is the great alarum bell clanging through the castle.

Doors start opening and Zada appears at the top of the stairs. 'Are we on fire?' she calls.

Adam turns to me. 'Get them all into the kitchen,' he says. 'I need a moment.'

Freda, who is as attuned to drama as the rest of the family, has started crying and is trying to climb up into my arms. I pick her up, while urging the others towards the kitchen and assuring Zada that fire is not the issue. Everyone else has noticed the policewoman standing by the front door, and that shuts them up.

Adam is standing by the back door. He waits for everyone to be still. He takes a breath. 'There's no easy way to say this, people, but you can forget about going home, at least in the immediate future. The police have been looking at Conrad's car. It was booby-trapped, apparently. They say someone tampered with the brakes. They're treating it as murder and we, of course, are their prime suspects.'

A moment's silence and then Zada laughs. 'Very good, darling. This is a wind-up, isn't it? You're 'avin' a larf.'

There is a breath of relief, an uncertain ripple of laughter, but Adam turns and opens the back door, pulling it back to reveal a policeman standing there. 'I assume you noticed the police presence in the hall as well. There's another of them in a car in the drive and one out on the verandah. *Resistance is futile; the house is surrounded.*'

'So what happens now?' It's James's voice, I think. I can't see well as everyone is standing and I'm only just inside the doorway.

'They want to interview us all. At the police station. Take statements. We'll have to wait and see what happens after that.'

'Do they want us to go right away?' Ray asks. 'And am I supposed to ferry everyone in the van or is there a fleet of police cars to take us down?'

'Don't be stupid, Ray.' Zada's voice is sharp. 'They're not arresting us for Christ's sake, are they, Adam? They just want statements, don't they?' She moves towards him. 'Did they say how long this will take?' she asks.

'Nope. They just said they wanted us to go now. If we go in the van, they say they'll lead the way. They trust us that far, anyway. So, get it organised will you, Ray?'

'Yessir.' He jangles his car keys. 'Come on you lot, let's be 'avin' you. At the double, quick march.'

There is, however, no *quick march* about it. For a start, the van will only take half of us at a time and Ray has to go and negotiate with the policeman in the car and return to say that we will be interviewed in alphabetical order, so top of the alphabet go on the first trip. We turn out to be less use than a bunch of primary school kids at putting ourselves into alphabetical order and Annie has to fetch a cast list and call us out: 'James Asquith, Adam Barrie, Emma Dalton, Clare Dartmouth, Sophie Forrester – and then there's me and Gina. That'll be the first lot.'

'And Freda,' I mutter. A morning in a police station with Freda. Such interesting challenges life brings.

Even now, we are hardly fast in getting ourselves organised. People wander vaguely, looking for jackets, bags and shoes; queues form outside the three bathrooms. Eventually we climb into the van, and we're all very quiet, busy in our own heads, so that it takes a while for me to notice that Zada is with us, sitting the other side of Adam, who is next to me.

'What are you doing here?' I mouth across to her, drawing a large P for Petrosian in the air.

She turns her soulful eyes to me. 'Had to be with Adam,' she mouths back, lifting a hand that is clutching his. It seems Adam isn't comfort enough, though, because in a moment she's on her phone, talking urgently in what I take to be Armenian. By the time she has finished, she is weeping again and everyone in the van is watching her. She shoves the phone into her bag, pulls out a handful of tissues and blows her nose.

'What?' Adam asks. His body language tells me he doesn't want to deal with this; he is edging along in my direction.

'My bloody father,' she storms. *'Make sure you have your papers with you, Zada*, he says, when he knows that all the *papers* I've got are a sodding Armenian passport.'

We all look a bit blank, not quite seeing the purport of this.

'I didn't think of passports,' Adam says. 'But it doesn't matter. We can always fetch them later if they need to see them.'

'That's not the point,' Zada storms. 'You've all got nice British passports. Mine's Armenian!'

'So?'

'So, it's weird. I'm weird. All my life, at airports, there's all the normal people going smugly through the EU passports channel and I'm in the other one, with the burkha women and the hairy men. I might as well be carrying a placard that says *Real Foreigner – probably terrorist.'*

'Americans go through the non-EU channel,' James remarks and Zada bares her teeth at him.

'Weren't you born in the UK?' I ask.

'No. My parents came here when I was two. Twenty years Daddy's been here and he won't apply for British citizenship.'

'Why?'

'It's a ridiculous affectation – it shows he's a patriot! If he loves Armenia so bloody much, why doesn't he want to be there? I mean, I don't mind that we have to celebrate the festivals and eat the peasant food that goes with them, but this passport thing – I knew it would be a disaster one day.'

'Couldn't you have applied for citizenship yourself?' Adam asks, 'Once you were eighteen?'

'Daddy said not. He forbade me to do it.'

There is a silence and she looks round at us all. 'All right, so I could have done it anyway, but I didn't. I was too feeble and now I shall pay for it. Can't you just see it? If things get really scary, they'll send the British ambassador to sort you all out, but me? Oh, Armenian – nothing to do with us. And I'll be the one that gets thrown to the wolves.'

'Hardly to the wolves, Zada,' Adam says. 'This is Denmark, after all. EU – Human Rights Act – all that.'

'But where there might actually be wolves,' I mutter under my breath.

'And you don't know much about the diplomatic service if you think an ambassador is going to be dealing with a group of students who've got themselves into a sticky situation,' says James. 'More likely some entry level graduate who's got no idea what's going on. And anyway, as you said, I believe, we're not being arrested. We're just witnesses. All we have to do is give our statements and that will be that.'

'But somebody did whatever they did to the brakes of that car, didn't they? And we're their only suspects. They're going to keep us here until they find someone to pin it on, aren't they?'

'What I don't understand,' Ray calls from the front, 'is why they're so sure it's murder. It was a bloody hire car, wasn't it? They've always got something wrong with them. I mean, I don't want to worry anyone but who knows what the brakes are like on this thing? And Conrad knew there was something wrong with it – that's why he was working on it. Only he was an idiot and didn't know wh –' He breaks off. *Nil nisi bonum* after all.

'Well, I assume the police know what they're talking about.' Adam sounds tetchy. 'If they say the brakes were tampered with they must have a good reason.'

Clare, who is sitting opposite me, murmurs something to Emma, who says, 'Yes. Why shouldn't the person who hired the car before Conrad have done it? I know you'd have to be a lunatic to just randomly make a death trap for the next

72

person who hired the car, but people do kill randomly, don't they?'

'They kill randomly, yes,' James says, 'but they want to be there to see people die. What you suggest would be very odd, wouldn't it? Because they'd never know what mayhem they'd actually caused, and that would spoil their fun.' No-one responds and after a moment he goes on, 'And anyway, it's obvious, isn't it, that the damage had to be done yesterday afternoon?'

'Why? I don't see why. The brakes could have been damaged but the car still driveable and then, bang, on the way home they went. Couldn't they?' Zada turns to Adam, but it's James who answers.

'No, they couldn't, because if there had been anything wrong with them yesterday morning, Conrad would have noticed it when he was tinkering so knowledgeably all morning with me as his faithful tool-bearer. Apply some logic, woman.'

'I am – and don't patronise me. Maybe, like Ray says, Conrad wasn't the expert he made himself out to be. You know how he was. Sorry, Sophie, but we have to be honest. I mean –'

'He knew what he was doing,' Sophie says very quietly, as though her throat is full of dust. 'He adored cars. He told me he didn't go back to LA last summer. He spent the long vac in Oxford. He got a job in a garage. He loved it.'

Zada, furious, throws herself back in her seat. 'Well, for fuck's sake someone else come up with an explanation,' she growls.

I summon to mind the pale blue Mustang as I saw it in the castle car park at lunch time yesterday, a sleek and exotic beast among the dusty camper vans and family saloons, attractive prey for thieves and vandals. As if she has read my mind, Clare says, 'Anyone could have cut the cable while it was parked. It doesn't have to have been one of us. And they could have hung around to see what happened when the driver came back, which gets over James's objection that they'd want to see the mayhem.'

'They'd need to jack it up,' Ray says. It'd be pretty obvious what they were doing. And they'd need to get the jack out of the boot. Are we sure that Conrad locked it?'

'I locked it,' James says abruptly. 'I put the tools and the jack away and I locked it. So,' he looks round us with an unamused smile, 'we seem rather to have run out of options.'

7

HOLIDAY

If you were in a hot air balloon, David Scott thought, they would not look human at all, these prone bodies, turning and shifting down below. It was barely 10.30 but the sun was high and fierce and bodies of all shades, from flawless black to freckled white, were laid out like sacrifices on the sand.

Holidays, in his view, were just weekends gone viral, the days multiplying to nightmare numbers. A weekend you could dispose of: lie-ins, leisurely breakfasts, domestic chores that couldn't be put off any longer, a long walk, a good book, a bit of TV, and there was always the option of going into the station and putting in some unpaid overtime. And recently there had been Gina at weekends. They hadn't been perfect, admittedly, but they weren't boring either. This two weeks' leave, though, was driving him up the wall. It was day four now and he had done everything on his mental to-do list, including things like mending the garden fence which he had never intended to get round to. By now he was ready to kill somebody in the hope of being called in to investigate his own crime. He could have been doing something interesting, of course. He could have spent this leave on a dig somewhere, as he had in the past, but by the time plans for the trip to Denmark with Gina had unravelled it had been too late to organise anything. 'Not going off somewhere with your other half?' one of his colleagues had asked him and he had failed to come up with a reply, so pole-axed was he by imagining Gina's response to being called his *other half.*

It was a riff she had done more than once – her *what are we supposed to call each other?* routine, in which he played the stooge. *Boyfriend?* 'Absolutely not for anyone over thirty.' *Partner?* 'Requires one to share a home, a child or a bank account – none of which we do or intend to do.' *Lover?* 'Implies a passion we may find it hard to live up to.' *Friend?* Too arch – as in *just good friends,* though it's the one I use for want of a better.' *Significant other?* 'Well you are certainly other, and I guess you're significant, but try using that in any normal sentence!' *Other half* he hadn't suggested, but he could supply her answer: 'I'm forty-eight years old and a complete person, thank you, David. I don't feel there are bits of me missing.'

He missed her. That was the truth. She was a hair shirt but he missed the itch. Announcing that he was cutting off email contact had been a tactical error, however furious he had been with her. He had, in fact, checked for messages since and found only the usual spam and scams. One thing to be said for Gina, she could tell a good story and he would have enjoyed her updates. He took out his phone and took a picture of the beach. He tried to think of an appropriate message and phrases from her email were offering themselves to him as ironic possibilities; *deciding to have a crap time* seemed the most appropriate but, on the principle that a picture was worth however many thousand words, he sent the photo just as it was.

It hardly constituted an apology, he reflected, as he turned into the town. If she answered at all, it would be to admonish him for sulking still, but at least it would be a response and he could take it from there. He headed for Dyke Road and a walk on the downs up above the town and away from the crowds. It was not a planned walk and he had no hat, no sun block and no water with him. *Autorhinectomy* Gina would have called it, and he would really have liked to hear her say it.

8

MORE FOUR

There is nothing either good or bad but thinking makes it so. 2.2

The *Politistation* is in a maze of streets in the middle of the town and is not at all what I envisaged. Cool, modern and shiny with glass was what I had in mind, but it is, instead, old and formidable with a square stone front outside and a high, echoing reception area inside. 'It's the Ministry of Truth,' Adam mutters as we are led along corridors and up steps, but the room we are taken to is reassuring. True, it has small windows set high in the wall, but it is furnished with decent chairs, magazines, a hot drinks dispenser and a fairly healthy plant in a pot. There is also, blessedly, a small play area with child-sized bean bags to sit on and, since we are in the birthplace of Lego, a plastic crate of the stuff.

As we settle ourselves to wait and Freda is absorbed in the novelty of the Lego (which won't last long – Freda is no embryo engineer, but for the moment she is enjoying bashing the pieces randomly together) I contemplate this little company of ours – seventeen of us originally, now reduced to fifteen. Fifteen may still seem too many people for you to take on board, I realise, even with a programme to help you, and in the interests of full disclosure, I should tell you that you have met all the really significant players in this drama already; the others are bit part players you don't need to worry about.

The interviews start slowly; James is away for a long time, and while he is out, the second group from the villa arrives, so the room is full when he comes back from his grilling. He looks superficially as cool as ever. His default expression is something close to a George Osborne smirk and that is still in place; I notice, though, that when he goes to get himself a coffee from the machine, his hand is shaking. No-one asks him how it went. Adam goes out to be interviewed after James and returns from his session looking furious – which is becoming his default mode at the moment. 'I'm out of here,' he says, picking up his jacket. 'Coming, James?'

'Did they say you could go?'

'Yes. Didn't they say that to you?'

James gives a bark of a laugh. 'No, they asked me to stick around.'

'Oh. Right. Well, I'm off anyway.'

Zada turns as if to protest but Adam stops behind her chair to pat her on the shoulder, as one might a nervous horse, and disappears. Zada jumps up and paces round the room. 'I need a ciggie,' she moans, 'and I can't even open a window and puff out of it.' She looks round the room. 'How many people are before me?' she demands. A few hands are waved at her. She counts them. 'Emma, Clare, Sophie, Marianne, Gina, Kelly, Alan. Six. And James and Adam were each in – what – half an hour? That's three hours. Aagh.' She throws herself back down on her chair. 'Three hours without a ciggie. That's just cruel. I shall be a nervous wreck by then. I'll be ready to confess to anything.'

If she was expecting a response, she'll be disappointed, and if she is wanting to be the centre of attention she's got competition from Freda, who has tired of the Lego and has devised a better game which involves crawling under people's chairs and tickling their legs. When reprimanded, she insists that she is 'just being a cat' and refuses to stop.

Emma and Clare are both in and out of their interviews quite rapidly but by the time Sophie goes in, Freda is rolling on the floor with boredom and no-one, not even Zada, has the will to distract her. I look across the room at Annie. 'Why don't I go in next?' I say. 'Then I can take Freda away. It doesn't matter which Gray goes first, does it?' She gives a non-committal shrug but when Sophie returns and the policewoman calls, 'Marianne Gray,' she's off, leaving me to pacify Freda as best I can by sitting her on my lap and playing *This is the Way the Lady Rides*, which is probably even more annoying to my fellow murder suspects than Freda's solo wrigglings.

When Annie gets back, I thrust Freda at her and hiss savagely, 'You look after her. I'm not taking her in with me. Don't go anywhere.' As I go out, I hear Freda set up a wail behind me, and Annie is, no doubt, sticking knives in my back.

By comparison with the waiting room, the room where I'm interviewed feels calm and airy. It's not one of those threatening, windowless places you see in TV crime dramas; it's more of an office, really, with a window open to the summer breeze. Because I experience life almost entirely through the medium of fiction, *The Killing* has been in my mind all morning and I have, of course, been half expecting to see Sarah Lund. And even when I don't find her here, I don't immediately think *Of course not, she's not real* but rather, *Of course not, she works in Copenhagen*. I'm admitting this to you though I wouldn't to anyone else because I know it makes me sound stupid.

Instead of Sarah, with her scruffy ponytail and laser eyes – and the jumper, of course – there is a man of fiftyish, tall and thin – almost cadaverous – with receding blond hair and small, humorous blue eyes. 'Anders Mortensen,' he says, shaking my hand, and I make a note to tell David that the Danish police really do introduce themselves by their first names; there's no intimidation by rank here. Mortensen has a young woman officer there with him but she is not Sarah either. She is square and solid, with red hair cut unattractively short. She introduces herself as Ingrid Larsen.

Mortensen starts with the expected questions: first, what I'm doing here in Elsinore, which takes a bit of explaining even to myself at the moment, and then when I last saw Conrad – or Wagner, as he refers to him. Had I seen anyone near his car? Was I aware of anyone having a grudge against him? When I give a breezy 'no' to this last question, he leans forward and looks at me over the top of his rimless half moon specs. 'But he himself had a grudge, I understand.'

'A grudge? Well, I suppose – yes. He just thought he should have been playing Hamlet.'

'And instead James Asquith plays Hamlet. How did he show it – this grudge?'

'Childishly, to be honest. Sniping.'

'Sniping? As with a gun?'

'No, no. As with words. Just nasty remarks. Nothing really. And then they seemed to have made it up, anyway.'

'Seemed?'

'Well, did. Only then –' I stop. I suppose I should tell him about the row by the car. 'Some of us went down to the car park to fetch Conrad and James for lunch. They seemed fine then, but the others went off for lunch and I was delayed – I've got a toddler with me on this trip – and I saw Conrad apparently lose his temper.'

'What exactly did you see?'

'Well, I thought for a moment that he was going to hit James with the jack he was holding, but actually he just threw it down and walked off.'

'And Asquith, what did he do?'

'Tidied up, put things back in the boot, locked the car, walked away.'

'In which direction?'

'Towards the castle.'

'Excellent.' Disconcertingly, he leans back in his chair and beams at me. He picks up a typed sheet from among the papers on his desk. 'An excellent witness. Your account matches exactly what the gatekeeper at the castle saw.'

'Is it his job to watch the car park?'

'He is not, I think, happy that your company is here. He was expecting trouble. And it seems he was right.'

I'm not sure I like the way this is going and while I'm in his good books as an excellent witness I decide to try and put him straight a bit. 'Look,' I say, 'they're not criminals. They're just young – twenty-one or twenty-two, stressed out after exams, hormones rampant, relationships in flux, egos a bit inflated – but I can't believe any one of them is a murderer.'

He looks at me for a bit and then says, 'But this is a case of murder. The damage to the car was not accidental and a young man died. Another young man was injured and could have been killed as well. If none of these young people are responsible, then what is your explanation?'

'Well, we talked about it this morning as we were driving in here, and it seems the damage to the car must have been done in the afternoon because otherwise Conrad would have seen it in the morning. He really did know about cars apparently – but I expect Sophie Forrester told you that?'

He says nothing and I plough on. 'So, somebody vandalised the car in the afternoon, but it wasn't one of us because we were all together, rehearsing.'

'And before that you were all eating lunch together?'

'Yes.'

'And James Asquith joined you for lunch?'

'No, he went back into the castle, but – well, I'm sure Ray

Porter was with him – they were together when the rest of us got back.'

He makes a note. 'Well, we shall be talking to Porter later on.'

He sits looking at me in a way that is making me feel uncomfortable, but it is Ingrid Larsen who rouses herself from her stolid silence and says, 'Virginia?' I open my mouth to say *Oh, Gina, please* but she is pressing on. 'I was surprised that you are so anxious to defend Asquith. No-one else we have spoken to this morning was interested to defend him, not even, I may say –' and here she glances at Mortensen, ' – Asquith himself.'

I don't think this deserves more than a shrug but just as I'm brushing it off she says, 'I am wondering what is your relationship with Asquith. Your daughter told us something interesting. She said you were happy to be here because you like being with young people.' She glances at her notes, but I think it's only for show. 'She said you have a boyfriend who was your student before.'

I am speechless for a moment as outrage at Annie's thoughtlessness and this woman's stupidity fight with one another. Then I laugh. It's not all that convincing as laughs go because it has to force its way past all the rage that's clogging my throat up, but it's good enough. 'Oh, language is such a trap, isn't it?' I say, addressing myself firmly to Anders Mortensen. '*Boyfriend*. Really, age thirty is the absolute upper limit for *boyfriend* and *girlfriend*, don't you think? We really don't have an appropriate term in English for later life companions. Do you have anything better in Danish? Well, anyway, I don't know what kind of theory Ingrid here is dreaming up about my hanging around with these students because I'm some sort of predatory cradle-snatcher, but when my daughter spoke of my boyfriend, she will have been referring to a good friend of mine who is forty-three years old and –' I am about to say that he's a

83

detective chief inspector in the British police force, but something warns me off; it might just alienate them '– and is a respected professional man,' I finish rather lamely. Mortensen smiles; Ingrid shrugs sullenly and busies herself with her notes. I turn to her. 'And if you were wondering about the three-year-old child I have with me, she's not a love-child of my hormonal middle age. I'm her grandmother. And that's a role I'm very happy with.'

This is not strictly true, of course – the being happy bit. I'm very happy to have Freda in my life but I do balk at the idea of *grandmother* being my primary descriptor. You see it in newspaper reports, don't you? *Grandmother on Drugs Charge.* As though being a grandmother is supposed to disqualify you from being anything else – criminal or otherwise. But the real point is, if I'm honest, that whenever I mention that I have a granddaughter, I do expect people to gasp in disbelief and cry, *But you can't be old enough.* It is disappointing how rarely this happens.

Mortensen steps in smoothly to reclaim the interrogation and takes me back to where we were before Ingrid stuck her podgy nose in. 'So you say none of your company can have damaged the car yesterday afternoon and yet, I have to repeat, somebody did damage it. So then I would have to think that Conrad Wagner had some enemy here in Elsinore, who is not a member of your company?'

He turns this into a question so I feel I have to offer an answer, though I really don't have one. 'It seems unlikely, I know,' I say reluctantly. 'I don't suppose he knew anyone here – why would he? Though –' I remember suddenly the way Conrad came across the courtyard, crowing, the day he got the car. He looked at James and said, *I got it from Karin's brother,* didn't he? I remember I thought Karin might be the woman I saw James talking to in the car park the day we arrived, but then everything got dramatic and I haven't thought about it since. '– well,' I end lamely, 'I think he may have known the man he hired the car from.'

'Really?' He looks genuinely surprised.

'At least, he seemed to know his sister.'

He makes a note, then sits looking at me in silence. It seems to be my turn so I ask a question I wanted to ask earlier but I got sidetracked.

'If the gatekeeper was so interested in what was going on in the car park, didn't he see anyone near the car that afternoon?'

'Unfortunately, he finished his shift at one o'clock. The man who replaced him was not so interested in the car park.'

He is looking at me again, as though assessing me. It's becoming more like a job interview than a police interrogation.

'I have asked everyone this,' he says, 'but I suspect that politics are not of much interest to these young people just now. What is your opinion about this new Harmony Party in the UK?'

This was the last question I expected.

'Why do you ask?'

He spreads his hands in an expansive gesture. 'I am trying to view the whole picture.'

'And that includes the political activities of James Asquith's father?'

'Certainly.' He leans back smiling, waiting.

'Right. Well, my opinion of the Harmony Party. You know what sort of party it is, do you?'

'I know absolutely nothing. Until this morning I had not heard of it.'

'Have you heard of the Respect Party?'

'Respect? No.'

'Right. Well, briefly, Respect is a new party, set up to appeal to disaffected Labour – left wing – voters, especially Muslims because it has an anti-racism stance and it opposed the Iraq war. It's had quite a lot of success in areas with a large Muslim population but its founder is a very dodgy character and many people can't stand him and there have been ructions in the party. I'm telling you this because I think Harmony is a sort of response to Respect. Sir Bruce Asquith, James's father, was a diplomat. He had postings all over, I think, but he was an expert on the Middle East. He speaks Arabic and has written books about the area.'

'And his son also studies Arabic and is preparing a thesis on a great work of Arabic literature?'

'I believe so, yes. Well, his father's aim in setting up this Harmony Party seems to be to get people in the UK to embrace Arabic culture as it was in its golden age, when the Arab world was an intellectual centre for science, medicine, philosophy and so on, and Europe was still in the Dark Ages. He wants to reclaim Islamic culture from the angry men with beards and set it alongside the Judaeo-Christian as a third strand in our cultural heritage.'

'And who will vote for this party?'

'Well, I wouldn't. I'm in favour of a party that looks forward rather than back. It's a general rule that the further back you look, the worse things are for women. But then Muslim women turned out in droves to vote for Respect, so who knows? But actually, there is a target electorate. Sir Bruce, I suspect, is pretty naïve about the realities of politics but he's got people around him who see a burgeoning Muslim middle class – small business owners, entrepreneurs, lawyers, doctors et cetera – who are natural Conservative voters economically but who see the Conservatives as exclusive and racist. They're the target. But small parties don't actually get anywhere in the UK, of course, because we don't have PR.'

'So, you would say this is not a serious party?'

'I think it's a bit of a vanity exercise. People like setting up small parties because they get attention. They get to go on TV.'

'Who would be financing such a party?'

'If I'm cynical, I'd say the Iranian government – through clever back channels, obviously – but I expect it's just Muslim millionaires.'

He takes a card out of his pocket. 'Well, that is most interesting. Thank you for your help, Virginia,' he says.

'Gina,' I say. 'I'm called Gina.'

'Gina. I'm afraid we shall have to take your passport from you, Gina, as we're taking everyone's, but in exchange here is my card. If you think of anything else to tell me, anything at all, please call.'

Annie rushes off as soon as I reappear in the waiting room, so I shall have to postpone shouting at her till later. I give a half-hearted tidy to the Lego, gather up Freda and head out in search of lunch. Freda is droopy and fretful with boredom, and she is probably hungry too. I'm certainly starving. Breakfast got aborted this morning and it has been a stressful few hours. I'm so hungry, in fact, that instead of going looking for an attractive café, I stop at an odoriferous stall in the pedestrian precinct and ask, 'How about a hot dog, Freda?'

Her face breaks into a beaming smile. 'With runny ketchup?' she asks.

'Certainly,' I say, eyeing the list of condiments on the stall. *Ketchup* is the same in Danish, as you might expect since it's an Indian word to start with, but some of the other delights on offer are mysterious. What is *sennep*? Or *løg*? I see that you can order *med det hele* and, assuming that this means *with everything*, I decide to go for broke myself, while sticking to ketchup for Freda. We sit down on a bench and my pungent bundle, oozing mustard, ketchup and some rather dubious dried onion flakes, has to be set aside because Freda needs all my attention. Hot dogs, I see now, are not designed for three-year-old mouths, and while she struggles determinedly to sink her pearly little teeth into it, the ketchup is dribbling all over her pretty pink t-shirt.

I am useless at this. I sit dabbing ineffectually with a tissue and crying, 'Oh do try not to tip it, Freda.' We are rescued by Clare and Emma, who appear from the direction of the market with bags of vegetables and take things in hand. 'Budge along, Gina,' Clare says, and sits beside Freda, taking the hot dog and – why didn't I think of this? – taking it apart and feeding it to her bit by bit. Emma, meanwhile, has produced a pack of wet wipes from her bag, with which everyone's hands get cleaned and the worst of the ketchup bloodstains are removed from the t-shirt. I take a few bites of my hot dog, which is getting cool and is really not very nice.

They are truly wonderful girls, these two. Before the possibility has even formed in my mind, let alone been phrased as a request, Emma says, 'Ray's given us the keys of the van. We're going to the supermarket for the rest of the stuff. Do you want to come, Freda?'

Does she want to come? Of course she does. Do I want a couple of hours to myself? Of course I do. Showering blessings on them, I watch them depart, swinging Freda between them. Then I consider what I'm going to do. I walk to the end of the precinct, to where the buses go from, thinking that I will just go back to the villa, but I see, when I get there, that buses run to the hospital from here too, and this confirms my niggling feeling that somebody really ought to go and see Jon. I guess Zada might do it – for the drama of it as much as anything else – but she will be stuck at the police station for a while yet, until officers Mortensen and Larsen work their way down to 'P', and I'm afraid no-one else will think of it. So, since there is a bus standing there at the stop, I hop onto it, giving the driver a hundred-kronor note for my fare, which he doesn't like.

On the bus, the woman sitting next to me scowls at the remains of my hot dog in its stained and greasy wrappings, gurgles something incomprehensible and points to a notice at the front of the bus which I take to be a series of prohibitions:

Rygning forbudt

Mad og drikke forbudt

Henkastning af affald forbudt

One of these – *mad og drikke*, I assume – forbids me to bring my undesirable lunch with me. I get up and drop it in the bin, where it will, no doubt, stink the bus out for the rest of the day.

I'm quite interested in all this forbidding that is going on. We in the UK, aren't often forbidden, are we? The most direct prohibitions we get are of the *no smoking* variety (and I'm told that when you get off the ferry on the Isle of Mull, you are greeted by no sign of welcome but by a notice bearing a large NO, followed by no fewer than twenty-one forbidden activities). More usually, though, we are told that activities are *not permitted*, or, more politely, that we are *requested to/not to*. Sometimes we may even be entreated, as in *Please do not walk on the grass*, or – a bit over the top, this – thanked, as in *Thank you for not smoking*. Forbidden we are not. Is that because we Brits are particularly averse to being ordered about or simply because we have a greater variety of linguistic strategies available to us? Years ago, when I was a teenager, I went to Switzerland on a school skiing trip. I was hopeless at the skiing – timid and reckless by turns – but I enjoyed the *après-ski*, and my friend Jessica and I acquired boyfriends of a sort, with whom we wandered the streets of Grindelwald hand in hand. If we ever attempted a snog, however, we would find a finger wagged at us by some Swiss *hausfrau* with the admonition, *Verboten auf der strasse!* We thought this was hilarious and wonderfully Germanic. *Verboten auf der strasse* was our catch phrase for the whole of the following term.

(The following year, we went on a cultural trip to Italy and, on a day excursion to Venice, I was bought a very expensive cup of coffee in Piazza San Marco by a charming young Italian, who kissed me on departure without raising any public protest. Calvinism has a lot to answer for.)

This train of thought keeps me happily engaged until we reach the hospital. If the police station was surprisingly old-fashioned, the hospital is all one might expect of Scandinavian design – its exterior white, spacious and gleaming and its interior cool, dim and hushed. I find a loo first of all and attempt to remove the remaining ketchup stains from my face and hands. My clothes, I'm afraid, are beyond help. I find a reception desk, give Jon's name and am given directions to his ward which, though given in impeccable English, sound impossibly complicated. I am rescued by a woman also making enquiries at the desk, who says she is going in that direction and leads me a good part of the way.

Jon is in a room on his own – are they all single bed wards here? The door is ajar and I can see him propped up in bed with one leg suspended in a sort of cradle. As I push the door open, I realise that there is someone else here too, sitting by the bed. She turns, looking murderous. She is Annie. Filled with confusion, I start to back out, apologising. 'Sorry, sorry. Didn't mean to barge in. Just wanted to know you were all right. I'll just...' I'm back outside again when he calls out, 'Don't go, Gina. It's kind of you to come. There's another chair here. Come and join us.' What a nice, civilised chap he is. I re-enter cautiously, my eyes on Annie. She, I can see, is swallowing her rage. Jon is a person around whom people like to behave well, I've noticed. Was that what Zada liked? Or didn't like?

He looks pretty battered, with a black eye and a nasty graze down one side of his face. It is his left leg that rests in the cradle and there is bandaging round his left wrist. I start with the usual enquiries about injuries and pain and he plays it all down in a blasé, medical kind of way. Then I edge onto more tricky territory. 'Sorry if you've covered this already,' I say, glancing at Annie, 'but have the police been to see you?'

'Oh yes. First thing this morning, while I was still dopey. I've just been telling Marianne, I thought they'd come to charge me with dangerous driving but I found they were treating me like a victim.'

'Did they tell you about the car's brakes?'

'They were pretty cagey, but Marianne told me. It's hard to take in, frankly. So it looks as though someone was out to get Conrad?'

'And you're in the happy position of being the only one of us who isn't a suspect,' Annie says, reclaiming the conversation from me. 'So what did they ask you about?'

'A bit about the accident itself. Why was I driving? Did I notice anything wrong with the car? What did I remember about the crash itself? That sort of thing.'

'And do you remember it?'

'I do, unfortunately. I imagine I'll be getting flashbacks for some time to come. I did think the braking was soft, but I've never driven anything other than my parents' cars so I didn't have much to compare it with. I wasn't worried, I was just aware of it. Then I got onto the dual carriageway and I started to pull out to overtake a transporter but I realised there was something coming up fast on the outside so I pulled back in and braked and – nothing. I remember standing on the brake, trying not to panic, and then I don't remember the next bit. Bang on the head. Shock. Whatever.'

Annie reaches out a hand to touch his. 'Sorry,' she says. 'I didn't mean to make you tell it all over again.'

'Don't worry. Won't be the last time, I expect. After that, though, the policemen's questions got very odd. They've got hold of the idea that I must be a friend of Conrad's – because I was driving him in his car, I suppose. Anyway, they kept asking me questions about him I couldn't answer. I didn't know him. Different college, different subject. And this is the first OUDS thing I've done. I've only done college stuff before.'

'I knew him a bit,' Annie says. 'What did they want to know?'

'Mainly to do with his father. I knew he was a Hollywood producer, of course, but they were interested in his political activities. He's a major donor to the Organisation of Zionist Americans, or something of the sort, apparently.'

'The Zionist Organisation of America,' I chip in.

'Exactly. And he's had death threats from Islamic extremists, it seems.'

'And they think Conrad was a victim of Islamic extremists?'

'It's a line of inquiry, they told me. They wanted to know if Conrad ever talked of getting threats.'

'Not that I ever heard,' Annie says. 'And I'm sure we'd have heard if there was anything to tell. Conrad wasn't one to miss out on being centre stage in a bit of drama. Attention-seeking doesn't begin to cover it.'

'*Nil nisi bonum*, Annie,' I murmur, and she has the grace to blush.

'So,' I say, 'it's possible the police are dreaming up a global conspiracy theory to explain Conrad's death. Do you remember the names of the officers who questioned you?'

'No. I was pretty dopey at that point.'

'A tall, skinny guy in charge? Receding hair?'

'Yes.'

'Anders Mortensen. I got the other end of this story. He wanted to know about Sir Bruce Asquith and the Harmony Party.'

'Which is pro-Islam, isn't it?' Annie asks.

'It is,' Jon replies, 'and I begin to see where this might be going. Can it possibly be that they are thinking of fitting James up as an Islamic terrorist assassin?'

'When in fact, the most likely explanation for the failed brakes is incompetence at the garage or random vandalism.'

Jon leans back against his pillows and closes his eyes. 'I don't know whether to laugh or weep,' he says.

'Oh, both,' I say. 'It's nearly always a matter of both, I find.'

9

AND MORE FOUR

Where be your gibes now? 5.1

I don't stay long, since Annie is clearly in occupation, but by the time I get outside I find a thunderstorm is well under way, rain falling in huge drops from a hot, heavy sky. I cram in with others under a shelter at the bus stop but my t-shirt is already soaked and my hair plastered to my head. It is not yet half past four on a July afternoon but the light is livid and, as I watch the rain bouncing off the road surface, I comfort myself with the reflection that this is, at least, the setting I expect for a Danish murder inquiry. Based on my assiduous viewing of *The Killing*, I believe that all police work in Denmark happens in the rain at night and by torchlight.

It's a long and tedious journey home with a change of bus back at Axeltorv, but it is enlivened when I turn my phone on. I do it in order to send a reassuring text to Ellie, since I know Annie's propensity to catastrophise and I worry about the tone of the emails she may be sending her. I find that I have a text message and that the sender is David. I have been determined not to contact him ever since he declared an email blackout and I feel so smug about his cracking first that I consider ignoring the message in case he thinks I've been checking my phone obsessively, waiting for his call. I see that the message was sent this morning, though, so I've made my point without even deciding to make it. I open the message to find that I have been sent a picture of people lying on a beach. I squint hard at it to see if any one of those people is David, but I can't spot him. I scrabble about in the virtual recesses of my phone to see if I have missed some accompanying text but find nothing. So, the picture is the message: *here is Brighton beach.* Does this mean, *I am here on the beach just like you advised* or does it mean *This is the beach – does it look any fun to you?* Apology or sneer? I've never been good at the visual – I'm illiterate with cartoons. I need words, as David well knows. He is deliberately putting me at a disadvantage. I decide to play safe. I press my phone against the bus window to take a picture of the streaming road through rain-battered glass and send it without a message. Let him work it out. *Wish you were here? You think you've got problems?* Or just *Piss off?*

I'm feeling clammy and shivery by the time I get back to the villa. I find the others gathered on the verandah at the back with the glass doors closed against the slanting rain and the sea below dense and metallic in the strange light. The air in here is heavily warm and damp and there is a powerful smell of garlic emanating from vast, sliced pizzas which are being eaten almost in silence and without benefit of knives and forks.

'No-one got much lunch,' Clare says, 'so we decided on an early supper.'

Freda is sitting up at the table, perched on a pile of cushions, munching pizza with grave concentration. She has tomato sauce in her hair. It occurs to me that her diet today has been less than ideal: cocopops for breakfast, hot dog for lunch, pizza for supper. And God knows how much ice cream and chocolate she has consumed in the course of the afternoon. I vow to do better tomorrow, give her a kiss and help myself to a slice of pizza. I am starving and it tastes delicious.

I take Freda upstairs for a bath when we have both had

enough, and I change my own wet clothes and dry my hair. Then we do bedtime story and the rest of the nighttime routine, which seems to gather accretions day by day. Eventually, I go back downstairs and find everyone still on the verandah. The pizzas have been demolished and lager straight from the can seems to be the post-prandial drink of choice. I take a can and retire to a shadowy corner where I hope my ineptness at slurping from it won't be noticed.

The conversation is about future plans and it is remarkably different in tone from the discussion at breakfast this morning. I gather quite quickly that all passports have been confiscated and that the police line is that we may have to be here for some time. Inevitably, then, they have come back to the question of whether to go ahead with the production. This morning there seemed to be the chance to cut and run; this evening they have to decide how to cope with staying. Actually, you can tell they nearly all want to do the play, but Zada is protesting that it would be *incredibly callous* to carry on with Conrad dead and Jon in hospital, and they have to find a way of presenting to themselves the decision to carry on in a form that makes them feel not shallow and unfeeling but mature and balanced. It is quite fun watching this and I'm glad to say that no-one attempts the *it's what Conrad would have wanted* argument, probably because everyone knows it isn't true.

They are manoeuvring neatly, speculatively recasting and rescheduling, the tone restrained and grown-up, when they hit a road block: recasting with the company already pared down to a minimum requires Stefan Pienkowsky, who plays Laertes, to double as Rosencrantz and he is resistant. 'Dead man's shoes,' he says. 'The guy isn't even buried yet. I don't feel comfortable about it.' They go quiet. They feel rebuked. They sip their beers, watch the sea, avoid looking at each other.

Then James, who has said very little so far, leans forward

to stub out his cigarette in a saucer on the table and says, 'For God's sake, people. Don't tell me this whole project's going to founder because we can't find someone – anyone – to do Rosencrantz. I know Conrad would have had us all believe that it's the key role of the play but actually any clown could play it – and better than Conrad.'

There is the sound of a gasp and everyone watches as Sophie stands up and walks across to stand in front of him. Then, she raises a hand and deals him a perfectly aimed slap across the face before running out of the room. It's a reaction both absurdly histrionic and perfectly appropriate at the same time. Someone attempts a laugh but it fizzles out into silence. James lights another cigarette. Adam waits a moment and then says, quietly, 'I think we should have a show of hands before we go any further. How many people, in principle, are in favour of carrying on?'

As far as I can see, everyone's hand goes up except for Zada's and Stefan's. He looks around and throws up both hands in a gesture of surrender. 'OK. I know I can't wreck it for everyone. Obviously, I'll have to do it.'

'Actually, I've got an idea.' The voice is Annie's. She was here when I got back from putting Freda to bed. 'I was thinking,' she says, a bit pink from being suddenly in the spotlight, 'that we could swap R and G round. I could do Rosencrantz and it wouldn't feel so odd because I'd do it differently, because I'm – you know – a girl.' There is a little cheer, and a whistle from Ray. 'And Stefan can do Guildenstern and he'll be stepping into a live woman's shoes.'

'OK, Stefan?' Adam asks.

'Yeah. OK. Thanks, Marianne.'

Adam jumps up and goes over to hug Annie. 'You are brilliant,' he says, and she smiles but not as adoringly as she might have done a few days ago. Mildly fractured heart on the mend, I think. Adam turns to Zada, picks up her hand and kisses it. 'And, you, darling? If I do Claudius, will you be my Gertie?'

She gives a smoky bark of laughter. 'Claude and Gertie,' she says. 'It sounds like a music hall act.' She looks up at Adam. 'Garn, then,' she says. 'Orright.'

'Excellent.' He drops her hand. 'Let's get down to it, then. A read-through-stroke-line-run. Off book if you're playing the part you were playing yesterday.'

People wander off to find scripts; James stays where he is, the red mark of Sophie's slap still visible on his face. Adam calls out to Annie as she is leaving the room, 'Can you read in Ophelia, darling, if Sophie doesn't come back.' She glances for a moment at James. 'If you like,' she says, 'but shouldn't someone go and see Sophie?'

I haul myself to my feet. It has been a wearing day, in the course of which I have been interrogated, starved and soaked. What I would really like would be to go to bed. 'Would you like me to go and talk to her?' I ask.

'No.' Adam looks at James. 'Thanks, Gina, but in the end it's James who's going to have to talk to her.'

'And say what?' James demands.

'An apology of some sort would be nice, don't you think?'

James raises his eyebrows in exaggerated surprise. '*She* hits me and *I* apologise? Political correctness gone viral, wouldn't you say? Besides –' he stubs out his cigarette '– I was only saying what everyone else was thinking – or everyone except Sophie.'

'Actually, not.' Adam moves towards James so that he is standing over him. 'We all bitched about Conrad but he's dead and the rest of us feel ashamed. Stupid, maybe, and pointless, yes, but – you know – human.' He turns to leave the room but stops and turns back. 'And if we're talking *realpolitik*, this show can't go on without Sophie and she won't go on without an apology. Not necessarily tonight, I would say – better to give everyone time to cool – but if you still want to play Hamlet, it's up to you.'

I decide not to go to bed. The bits of rehearsal I've seen have been randomly disjointed and I would like to hear the play from beginning to end. And without moves it will be short; it has been heavily cut anyway. I settle back with my can of beer to listen.

Hearing it like this, cut and trimmed, without moves, without thoughts about costume to distract me, I hear the play quite freshly, and what strikes me most – not surprisingly, I suppose, in the light of recent events – is just how callous everyone is about death: Claudius seeing the deaths of Polonius and Ophelia only as political difficulties; Hamlet joking grimly about Polonius being at supper – 'Not where he eats but where he is eaten'; the gravedigger's detached professional interest in 'how long a man may lie in the earth ere he rot'; above all, Hamlet's contempt and pleasure as he plots the deaths of Rosencrantz and Guildenstern. I listen to James.

'And my two schoolfellows,
Whom I will trust as I will adders fang'd,
They bear the mandate...
...Let it work;
For 'tis the sport to have the enginer
Hoist with his own petard, and it shall go hard
But I will delve one yard below their mines
And blow them to the moon.'

It's a nice ambiguity in the play that we don't know whether R and G are aware that the letter they are given to take to the English king is an order for Hamlet's death, but Hamlet doesn't care anyway. When he tells honest, decent Horatio what he did in substituting for his own death warrant an order for the execution of R and G themselves, Horatio comments, 'So Rosencrantz and Guildenstern go to it' and Hamlet sneers, 'Why man, they did make love to this employment; they are

99

not near my conscience.' I hear the hard, dismissive edge in James's voice now as he delivers the line and I wonder if he would have said it any differently if he'd seen Conrad's body as I did last night. Poor, stupid Conrad with his pretensions to be an actor and his jibes at James, his pride in his car and his little-boy showing off. I feel stupid tears welling up and I start grubbing around in my bag for a tissue.

The front door bell rings, loud in the hushed atmosphere of the reading. No-one else makes a move to get up so I go and am utterly unsurprised to find police officer Ingrid Larsen on the doorstep with another officer – a young lad in uniform – standing behind her. I look into her impassive face and I feel a powerful urge to slam the door in it. Why do I dislike her so much? Is it just our run-in this morning when she accused me of being a predatory older woman – a cougar, in fact? The thought of myself, standing here in baggy pedal pushers and a washed out t-shirt, as sleek, sexy and powerful makes me start to laugh and I have to cover it with a wide and insincere smile of welcome.

'Good evening,' I say

Her face doesn't move. 'James Asquith?' she asks.

Well, that's why I can't stand her. It's not just that she is stupid and insulting; it's her determined gracelessness. How does Anders Mortensen, who is politeness itself, put up with her? Does he need someone to be rude for him?

I laugh. 'Well, I'm not James Asquith,' I say. 'Obviously.'

'He is here?'

I say nothing but I don't shut the door on her. I turn to walk back to the verandah and she and her sidekick come tramping after me.

On the verandah, Zada gives a wail at the sight of them and rushes out of the room. Ingrid Larsen pays no attention to her, but surveys the ring of faces turned towards her and says, 'James Asquith, come with us please.'

James doesn't get up. In fact, he leans back in his chair. 'Are you arresting me?' he asks quietly.

'Not at the moment. We have more questions for you.'

'And they can't wait till the morning?'

'No.'

He looks around, gathering up his cigarettes and his lighter, which are lying on the table in front of him. 'So can I expect to be spending the night at the police station?'

'That would be a good expectation.' She turns to go. 'Come,' she says over her shoulder, and he gets up, looks at nobody and follows her. He is almost out of the room before a few people call out, 'Bye James' and, 'Good luck' half-heartedly, almost in whispers. I follow with the vague sense that I ought to see him off and I stand at the door, looking out into the rain-sodden evening, watching the car lights circle and disappear. Then because I can't face any more talk, I go upstairs.

I had forgotten Sophie. I find her not in her own bed but in mine, curled around Freda. In the pale light leaking in from the landing she looks, lying there with her blonde head next to Freda's, like another child. I wonder who was comforting whom that they ended up like this, and I feel another lurch of guilt about Freda being mixed up in the drama. I would pack up and take her home if I could but Anders Mortensen has my passport. It occurs to me that the only person in our company who still has access to her passport is Freda but she can't go home because I can't go home. It's time, I decide, to let Ellie know what's going on. Better by email than by phone, I think – less alarming and allowing more time for thought – so I start rummaging in my case for my laptop.

'What's happening?' a voice says behind me, and I turn to see Sophie sitting up in bed, eyes huge in the darkness. 'Who was at the door?' she asks.

'The police,' I say with as casual an intonation as I can manage, but her voice is sharp with alarm.

'Why?'

Freda stirs. 'Outside,' I mouth at Sophie and the two of us go along to the end of the landing, where we sit down on the floor outside the bathroom door and I say, 'They just want to ask James some more questions.'

'But why? He was in with them for ages this morning. What else do they want to know?' Her voice has a panicky edge to it.

'I don't know.'

'Are they talking to him here?'

'No. At the police station.'

'So they've arrested him?'

'No, but it looks as though they'll keep him there over night.'

She has been sitting with her knees pulled up under the oversized t-shirt she sleeps in and her arms round them. Now she drops her head onto her knees and starts to cry, quietly and hopelessly, making no attempt to stop or even to wipe away her tears. Oh really. When I said at the beginning of this misbegotten adventure that I was afraid I was going to be pushed into the role of mother hen, wiping noses et cetera, I meant it metaphorically. I really didn't expect to need a box of Kleenex with me wherever I went. I sit beside her and try to work out what, exactly, she is crying about. Eventually it seems that I shall just have to ask. I put an awkward arm round her and ask, as gently as I know how, 'Is it Conrad or is it James?' Then, when I get no response, I add, 'Or both?'

She mutters something into her knees and I lean close to hear her but all I pick up is, '...and there's no-one now.'

'I know it's been hard for you,' I say tentatively, not really knowing where I'm going with this, 'things difficult between you and James, and then Conrad. It's a terrible shock but –' but what?

I'm saved from having to go on by Sophie, who lifts her

streaked face and wails, 'Conrad's dead and James is going to prison so what happens to me?'

The temptation is to say, *You're twenty-one years old. You haven't started yet. You go home, get a job and eventually meet someone else. That's what happens to you.* This bracing approach has always worked fairly well on my own daughters but I'm not sure it's for Sophie, so instead I say, 'James won't go to prison. They don't send innocent people to prison in Denmark.'

She sits up straighter and pushes strands of wet hair off her face, wiping her eyes with the heels of her hands. 'And what if he isn't innocent?' she asks.

I gape. 'You don't think James killed Conrad?' I croak. 'What reason would he have?' And then it strikes me that she has been James's girlfriend for the past two years and would know, if anyone does, if he's an Islamist agent. 'Don't tell me,' I whisper, 'that the police are right about their anti-Zionist conspiracy theory?'

She leans her head back against the wall and shakes it fretfully. 'No, of course not. They don't understand, this Islamist stuff with James and his father, it's all academic – academic and romantic. It's not about bombs and suicide vests.'

'So why would James kill Conrad? You don't kill people for being annoying – at least not in cold blood.' *And James has plenty of that,* I think, which would also rule out a *crime passionel.* I look at her. 'You're not thinking, are you,' I ask, 'that James did it because you and Conrad –'

'No!' She yells it suddenly, her face scarlet. 'I'm not stupid, though you all think I am. I know James doesn't care about me. What you don't know – what none of you know – is that Conrad was trying to blackmail James. So there's your motive for you.'

Before I've even got my mouth open for a question, she is

on her feet and heading back down to our room, and as I'm struggling to get up, the bathroom door beside me flies open and Zada emerges, still dressed but with her hair wrapped in a towel and holding to her eyes pale green pads designed to look like cucumber slices. She lifts them off and smiles wanly at me. 'Been blubbing again,' she explains, waving the green pads at me, 'and trying to repair the ravages.'

If she wants a heart-to-heart, I'm not offering one. I need to pursue Sophie and find out what the hell she's talking about. 'Well, you know, *this vale of tears*,' I say vaguely and depart as fast as my stiff knees will take me.

Sophie is in her own bed with her back turned when I get back to the room. I lean over her. 'Are you serious?' I hiss. 'What do you mean?'

She keeps her eyes closed. 'Nothing more to say,' she says. 'End of.' And she pulls the duvet over her head.

So that's that. Any further attempts to get some sense out of her will only wake Freda, who is stirring already. On the other hand, there is no point in my going to bed because I'm fizzing with questions. I get my laptop and go downstairs, where I find a largish group still on the verandah and another group sitting round the kitchen table eating toast. The splendid salon, however, is empty. Hardly anyone ever sits in here – it overwhelms with its size and splendour. I find a chair in a corner, switch on a standard lamp, open up my laptop and click onto my emails. Ignoring the many messages in my inbox since none of them is from anyone I love, I start typing. I type furiously for twenty minutes, don't read my missive through and click *send*. Then I fish out my mobile from my bag and write a text message. *Murder mystery. Read your emails*, I write and despatch it into the ether.

10

DAY FIVE

When sorrows come they come not single spies
But in battalions. 4.5

Some sort of crash wakes me out of that exhausted sleep that can come out of hours of wakefulness and I see Sophie scrabbling about under the little dressing table in the corner of the room. I reach for my phone to check the time. It is 7.30. What is the matter with this girl? Every other morning she has been dead under the duvet, and now she's up at what I might hyperbolically call the crack of dawn if this weren't Denmark at midsummer.

'What the bloody hell are you doing?' I enquire pleasantly.

She starts, jerks her head up, bangs it on the dressing table and scrambles to her feet, scarlet-faced, but before she can say anything, Freda sits up. 'Something breaked,' she says, and the two of us turn accusing eyes on Sophie. She looks terrible now the flush has faded from her face but she is dressed and has washed her hair and made an effort with some makeup. She picks up her bag and hugs it to her.

'Sorry I woke you,' she whispers. 'Nothing's broken. Just dropped my bag.'

'Where are you going at this hour?'

'I'm – I just need to get out for a bit. I thought I'd go for a cycle ride, actually.'

'Has the rain stopped?'

'I think so. See you later.' And she's gone.

I climb out of bed and stand on a chair to peer out of our high little window. The rain does seem to have spent itself and the sky above the trees is already a promising blue. I push the window open and lean out, savouring the damp, salty air. Then I hear footsteps on the gravel and see Sophie come out, run to the summer house at the side of the drive and emerge wheeling a bike. Several bikes came over on the ferry, strapped to the back of the van, though I have yet to see anyone ride one. I remember vaguely being told a story on my first evening here about Zada's bike. I forget the point of it exactly but I think the joke was that it is a state-of-the-art machine that has never been ridden by its actual owner. I wonder if it's Zada's bike that Sophie has taken now, following the ancient Oxford custom of regarding the bike as what economists term a free good – a resource needed by the society and available without limit at zero cost.

I watch Sophie mount the bike, pedal over the gravel to the gates and turn left towards Helsingør, and I think how appealing the idea of a day out on a bike is. I should have to take Freda, of course, and none of the bikes here will have a child seat, so it would mean going into Helsingør and hiring one. Not impossible – I've seen a garage near the castle with a *Cykler til leje* sign, which I take to mean *Cycles for hire*. With James at the police station, there will surely be no rehearsals today, and the likelihood is that the others will sit around here annoying each other, like bored kids on a long car journey. I look at Freda.

'What do you think,' I ask, 'of going for a picnic?'

She looks puzzled. 'A breakfast picnic?' she asks.

'No. We'll have an adventure,' I improvise. 'We'll go on the bus into the town and we'll have breakfast in a café. Then we'll get a bike just like my bike at home, with a little seat for you, and we'll go to the beach for a picnic.'

She lies down and puts her thumb in her mouth. 'Want to go on your home bike,' she says, indistinctly.

I sit down on the bed beside her. 'But my home bike is in England, sweetheart.'

'I want to go in England.'

Her face is crumpling into tears. I scoop her up and sit her on my lap. She turns her face to mine. 'I decided,' she says, 'I don't like ventures.' *You and me both, sweetheart,* I think, *and at this moment you speak for everyone in this house, I imagine.* The familiar wash of guilt hits me. I didn't email Ellie last night as I meant to. I got distracted by Sophie. With so many adults behaving like children, I lost sight of the actual child, didn't I?

I never had much in the way of strategies for dealing with my children and I'm no better equipped to deal with Freda. Bracing or bribery is all I have and bracing will hardly do for this poor little scrap who is actually trying quite hard to be brave and reasonable. I put my lips close to her ear and I murmur, 'How about pancakes for breakfast, and after that we'll phone Mummy and see if she's having a nice holiday.'

'Will you make the pancakes?'

'If we have them at a café, there'll be syrup,' I wheedle.

'All right.' She gives the glimmer of a smile. 'I might get sticky, though.'

'So might I,' I say, and she starts to giggle.

Taking advantage of this temporary lifting of spirits, I scramble us both into our clothes, throw a few child-related necessities into a bag and march us out of the house. On the drive we meet Ray, who is just getting into the van.

'Not taking the van to get the pastries this morning, surely, Ray?' I say. 'What's happened to the fitness regime?'

He laughs. 'Already been for my run. I'm off to pick James up. He just rang. They're letting him out.'

'Really? So rehearsals today then?'

'I assume.'

'Well, change of plan then. Freda and I were planning a day out, but if this thing is actually going on, people need to start getting used to their costumes.'

Of course I'm glad that they've released James but I really could have done with a hike on a bike, and I feel bad about disappointing Freda, though she is actually more fixated on the pancakes; she has been chanting *pancakes, pancakes, pancakes* for some time and with mounting ferocity. In fact, I see a tantrum in the offing if we don't get moving; any moment she will be lying on the drive eating gravel.

'You couldn't give us a lift into town, could you, Ray?' I ask. 'I've promised Freda a pancake breakfast.'

Ray offers us seats on the bench beside him at the front but I'm playing safe in the light of recent events and I put us in the back, with our lap straps on. As we approach the town, Ray says, 'Jim'll be waiting so I should pick him up right away. There'll be a café round the corner in the market, won't there? OK?'

I remember our experience with the hotdogs. 'Actually,' I say, 'I was planning on going to the castle café.'

'The castle café?' He sounds surprised. 'Expensive there, isn't it?'

'But good. And child-friendly. But don't worry. I wasn't expecting you to take us there. We can walk from here.'

He says nothing but when we get to the police station, he parks right outside in a space that says *parkering forbudt* and he says, 'Stay here, will you, and argue with anyone who kicks up a fuss? I'll only be two ticks. Then I'll drop you at the castle.'

'But Ray –' I protest, but he's gone, taking the steps up to the doors of the police station two at a time. Damn. Do I look like a woman who is good at arguing with traffic wardens? Well, perhaps I do to those who don't realise that I'm one of the developed world's last pedestrians. I peer down the street looking for signs of a uniform.

'Tell me if you see anyone wearing a hat,' I instruct Freda, but she is looking mutinous. 'We'll count to a hundred,' I concede, 'and if Ray's not back we'll walk to the café.'

We sit and watch the street while I count at a brisk pace. I'm just at fifty when I see not a uniform but a woman I recognise, the mystery woman I saw James talking to on the day we arrived – the woman I connected, on no very good evidence, with the Karin Conrad talked about, Karin whose brother loaned him the fatal car. She is not very distinctive looking – average height, slim, dark blonde hair – but what makes her noticeable is that she is wearing, as she was when I saw her previously, denim dungarees of the kind I remember being worn for a while by über-feminists in the 80s but which are now, I feel sure, genuine work clothes. Hence my leap to Karin and the garage.

As I watch her, she walks briskly past the van, stops at the police station, takes one step up and then freezes for a moment before turning and heading back fast, but not quite at a run, in the direction she has just come from. I watch her for a moment and then see that James has materialised on the pavement looking at her too. She was planning to go into the police station but changed her mind when she saw James. Why?

James and Ray get into the front seat of the van and Ray says, 'Gina's going out for breakfast, Jim. What say we do the same?'

James twists round to glance briefly at me but then turns back to Ray. 'Yes,' he says. 'I wouldn't mind delaying our return to the madhouse.'

Ray drops us at the castle entrance and goes off to park the van. Freda, finding herself walking between two adults, demands to be swung along and James participates awkwardly. Small children are clearly outside his comfort zone. The café is just opening up as we arrive and we are the first people in. It's small and furnished mainly with tables for two. Without discussion, Freda and I take one table and James seats himself on the opposite side of the room. We are by the window, where we can take an interest in the world; James (or Jim – who else but Ray would think of calling him Jim?) lurks in a corner. When Ray comes in, he looks surprised to see us sitting separately but I am quite happy not to eat my pancakes in the company of James and his black dog aura when I have the potentially entropic combination of Freda and syrup to deal with.

Actually, we have a lovely breakfast. The pancakes come nicely doused in maple syrup and accompanied by rashers of bacon, American style. Freda doesn't care for the bacon so I get double, which suits me. I have remembered to bring a scrunchie to tie Freda's hair back, so stickiness is confined to her face and hands. The coffee is wonderful and I order a second pot while I reorder the day in my mind. I shall have to stay here and start the business of trying on the costumes. If things don't fit, I need to know now. I'm hoping that Freda has forgotten about the proposed bike ride, or was never very keen on it anyway. I shall just have to keep her here with me, and hope to keep her entertained. And I haven't forgotten that I promised her we would ring Ellie, but I need to wait until there are other people around to distract her, so I can have a quiet word with Ellie about what is going on here. Anders Mortensen may have let James go but he has got his teeth into this case and there's every possibility that he will arrest each of us in turn until he finds his murderer.

James and Ray are still making their way through a multi-course breakfast when we leave and Ray lifts a laden fork in a farewell gesture. Although the grounds and the café are open, the castle doesn't open till ten o'clock – another fifteen minutes – but Adam has negotiated access for the company from nine each day so I stop at the gatehouse to ask the gatekeeper to unlock the door into the courtyard.

'I'm afraid we're the early birds,' I apologise.

'No,' he says. 'I already unlocked it for the girl.'

I've no idea who he means but I smile and thank him and through we go. As we're crossing the courtyard, I start to feel in an inner pocket of my bag for the key to the cellar which is my costume store, but before I even start feeling for it I know I'm not going to find it. It is a huge iron key on a heavy ring and I have been conscious of it clanking about in my bag ever since it was handed over, grudgingly and disapprovingly, by the gatekeeper on the day the costumes were delivered. This morning, I realise, there has been no clanking, and I haven't felt the weight of it on my shoulder. I rummage anyway, even to the extent of sitting down on the flagstones and emptying out my bag, willing it to be there and knowing it's not. I sit, surrounded by the detritus of my daily life and consider possibilities.

I have been neurotic about this key, lending it to no-one, replacing it in its designated pocket in my bag, terrified of losing the damned thing and having to face the wrath of the surly gatekeeper. I rewind to the last time I had it in my hand. It was, I suppose, shortly before Conrad made his dramatic appearance on Wednesday afternoon. No, I had it after that. I remember going back to lock up when Ray set off carrying Conrad. So I must, at some point, have taken it out of my bag, but if I did I have completely blanked it out, which says something worrying about my mental state. Well, there's only one thing to be done.

'Sorry, Freda,' I say, bundling everything back into my bag, 'Granny has to go and grovel.'

'What's *grobel*?' she asks.

'Watch and learn,' I say.

The door to the courtyard opens as we approach, on the

stroke of ten from the courtyard clock. I return to the gatehouse, intending to confess all, but I lose my nerve when I look into the gatekeeper's stony face and instead I smile brightly. 'I am SO sorry,' I say, 'but I've forgotten to bring the key to the cellar. Do you think you could possibly let me in?'

He frowns and I feel a blush rising from my throat into my lying face. *He knows. He knows I've lost it.*

'Just this once?' I add, weakly.

He gives a puff of irritation. 'But the girl has it,' he says. 'I told you.'

The girl. Who does he mean? 'But I haven't given the key to anyone,' I protest.

For an answer, he turns and calls out something into an inner office behind him, then comes out and takes hold of my arm – something I really dislike and I would object to if I weren't feeling so firmly in the wrong at this particular moment. He steers me at speed across the courtyard while Freda hangs onto my other hand and runs to keep up with us. At the cellar door, he stops and points at the handle. 'Open it,' he commands, so I turn it and the door creaks open. 'You can go in,' he says, and gives me an unfriendly little push.

'So kind of you!' I say as I step inside but I fear the irony is lost on him. I am conscious that he is standing at the open door watching me as Freda and I negotiate the uneven steps down into the cellar. The light is on and I can see who is down here. Sophie is standing in her mad scene costume – her tattered bride's dress – scarlet-faced and guilty, just as I've already seen her look today.

'You stole the key!' I yell at her. 'You stole it out of my handbag. That's what you were doing this morning. Stealing the key out of my bag.'

She flares back. 'What are you talking about? I didn't steal anything. I just borrowed it.'

I hear the heavy door close above us and shut the sunlight

out as the gatekeeper leaves. Sophie says, 'You were asleep. I was going to leave you a note.'

'I woke up!' I roar. 'We had a conversation. Why didn't you ask me for it?'

'I was embarrassed.' Her voice wobbles. 'And you've made such a big deal about never letting it out of your sight.'

'For a good reason. It was entrusted to me. I was worried sick when I thought I'd lost it!'

'Well some people have more important things to be worried sick about!' she yells back. 'Try thinking about that.' Then she sits down on a trunk and starts to cry. *Dear God, not again.*

'Why,' I ask more quietly, 'did you want your costume anyway?'

She gets up and starts pacing about. 'I don't know,' she says with her back to me. 'It'll sound stupid when I say it, but I just wanted to get away from all the crap at the villa and just get into role. You know, put the costume on and be Ophelia. Do some of the speeches. I'm good in the part, I know I am, when there isn't all the other stuff to think about. I wanted to feel I was good at something, that's all.'

'But why be so furtive about it?'

She turns on me. 'Why can't you stop asking bloody questions?' she screams. 'Sod you and your fucking costumes.'

Then she's away, taking the steps at a run and leaving the heavy door hanging open.

'Freda,' I say, 'Sophie said some nasty words just then. It's not a good idea for you to try saying any of them.'

She nods solemnly then starts climbing the steps. 'Shall we go on a bike now?' she says.

I look around at my costumes. I'm sick to death of all this – the on-off rehearsals, the egos and spite, the tantrums and tears, the mistrust and the lies. Sophie was lying to me, I'm sure. It was a feeble story, insulting in its feebleness. What point was there in rehearsing a part she didn't expect to play? As far as Sophie knows, James is still at the police station and as she told it last night, she thinks he's going to prison. No more Hamlet and no more Ophelia. So why all this – slipping out of the house, stealing the key, dressing up? What the hell is she up to?

Freda is now at the top of the steps, teetering dangerously.

'Sit down, Freda,' I bark, more fiercely than I intended to because I'm scared.

She sits down, startled, and her thumb goes into her mouth but she doesn't cry. She has more spine than most people round here. I spot the key lying beside a pile of Sophie's discarded clothes. Well, I'm going to lock up and she'll have to get round the gatekeeper if she wants her clothes back. I pick it up and go up the steps to Freda. I pick her up. 'Sorry I shouted,' I say. 'Let's go and find a bike.'

'Can I have a carry?' she asks, milking the moment.

'Just as far as the bridge,' I say, and I carry her across the courtyard in the sunshine. I go through the gatehouse, avoiding the eye of the gatekeeper, and when we reach the drawbridge I am about to put Freda down when, out of the corner of my eye, I see a large white object falling from the battlements towards the moat. It is only when it hits the water that I see that it is a body wrapped in the floating draperies of a wedding dress.

11

TRAFFIC

Scott heard the text message come through on his phone at some time after midnight and turned the bedside light on to look at it. *Murder mystery*, he read. *Read your emails*. Even if his phone hadn't told him the message came from Gina, he would have recognised it – bossy and infuriating – as unmistakeably hers. The morning was soon enough, he thought, and switched out the light.

An hour later, he admitted that sleep was not going to come until he'd read the wretched email and he got out of bed and opened up his laptop. Four days it had taken for her to break her silence and he assumed that what she was sending now would turn out to be a joke, a clever take on Scandi crime – not an apology but a peace offering of sorts. So he was not prepared for the message he found, a message that reflected Gina at her best, just as her text message displayed the worst.

Her email told a complicated story well. It was pithy and remarkably objective; it was also rather appealingly academic in its attachments, offering potted histories of the major players, enhanced by Gina's own thumbnail sketches, and a *Hamlet* cast list for good measure. It was also deeply alarming to anyone who knew Gina. Whatever was going on here – misadventure, negligence by the garage, a lethal practical joke or, just possibly, murder – Gina would be right in there trying to work it out. He was not deceived by the apparent objectivity of her account; she would have a theory and she would be pursuing it.

He clicked *Reply* and typed furiously.

David Scott

From "David Scott" D.S.Scott@mailcon.co.uk
To "Gina Gray" gina.gray@freenet.com
Sent 17th July 2011 01.48
Subject DON'T

Gina –

Do you know what the chances are of you walking into another murder case? I don't either, but the odds against must be astronomical, so I refuse to believe that it's murder. I don't think this is a murder case and, reading between the lines of your account, I don't think you do either. The police have to treat it seriously but in the end it will come down to forensics and the police will know that a good defence team will find someone to cast forensic doubt on whether the brake cable was really cut, so they'll give up on it as a murder case. There might be a negligence case to be made out against the garage but that doesn't affect any of you. My guess is you'll soon get your passports back and be able to come home.

In the meantime, the important thing – and I can't emphasise this enough – is that you personally DO NOT GET INVOLVED. You've got used to muscling in on my investigations but the Danish police won't like it and you'll make them suspicious, so keep a low profile and your head below the parapet, don't stick your oar in, lie doggo and whatever other metaphors you want to dream up – I'm sure you can find a lot more than I can. Don't be a know-all and don't treat the police as though they're stupid. It never works well. Let them sort it out. It's what they're paid for.

Look after yourself and Freda and Annie, and try not to become everyone's mother.

If you're back earlier than expected, I at least will be pleased.

David

Then he reached for his phone, sent a single-word message: *Ditto*, and went back to bed.

12

FIVE LIVE

Of accidental judgements, casual slaughters. 5.2

My first reaction as I see Sophie hurtling into the moat is to press Freda's face into my chest. This is so she can't watch – and perhaps it's also a knee-jerk urge to keep her from whatever harm is happening here. People start running towards the water but I look up to the place from which the bizarre white bundle came floating down. I just catch sight of a figure that turns away and disappears from view but it's too brief a moment and I look back at the water, where someone has dived in. Freda is struggling to release herself from my grip in spite of my exhortations not to look, and I realise that I can't prevent her from seeing this. I can't go away and I can't blindfold her so I set her down and we stand, hand in hand, watching.

The diver gets Sophie to the surface quite easily, it seems, which means, as I know from my obsessive watching of police dramas, that she has probably got air in her lungs, and that's encouraging. He is struggling to get her out of the water, though, in spite of the efforts of bystanders to help, and it is the surly gatekeeper who saves the day, appearing at speed and hauling her up the bank. I catch a glimpse of her face, which looks very white and very dead, but when he turns her onto her front and hits her hard on her back, something gushes out of her mouth. Then he rolls her onto her back and starts mouth-to-mouth respiration, which I've never seen done in reality and can't quite believe. I look at Freda, who is watching with interest but without alarm, though to me it seems rather terrible, this parody of kissing. At one point there is another spurt of watery vomit but I'm not close enough to see if her ribs are moving at all. What I do see now, though, is that a dark red stain is spreading through the tangled, wet hair at the side of her head.

Now things speed up. An ambulance and two police cars arrive and suddenly there seem to be police everywhere. Sophie is lifted, with brisk professionalism, onto a stretcher and into the ambulance and I'm wondering if I should offer to go with her, which is a stupid idea since I've got Freda in tow, when I get a tap on the shoulder. Ingrid Larsen is standing there.

'Get in the car, please,' she says.

'What?

'In the car. We need to ask you some questions.'

'Can't you ask them here?'

'No, we can't.' She doesn't waste words, this woman.

'Why not?'

'It will take some time.'

'Really? I haven't got that much to say.'

'We will decide that. Come.' She jerks her head towards the two police cars and I can see that James is sitting in the back of one of them.

'I assume I'm a witness, not a suspect?' I say.

She says nothing.

'Well, what about Freda?' I protest, picking her up.

Ingrid Larsen looks at Freda and shrugs. 'She comes too,' she says.

'No, she doesn't,' I hiss. 'She's had quite enough of all this.

119

I need to make a phone call and get someone to come and fetch her.' I set Freda down at her feet. 'Watch her,' I say, 'while I make a call.'

Both she and Freda start to protest but I turn away and dial Annie's number. 'Annie,' I say. 'Just listen to me and don't argue – I've only got a minute. Sophie's had an accident at the castle. The police are here and I have to go and answer some questions. It'll take a while and Freda's had enough of the police station. You'll have to come and get her and look after her for the morning. No! Don't argue, Annie. Just do it. Is Ray back with the van? Well, if he's not, get the bus. Give Freda a treat – I'll give you some money – take her to a playground, take her shopping, buy her ice cream. All right? I'll expect you at the police station in half an hour.'

I glance over my shoulder. Ingrid Larsen is crouched down talking to Freda and looking almost human. I risk a second call. *Hi, this is Ellie's phone*, the cheery message tells me, *I'm sorry I can't talk to you right now but leave me a message and I'll get back to you*. 'Ellie,' I say 'I don't want you to panic. Freda is fine – absolutely fine – but things have got weird here. Not just the car accident but now something else. It's all a bit crazy and not the best atmosphere for Freda. I would cut and run and take her home but I can't. Did Annie tell you the police have taken our passports? I've got to spend the morning at the police station so I won't be reachable for a few hours. Phone Annie if you want to know more. She'll have Freda with her. Sorry to be a blight on the honeymoon but I thought you'd want to know. Speak to you soon.'

I switch off the phone and turn round. 'OK,' I say. 'Let's go.'

We pass the car James is sitting in and I can see him, sitting very upright with his head leaning against the back of the seat. He seems quite impassive except that there are tears running down his face. I bend down and mouth, 'What happened?'

through the window but Ingrid Larsen hurries me past and into the other car. No-one, I'm glad to say, puts a hand on my head to push me into the car, as they do when people are arrested on television, but I'm in no doubt that I am not here just as a witness, and I find that I'm feeling a bit shaky. It's shock, of course but, if I'm honest, I think it's also fright. I look at Freda, who is sitting up, taking an interest in the world outside the windows. 'Well! A ride in a police car!' I say. 'This is fun, isn't it?'

Shortly afterwards my phone rings. I answer it without looking at the caller ID assuming it's Ellie. 'Hello darling,' I say. 'I'm sorry about all this.' There is a pause on the other end and then a very deep male voice says, 'Is that Mrs Gray? Here is Theodosios Christodoulou.' *Christodoulou!* Do you remember him? Father of the infuriating and unfortunate Anastasia whom I left recovering from an overdose in Marlbury Hospital five days and a lifetime ago? 'Mr Christodoulou,' I say.' I'm so sorry. I thought it was my daughter calling.'

'No problem.' He chuckles happily. 'Mrs Gray –'

'I thought she would be calling,' I interrupt, 'because we have something of a family crisis going on at the moment, so –'

'– I have wanted to speak with you,' he continues, unperturbed, 'because –'

'– I really think it would be better to have this discussion –'

'– I wanted to say –'

' – later. Later, Mr Christodoulou. I am at this moment in a police car in Denmark, so this is really neither the time nor the place. I have your number and I will call you as soon as I'm free.'

There is a pause. 'Well, I wanted to thank you,' he says, 'but if you don't wish –' and he hangs up.

He doesn't believe me, of course. He thinks I have invented an insultingly implausible story to fob him off, and he is offended. But for what can he possibly be thanking me?

I wait a long time for my interrogation, not in the big room with the coffee machine where we waited before, but in a small, airless room which I tell myself not to think of as a cell. When Annie turns up, she is less cross than I expected and more intrigued. We are being watched closely by the young policewoman who is in charge of me but I manage to murmur some minimal information while making a performance of counting out twenty-kronor notes. 'Sophie in the moat,' I mutter.

'Dead?' she mouths.

I make a *could go either way* hand movement and she mutters, as she folds up the notes, 'Zada's acting weird.' Then she turns away. 'OK Freedie-weedie,' she says. 'I've stolen all Granny's money and we're going to have a girls' day out.'

Freda is doubtful. 'Why isn't Granny coming?' she demands.

'Because,' Annie says, picking her up, 'Granny is old. She needs to stay here and have a rest.' And she marches out.

I feel bereft – ready to weep, in fact – so I get assertive and request coffee. My request is turned down but making a scene about it proves a useful distraction. When that fails, I rummage about in my bag for reading material. I am threatened by another pang of self-pity when I come across the emergency supplies I gathered so hopefully this morning for a ride to the beach, but among them I find not only *The Very Hungry Caterpillar* but my copy of *Hamlet*. Appropriate reading enough, even if this production of ours will never now stalk the halls of Kronborg Castle. '*What have you, my good friends,*' Hamlet asks Rosencrantz and Guildenstern, '*deserved at the hands of Fortune that she sends you to prison hither?*' It's a question I could ask myself and I would have to say that all I've done to tempt fortune is to allow myself to be bullied by my daughter. Imprison every woman guilty of that crime and you couldn't build jails enough to house them.

I turn to Ophelia's first mad scene, though it's painful to

read it now, remembering how well Sophie played it and how pleased I was with the torn wedding dress idea to match her song, which is all about ruined maids and broken promises. It takes me down a long, confused and not very fruitful thought train, from which I am summoned to my interview with Anders Mortensen.

We are not in the pleasant office this time but in a proper, windowless interview room, and my bag is taken from me before I go in. Anders Mortensen and Ingrid Larsen sit facing me across a table.

'I asked you,' Mortensen says without social preamble, 'to inform me if you had any more information about the death of Conrad Wagner. Is it possible that you lost my card?'

I am completely wrong-footed – as I suppose I'm intended to be. 'Well,' I stutter, 'if you mean this morning – the – seeing Sophie fall off the battlements – I haven't had –'

He cuts me off. 'No, I shall want to hear about that later. I mean the information – significant information – that Sophie Forrester gave you yesterday.'

'Information?' What is he talking about? I can't seem to make my mind work. It's like one of those dreams where you're trying to run but your legs won't work. *I must not cry.* 'I'm sorry,' I say, as briskly as I can, 'but I don't know what you're talking about. I know violent incidents are all in a day's work for you but for the rest of us they're rather shocking. I saw someone I know nearly drown – and for all I know she may be dead. Is she dead? You won't tell me that, will you? The information here has to be all one way, doesn't it? Well, I've had no time to recover, I've got bundled into a car and brought in here, no-one has told me anything, I've got a three-year-old child I'm responsible for, she's had a shock too and I haven't been allowed to –' I stop because he is speaking, not to me but to Ingrid Larsen. I'm pretty sure I catch the word *kaffe*. She gets up and goes out of the room and I feel a whole lot better not only at the prospect of coffee but at seeing her being sent off to fetch it.

Mortensen says nothing while she is gone. I look for my bag, remember it has been confiscated and rummage in my jacket pocket to find a crumpled tissue, on which I blow my nose. Ingrid returns with the coffee and a sachet of sugar, which I stir in, and Mortensen lets me take a swig or two before he says, 'I will explain.'

'Thank you.'

'You had a conversation with Sophie Forrester yesterday evening.'

'Yes. I did. She was upset and I –'

'Where did you have this conversation?'

'In the corridor at the villa where we're staying. Sophie shares a room with me and my granddaughter and she – Freda – was asleep in there, so we went outside to talk.'

'What did you talk about?'

'Sophie was very distressed.'

'About what?'

'Well, I'd just told her that you had taken James Asquith in for questioning.'

'And that distressed her?'

'Yes.'

'Why?'

'Well, she was already upset by Conrad's death and now James… I mean, she and James were – are – going through a bad patch but I think she still hoped they'd get back together and now suddenly it looked as though you were going to charge him with murder.'

'Why did she think we would charge him with murder?'

I laugh. 'Well, you'd taken him in for questioning – and this morning you've done it again!'

'Did she say anything to you that suggested she thought he was guilty?'

124

I stare at him. 'She was very upset. She wasn't really thinking what she was saying.'

Ingrid Larsen gives a little huff of impatience and Mortensen leans forward across the table. 'That is not an answer to my question, is it?' he says, looking hard into my face, which starts to go hot in response.

'She said something wild about Conrad blackmailing James,' I mutter.

He leans back in his chair. 'And here we have it,' he says. 'An interesting information which you have known now since last night but which you did not pass to me.'

I want to tell him that *information* is an uncountable noun, so you can't talk about *an information* but I realise that this is not the time. Instead, I ask, 'Who told you about our conversation?' This is, of course, almost equally unwise as a response since it suggests that I was hoping to keep it secret. He just looks at me but he doesn't need to answer since I've worked it out. *Zada's acting weird*, Annie muttered. Of course she is. She heard us when she was in the bathroom and she's ready to sell anyone if it will get her passport back and a flight home to Daddy.

'Something wild?' Mortensen enquires softly.

'Yes. She just blurted out that Conrad was trying to blackmail James and then rushed off to bed and refused to say any more. I asked her to explain but she wouldn't.'

'So you decided to forget about it.'

'No. No, I didn't. In fact, I –' I stop. Actually, best not to say that I included it in an email to my policeman boyfriend. 'I lay awake thinking about it,' I say – truthfully, as it happens.

'Did you come to any conclusion that you would like to share with us?'

'In the end I decided that I didn't believe it.'

'Really? Why was that?'

'I couldn't see what anyone could blackmail James about.

What could he have done at twenty-two with a background like his that he could be blackmailed about? People get blackmailed over adulterous affairs or criminal activities, don't they? And I can't see James involved in either of those. And anyway, there are no secrets any more for the young – every last detail of their lives gets laid out on Facebook. James seems completely conventional: good school, good 'A' levels, good degree, one girlfriend. And he strikes me as a careful young man – not someone to get led astray or go in for risky behaviour.'

'But he smokes heavily.'

'Well, yes, but –'

'So much that he becomes very uncomfortable if he is deprived of cigarettes.'

I laugh. 'Well, I've been a smoker myself and I know what that's like. It didn't make me a criminal, though.'

'I think,' he says, leaning back in his chair, 'that you are missing my point.'

'So what is your point?'

The question comes out quite rudely and he says nothing – just goes on leaning back in his chair, tipping it so that it balances on two legs. The teacher in me wants to tell him off – *it'll slip and you'll end up on the floor* – but I restrain myself and eventually he says, not answering my question, 'If there was no blackmail, why did Sophie Forrester say there was?'

I shrug. 'I don't know.'

He leans forward suddenly. 'That's not good enough. You say you thought about it. You have surely some explanation.'

'I thought she was dramatising – just speaking for dramatic effect. After all, we came here to do a play. They are all actors of a sort, these students.'

'But not you. You are not a good actress, I think.'

I'm about to say something flippant in reply but I'm disconcerted by the distinctly chilly look he's giving me. I feel

126

the beginnings of a sort of panic. I felt quite comfortable in my first interview with him, felt that he quite respected me and my views, felt that we were speaking as one adult to another in a crowd of overgrown children, but that's gone now. And just when I need my mind to be at its sharpest, it has gone sluggish and distracted. I can't work out where he's going. He suspects me of something, but what? Playing for time, I reach for my coffee cup and drink down the cold, bitter dregs. Then as it usually does in a tight spot, anger comes to my aid.

'No, I'm not an actor,' I say, putting the cup down and giving it a shove across the table, 'and I'm not trying to deceive you. I have nothing to hide and I resent the implication that I have. Like everybody else involved in this, I'm just trying to keep my head above water.' (This is a bad metaphor in the circumstances and realising this nearly derails me, but I'm gathering momentum and I speed on.) 'I am perfectly willing to answer any questions you like but it's been a difficult day so far and I'm not up to coping with hints and suggestions and sneers and nudges and all the rest of it. I'm sure you think you're being very clever but you're just taking us round in circles. I'm not a suspect, I'm a witness. I can't be a suspect. If any crimes have been committed at all – and I'm not sure they have – I was accompanied by a three-year-old child at all the relevant times. So why don't you just ask me your bloody questions and I'll answer them.'

'Why was Wagner blackmailing Asquith?' He shoots the question straight at me without a moment's pause.

'I don't think he was and if he was I don't know why.'

'Did you ask Sophie Forrester why?'

'Yes, but she refused to answer.'

'Did you press her for an answer?'

'No.'

'Why not?'

'My granddaughter was asleep in the room and I didn't want to wake her.'

'Did you ask her again this morning?'

'No.'

'Why not?'

'We talked about other things.'

'What other things?'

'I asked her why she was up so early.'

'What did she say?'

'That she was going for a bike ride.'

'Why didn't you ask her about her blackmail story?'

'I told you, she –'

'Why didn't you ask her?'

'Because she didn't give me a chance.'

'Why didn't you ask her?'

'Because I didn't!' I yell.

'That's a child's answer. Why didn't you ask her?'

I take a deep breath. 'Because I thought I might have worked out what she meant.'

'And what was it you thought you had worked out?'

He is speaking softly and I try to moderate my voice to match.

'I thought,' I say slowly, conscious that the story I told myself in the turmoil of my nighttime reflections will probably look lame and ill-formed in the light of day, 'that she was using *blackmail* loosely. We all knew that Conrad was furious that James had been cast as Hamlet and he was doing everything he could to undermine him. I thought maybe Conrad knew something, something not criminal but embarrassing about James and was using it to try to get James to give up the part.'

'Something embarrassing?'

'Yes.' I'm sweating now with my own embarrassment as he starts to pick away at my threadbare story. 'Conrad and Sophie were seeing a lot of each other and I knew Sophie was very angry with James. I thought maybe she'd told Conrad something embarrassing – something private – that James wouldn't want spread around. He has quite a sense of his own dignity, James.'

He gets up from his chair and takes a turn round the room. 'And that would mean, of course,' he says from somewhere behind me, 'that Asquith would have no real motive for killing Wagner.'

'No.'

'You are very anxious to be helpful to Asquith, aren't you?'

Ingrid Larsen, who has been slumped in her seat, taking no obvious interest in the proceedings, looks up sharply. So we're on to this again. I resolve not to rise to the bait.

'I'm anxious to prevent an injustice,' I say.

'You don't think that is our job?'

'I think you're not making a very good job of it,' I retort, rudely, though I know it's a bad idea to be rude to policemen. *Sorry David.*

Mortensen sits down again and pulls a sheet of paper towards him.

'What were you doing at the castle this morning?' he asks.

'Having breakfast, initially.'

'Why there?'

'I was giving my granddaughter a treat. We were going out for a bike ride afterwards.'

'And Asquith and –' he consults the paper in front of him '– Porter, were you giving them a treat too?'

'No. Ray Porter offered me a lift into town as he was going in to pick James up from here, I said we were going to have breakfast in the café at the castle and they decided that was a good idea.'

'And you all had a happy breakfast together, I suppose?'

'Not at all. We sat at separate tables. We didn't even speak to each other.'

'Really? Wasn't that a little unfriendly?'

'You mean, considering that James is my special friend?' I dart a vicious glance at evil Ingrid. 'It does rather undermine that theory, doesn't it?'

He makes a note. 'We can check that,' he says. 'Who left the café first?'

'Freda and I did.'

'To go off for your cycle ride?'

'No, I went in to the king's wine cellar, where our costumes are being stored.'

'And where you knew you would find Sophie Forrester?'

'No! I didn't expect Sophie to be there. I just found her there. She said she wanted to try her costume on and practise some lines. She'd taken my key to the cellar. I was furious.'

He gives me a long look. 'As I hear the story from you,' he says, 'everyone's actions are strange and changeable. Sophie Forrester told you she was going for a cycle ride but instead she went to the castle; you planned to go for a cycle ride but instead you went into the castle; Sophie Forrester had the key to the wine cellar but you told the gatekeeper that you had left it at home; Porter came to take Asquith home but instead they went to the castle and, even after they had eaten their breakfast, Asquith was wandering about the castle battlements; Sophie Forrester went to the castle to try her costume on and fell into the moat. Does that sound normal to you?'

'Pretty much run of the mill, I would think,' I say flippantly. 'Very few of my days end up going the way I intend when I wake up in the morning. Do yours?'

He leans forward. 'You are very quick with your jokes,' he says. He pronounces *jokes* to sound like *yolks* and I have to press my lips together hard to stop myself from giggling stupidly. 'But when I hear this story, I hear a quite clear set of intentions and suddenly everyone is behaving rationally.'

There is no doubt about his seriousness, nor about the malice in his tone. I am teetering on the edge of a nasty fall and the trick is not to look down. I stare back at him. 'Do tell,' I say.

He stays leaning forward, hitting the table with his forefinger as he lays out each piece of his story. 'Sophie Forrester asks you for the key to the wine cellar and you give it to her. You then set out to follow her to the castle. She is an angry young woman and she has damaging information about the relationship between Asquith and Wagner. Somebody, you think, needs to keep an eye on her. You meet Porter, who tells you that Asquith is to be released, and you persuade him to take you with him to collect Asquith. This gives you the chance to tell Asquith about the threat from Sophie and you all go to the castle on the pretext of having breakfast. Then you go to find Sophie. You fabricate an argument about the key and force her out into the grounds of the castle, where Asquith is waiting to deal with her. By chance or not, you leave the cellar and arrive at the bridge in time to see her go into the moat.'

One could almost laugh to hear one's most innocent actions turned to conspiracy, but the look on his face takes away any thought I might have of laughing.

'Why?' I ask, and my voice sounds oddly croaky. 'Why would I? Why would I be going to so much trouble to protect James? And don't tell me that I'm harbouring some menopausal passion for him. Has anybody – anybody – suggested that there is any relationship of any kind between us, or even that we have ever said more than the most commonplace things to one another?'

That feels a bit better but he is unmoved. 'I have been finding out a little more about you, Gina Gray,' he says. 'I find that you are not only the director of the English Language Department at Marlbury University College, but that you have written articles for professional journals on the theory and practice of language teaching. You are an authority on *cross-*

cultural pragmatic competence and you recently wrote an article entitled, *Undiagnosed Cultural Dysfunction and the Ailing Language Learner.* Your concern in this article, it seems, is mainly with Muslim students who, you argue, feel that although provision is made on university campuses for their worship and their dietary laws, their culture and social attitudes are in fact disrespected by the dominant student culture, and that this hampers their ability to learn.'

'Well, yes,' I say, 'that's it roughly. You have rather taken the nuances away but that's the bottom line.'

'So that takes me back to the conversation we had yesterday. You were very well-informed about the Harmony Party – others I asked have barely heard of it – and though you claimed you are not a supporter, I wonder now if that is true. If you care so much about the disrespect that your Muslim students suffer, is this not exactly the party for you? And if it is, you would be anxious, wouldn't you, to stop any disgrace falling on its founder's son at this delicate time?'

'There is a difference,' I say, and David would, I think, be impressed by the quiet reasonableness of my tone, 'there is a difference between professional concern about anything that gets in the way of effective learning and a personal commitment to a fringe political party. As I said before, I think Islam in most of its current manifestations is deeply antagonistic to women's rights and progress – and participation in the world, frankly. Any religion-stroke-cultural norm that allows gangs of men to go round beating up women because they don't like their clothes doesn't get my vote, but that doesn't stop me from wanting my Muslim students – men and women – to do as well as they can. I am not a member of Harmony, and it should be quite easy for you to check that out. On the other hand, I was a paid-up member of the Labour Party for twenty years.'

'Was?'

'I left when Tony Blair invaded Iraq.'

The words are out of my mouth before I see their consequences.

'Yes,' he says.

'A lot of people resigned over that. They haven't all signed up to Harmony!' I'm beginning to shout again. I take a breath. 'Anyway, this fabrication of yours about what I did this morning,' I say, hoping to change the subject, 'point one, Sophie did steal the key from my bag and she will tell you so when she's able to.' I scan his face for evidence of how likely he thinks this is to happen, but it tells me nothing. 'Ditto she did say she was going for a cycle ride – and I saw her set off on a bike. Also, how was it that I planned a murder with James when Ray and Freda were with us the whole time? And, in fact, does it seem at all likely that I would have got involved in any of this dreamed-up conspiracy when I had Freda with me? And as for your suggestion that I went down to the drawbridge in order to see Sophie go into the moat, what possible reason could I have had for taking a three-year-old to see that?'

'Yes,' he says, making a note, 'your granddaughter. We may, I think, need to speak to her. We do it very carefully, we have specially trained women officers who –'

I am on my feet and incoherent with rage. 'You will not!' I gasp. 'You will not talk to Freda!' I see Ingrid Larsen get up and start to move towards me. If she's planning to wrestle me back into my chair, then bring it on. At this moment I'd really like the opportunity to hit someone and she's a prime candidate. Mortensen gives her a glance, though, and she stays still, so I carry on. 'This is a pathetic attempt to get me to "confess", isn't it? You know no court would accept the evidence of a three-year-old. You're just using this as a threat to bully me and I –'

I am stopped by the ringing of the phone on the table. Mortensen picks up and listens. He barks a couple of short questions which I don't understand then puts down the receiver and looks at it for a moment. Then he looks up at me.

'I wonder why,' he says, 'you did not tell me that Sophie Forrester was pregnant.'

It is another two and a half hours before I stumble down the steps of the police station into the light of day. At the end of it, after all the threats, assertions, demands and general harassment, Mortensen was forced to admit what I kept grimly insisting – that there was not *as yet* a single piece of evidence to link me to anything criminal at all. And what I have kept thinking – what has kept me sane, in fact – is that this is how policing works in Denmark, isn't it? I have seen Sarah Lund work like this in *The Killing* haven't I? She gets a theory and pursues a suspect until either the suspect produces a cast iron alibi or the evidence can't be made to fit or another suspect appears in the frame. Then the first suspect is off the hook and the next one is reeled in. So, I've had my turn and now I'm off the hook, I tell myself as I stand blinking in the late afternoon sunlight.

They have taken my phone, though. In theory, I surrendered it voluntarily but I think they would have arrested me if I hadn't. I mind losing the phone more than I minded losing my passport, really. The passport is symbolic, of course, but practicality trumps symbolism almost every time and being without my phone is wretchedly inconvenient. I shall have to borrow Annie's phone to talk to Ellie. Mr Christodoulou will have to wait, though I would like to know what he wants to thank me for. Is it possible that he was being ironic?

On the bus home I'm still fizzing with adrenalin and caffeine (I got a second cup of coffee this afternoon, but I've had nothing to eat since the breakfast pancakes). At some point I shall feel exhausted, I suppose, but at the moment I'm busy composing my account of my interrogation to email to David later on. As I tell it to myself, it's really quite amusing and I manage to omit any suggestion that I was, at any time, at all frightened.

Back at the villa, I find Annie and Freda on the beach. Freda is working industriously to bury her aunt in damp, gravelly sand. At the sound of my voice, Annie sits up and springs to her feet, shaking sand off herself like a wet dog. She looks at her watch and scowls at me.

'Sorry,' I say. 'I've been in the police station all day and they've taken my phone, so I couldn't let you know anything.'

'Taken your phone?'

'Yes. So I wondered if I could –'

'I'm going to have a shower,' she says, not listening, 'and then I'm going up to the hospital.' She moves away and then half turns back. 'Ellie'll be here tomorrow evening,' she says and runs up the steps into the garden.

Freda brandishes her spade at me. 'Shall I bury you?' she asks.

'Freda, my darling,' I say, 'that's the best offer I've had all day, but I am very hungry. I haven't had anything to eat since we had our pancakes. Shall we go and find some tea?'

'I'm not hungry,' she says, but she takes my hand and we walk into the house.

'Did you have yummy food with Auntie Annie?' I ask as I scour the kitchen cupboards for something quick and comforting.

'Yes,' she says, but then adds, 'but I can't remember what I had.' This I take to mean that I would disapprove of her day's food intake and she has been sworn to secrecy. *Sorry, Ellie*, I apologise silently.

I find a stash of baked beans and make myself a plateful of beans on toast with a lot of butter on the toast. I persuade

Freda to drink a glass of milk and to share an apple with me for pudding, which makes me feel a bit better. As we are finishing, Adam comes in.

'Ah, Gina,' he says, 'I haven't seen you all day.'

'No. I've been at the pol –'

'Anyway, I've found you now.'

Why is it that I've become inaudible all of a sudden?

'The thing is,' he says, 'Sophie's mother is arriving tomorrow and –'

'Has there been any news of Sophie?'

'What? No, nothing. But her mother rang to say she's coming and I wondered if you could – you know – take charge of her.'

'Take charge of her?' I ask, busying myself with washing up my plate and glass.

'Well, she sounded pretty anxious on the phone and she hadn't thought about where she was going to stay or anything, and I just thought if you could –'

'Take charge of her.'

'Yes.' He runs a hand over his unshaven face. 'The thing is, Conrad's father is arriving on Sunday.'

'J.C. Wagner in person?'

'Yes. I knew he wanted the – Conrad's body taken to Oxford for the funeral. The police told me that. I assumed he would send a minion to deal with it but he's in Europe already, apparently. It seems he had been planning to come and see the show.'

I suddenly remember Conrad's text message. 'Oh, yes,' I say, 'I knew that.'

'You knew? Conrad didn't say anything.'

'He had a text message and I happened to see it. Everything that's happened knocked it completely out of my head.'

'Well, he's coming on Sunday. I assume it'll be a flying visit – literally, in his private jet. I've no idea how you deal with a

136

bereaved film mogul but I feel, you know, that I should give him my full attention.'

'I wonder how much he cares.'

'I don't know. He's got half a dozen other children, by various wives.'

'Still, he is coming himself to take his son home. Or to Oxford, anyway. I wonder why Oxford.'

'The only place Conrad ever really lived in, I think. His mother took to booze and pills after the divorce; Conrad was packed off to Eton and spent holidays with whoever would have him. He spent a couple of holidays with James, you know, in whatever embassy his father had at the time. Cairo, I think.'

'The development people in Oxford will be excited. They'll be hoping for a Wagner College.'

'So you'll look after Mrs Forrester?'

'I will. Come on, Freda. Bath time.'

I feel honour bound to give Freda full value in the bedtime ritual since I haven't seen her all day, and she milks my guilt for all it's worth. Settled in bed, finally, read to, sung to and kissed, she declares that she can't sleep because the room is *too messy*. When I point out that she won't be able to see the mess in the dark, she buries her face in her pillow and says she doesn't like Sophie's things, and now I look at them, I don't either, really. Sophie's stuff is everywhere, crumpled up on her bed, strewn on the floor, draped over chairs, spilling out of her suitcase, and there is something pathetic about these things, something expectant, as though they are waiting for their sad little owner to return. Why haven't we had any news about Sophie? Has anyone rung the hospital? Annie obviously went there to see Jon not Sophie but will she bring back news?

'I'll pack it all up,' I say, 'and put it in her case.'

'And then you can take it to the hospital,' she says, turning her back to the room and finding her comforting thumb.

137

I haul Sophie's suitcase up onto her bed and open it up. It's a square, old-fashioned, leather case and inside the lid it carries an inscription in red ink, *Sophie Jane Forrester, Venn House, Ashenden School, Dorset.* Inside is some rather grey underwear and a small, bald, teddy bear wearing a blue knitted scarf. Unmethodically, I start collecting up Sophie's belongings and packing them into the case. They look as limp, unwashed and forlorn as Sophie looked in the past few days. I survey the grubby bras, the saggy t-shirts yellowish under the arms, the scuffed shoes, the squeezed-out tubes of sun cream and concealer, and the truly filthy brush and comb. I picture the case as it might have looked when it made its first journey with Sophie to her expensive new school. I see name-taped piles of navy blue knickers and grey socks, crisply-folded white blouses and fleecy pyjamas, pleated skirts, a shiny striped tie and, in the corner, the teddy bear, slightly less bald, wearing his blue scarf. Oh, hell, I'm going to start crying. I move briskly over to the dressing table and sweep up the litter of bits and pieces there to put into the case. A square of card flutters to the ground and I pick it up. *Conrad Wagner, Christ Church, Oxford* it has embossed on the top, and underneath, handwritten, is *Ro i Sindet, København* and a phone number written European style with crossed sevens. I pile it with the other odds and ends into the case, jam the lid down and stand the case by the door. Then I pick up my laptop, kiss Freda once more, turn off the main light and slip outside.

Out in the corridor, I sit down on the floor and go into my emails. There I find a message from David, sent in the early hours of this very long day and now sadly out of date. Its warnings against getting involved with the murder inquiry and admonitions not to let the police know I think they're stupid ring with an irresistible tragicomic irony. I would laugh if I weren't too tired. I ought to reply but I haven't the energy now to tell him the whole story. If I had a phone I would ring him but as it is brevity will have to do.

Too late, cock! I write. *Second incident and I seem to be a suspect so am involved will I, nill I. Would talk but phone is in custody. It just gets better and better. xG*

I go and clean my teeth and then I sit back on the floor, lean my head against the wall, close my eyes and wait for a reply. It's not long before I hear the beep of an incoming message. *I could come over,* it says. *Do you want me there?*

Do I want him here? More than anything in the world at this moment I want him here. I want him to jump out of a taxi here, in front of the house, looking tanned and good-looking and grown-up, and sweep me into his arms, laying to rest once and for all any suspicions anyone in this house may have that I'm only here because I'm a sad old bag without a life. Then I want him to sweep into Helsingør police station and do much the same thing there, making it clear, additionally, that I have no reason to be preying on beardless youths. After that, I want him to solve these mysteries with a dazzling display of professional brilliance, leaving Mortensen and Larsen amazed and shamed. And finally I want him to carry me off to the Marienlyst hotel, where we will dine under the stars and make love in a cool, blue room with its windows open to the song of the sea. I settle the laptop on my knees and I type:

No need.

Am coping fine.

But thanks anyway.

G

Then I switch off, carry it into the bedroom, pull off my clothes, climb into Sophie's bed and weep.

13

DAY SIX

A mote it is to trouble the mind's eye. 1.1

Cycling up a steady gradient with cramp in one's legs and the sun on one's back is not conducive to logical thought. Even less conducive is freewheeling down a gradient with the sea breeze deliciously cooling on one's sweaty arms and face. The ride north along the coast from Helsingør to Hornbæk offers both of these sensations and I'm quite happy, for the moment, to block out thought of any kind. In my sleep, I pursued crazy, repetitive lines of thought endlessly and woke feeling sick and exhausted. The idea of the cycle ride, which I had promised Freda we would definitely do today, seemed impossibly strenuous, but in the end hanging around here, coping with her boredom and disappointment, seemed even worse. So here we are.

I'm not used to cycling so far, and with solid little Freda on the back, but I keep going resolutely, absorbing the intense glitter of the sea and the shimmer of the white houses, which have an almost Mediterranean feeling today but for the clarity of the northern light and the briskness of the breeze that ruffles leaves and flags along the road. There is enough here to stun the senses and daze me into thoughtlessness and I carry on until the point where I feel I might bring us both crashing to the ground and I slither to a halt, climbing off cautiously on cotton wool legs. I lean the bike against a tree, lift Freda from her seat and sit down on the roadside grass for a minute to recover. Then I haul myself to my feet and wheel the bike into the stretch of dark conifers behind us, strung out between the road and the sea. We proceed slowly – I am amazed at the jelly-like consistency of my leg muscles – but soon we emerge again into the sun and reach the sand dunes, where Freda throws herself down in the warm sand and I'm happy to do the same.

We drink cartons of apple juice and we each eat a banana (if I make this, at least, a healthy eating day, I may be able to look Ellie in the eye this evening). Then Freda gets out her bucket and spade and starts transporting buckets of sand from one place to another with an air of serious intent. Since she is happily occupied and I have scanned the area for potential hazards and found none, I am freed for thought, so think I must. First of all, before I get to any of the substantive issues, there is the oddity of what happened this morning at the garage where I hired my bike. When I walked in, who should be at the desk in the office but the young woman in dungarees whom I last saw changing her mind about going into the police station? And she was wearing a badge which told me she was Karin Møller, so I think I'm right about her being the Karin that Conrad and James both knew. Anyway, the thing is, she looked as though she'd been beaten up. She had a really painful looking black eye and a vicious graze all down one side of her face. While a man (Karin's brother, as mentioned by Conrad? His badge says *Jonas Møller*) went to get a bike for me, I said, 'You've been in the wars, haven't you?'

She said, 'Oh, I got knocked off my bike, that's all,' and I, being me, didn't let it go at that.

'By a car?' I asked.

'By a – yes, by a car.'

She was obviously uncomfortable and I should have

dropped it but I didn't. 'They get too close, don't they?' I burbled on. 'Or they come speeding out of side roads. I'm a cyclist myself. I know how it is.'

She started looking busy with some papers. 'I hope you reported it to the police,' I said, and then the chap with my bike came in and said, quite aggressively, 'She doesn't need the police. She's fine.' And, of course, it went through my mind to wonder whether he had, in fact, beaten her up and the bike accident was just a cover. But they got very businesslike over the hire arrangements and that was that. Still, I can't help wondering.

And now there's Sophie to think about. Annie did manage to get some information yesterday, though not directly; there was a police guard on Sophie's room, apparently, and no-one was giving anything away. Jon, though, had managed to charm one of the nurses looking after him and convince her that he and Sophie were bosom friends. She reported that Sophie was *seriously ill but not in danger,* so that's something, though I guess it will be a while before she's able to say what happened to her.

I came to a view in the night which made sense then, though I'm not sure how it will look in the light of day. Given that I know that I didn't tell James that Sophie was talking about blackmail in a way that put him back in the frame for Conrad's murder, and that I didn't tell him that Sophie was in the castle because I had no idea that she was, I can't see how James could possibly have been the person who pushed her in the moat. So who did, if anyone? I keep picturing her as I found her in the wine cellar, dressed in her ragged white dress and looking really very pretty with makeup on and colour in her face and her gingery-fair hair in little ringlets round her head. She looked ready, in fact, to pose for any pre-Raphaelite painter as a model for drowned Ophelia. Could that be what she was doing? I didn't buy her story about wanting to come

142

and rehearse in her costume; it made no sense because, as far as she knew, James was in police custody and there was going to be no play. On the other hand, her despair last night – *There's no-one now* – does make sense, now that I know that she was pregnant. *Was* pregnant or *is* pregnant? Mortensen said, 'Why didn't you tell me that Sophie Forrester was pregnant?' I couldn't get him to tell me anything more and I don't know how to interpret that *'was* pregnant'. My immediate fear was that it meant that Sophie was dead, but then I realised that it might mean just that she wasn't pregnant any more, and finally I wondered if it might actually just be a grammatical thing – correct sequence of tenses in indirect speech – 'Why *didn't* you tell me' in the past tense and therefore 'that she *was* pregnant'. We are pretty slack in English about following sequence of tenses but non-native speakers tend to be more accurate; it would rather depend on how it's done in Danish, I suppose.

Well, she was pregnant, and supposing the break-up with James was because of the child? James looks cold-hearted enough for that. Then where did Conrad fit in? As a new boyfriend ready to father the infant? Or as provider of the money for an abortion in a nice private clinic? I try to dredge up what I know about Sophie's background. Earlier this year, I went to Oxford to see Annie in a strange play about cockroaches written by a student. Sophie was in it too and I was introduced to her mother, up from Sunningdale for the weekend. She was a very quiet woman with a clipped accent that was old-fashioned RP even for Sunningdale. She had an anxious, nervous manner, as though she found the vulgarity of the world too much for her, and she made me feel loud and brash. She could have been a cathedral canon's widow except that she is, in fact, the widow of an army officer, killed in a helicopter crash when Sophie was quite young. Sophie, she told me, was an only child and her father would have been

143

terribly proud of her. But not of an illegitimate baby, I suppose. Was that enough to have made Sophie actually suicidal about her pregnancy? I can hardly believe that a young woman with an Oxford degree at the beginning of the 21st century could be that desperate, and yet I can't shake off the sense that Sophie was dressed to be seen, to embody her own misery as the ruined maid of whom Ophelia sings and to go to a watery grave in the person of Ophelia.

And here's the thing – the thing I haven't admitted yet – if Sophie was trying to kill herself, how can I not be to blame? She had shared a bedroom with me for four nights and I could see that she was unhappy but I never really tried to find out why. And when she came close to telling me something with her pathetic little cry of *there's no-one now*, I fumbled it. Some mother hen I turned out to be.

Conrad's death I can look at with more detachment, at least, and I have the feeling that last night, at some point, I had the glimmering of an idea about that too. It was to do with that text message on his phone, though now I can't remember what it was, and it was probably nonsense anyway. There was something Annie said this morning as well, though. It was at breakfast and she had passed on the news about Sophie and then I asked how Jon was, and she said, 'Oh fed up with being hoist.' I didn't know what she meant and she got snappy and said, 'You know, having his leg held up in that thing. It's called a hoist, isn't it?' So now I'm putting that together with the text message and Karin and the man in the garage and I have an idea. It's wild, certainly, and I can't imagine myself telling Anders Mortensen, or even David, about it but the more I think about it the better it seems, so I lie in the sand and watch Freda through half-closed eyes and try fitting everything else in around it until Freda comes and pokes me quite hard with a stick and tells me that she's hungry and she needs a wee.

I purchased our healthy lunch at the shop attached to the

garage and I unpack it now with some pride: ham and cheese in slightly sweet little rolls rather like old-fashioned bridge rolls, sticks of celery and plastic tubs of cut-up fruit, which I usually despise as being there to tempt the idle and profligate but which are perfect for today – and Freda likes the little plastic fork that comes with hers. In fact, Freda likes all of it. She asks rather doubtfully, 'Do I like cerely?' but she crunches away at it when told firmly that she does. My self-esteem as a grandmother, at least, begins to rise. And I have provided a treat to round off this sensible meal: a small bar of fair trade chocolate – the only kind I allow myself to buy since I learned that the production of all other chocolate involves an element of labour by trafficked children. Did you know that?

After lunch, we paddle for a bit and then, mindful that Susan Forrester will be arriving, I pack us up and start the ride home. It is less fun that the outward journey because I'm tired and I don't want to go back to everything that's waiting for me back in Helsingør, but I get us back to the garage in one piece, hand the bike back to the man who may or may not be Karin's brother (she is nowhere to be seen) and catch the bus along the coast to the villa.

As we walk in through the gates to the villa, someone is getting out of a hire car from Copenhagen. It is, astonishingly, David. My fantasy scenario of last night (the sweeping into arms et cetera) cannot come to pass, however, for a number of reasons. The most important is that I am in a disgusting condition; I am salty, sandy, sticky, sweaty and smelly, wind blown and frizzy-haired, and wearing a pair of shorts such as no woman of my age should be seen in ever, anywhere. It looks as though David may be going to attempt something like the sweeping thing anyway but I stop him in his tracks. 'I thought I told you not to come,' I say, and I sound more unfriendly than I expected to, even to myself, so he sweeps Freda into his arms instead, where she jigs up and down with delight. A second reason why it is hardly the moment for me to melt into his arms is that he seems to have brought a woman with him. The passenger side door of the car has opened and a woman of about my age has climbed out and is advancing towards me. She has to get quite close before I recognise her as Susan Forrester.

'David and I met on the plane from Gatwick,' she says in her hushed, lady-like little voice, politely ignoring my unseemly get-up and bravely putting out a cool hand to shake my hot one. 'I think we probably got the last two seats right at the back.' She sounds composed for a woman whose daughter's life may still be hanging in the balance, but her eyes fill up as she says, 'David has been so kind, driving me here from Copenhagen. I don't know what I'd have done without him.'

David looks uncomfortable, as he always does when people are nice about him, and says, 'I'll be happy to take you to the hospital as soon as you're ready.'

She gazes at him with something close to adoration, this polite, kind and competent man. I wonder if he has told her he's a chief inspector; that would be the icing on the cake. Anyway, she can borrow him for a bit, since her need is greater than mine, but I may have to make it clear at some point that he's spoken for. In the meantime, I am truly sorry for her and I'm happy to be generous.

'I am so sorry about Sophie,' I say, giving her hand a sticky squeeze. 'Have you spoken to the hospital recently? We haven't been able to get much information, not being family.' (I don't add, *and possible murder suspects*.) 'How is she?'

'She's in what they call *a medically induced coma*,' she says, 'because of the head injury. But they say she is stable and I can go and see her.' She looks at David and then at me. 'Perhaps we could have a cup of tea?' she asks. 'And then go?'

I usher them out into the garden, where they settle on a

bench under a tree, Freda still clinging to David, and then I go into the kitchen, where Emma is washing vegetables, and ask if she could possibly make a cup of tea while I go and shower. Upstairs, I find our room in chaos. Drawers have been emptied, the beds have been stripped and the contents of Sophie's suitcase are lying in a heap on the floor. I haven't got time to wonder about this now. I bundle stuff back into the drawers and into the case and leave the beds till later. Then I wash my hair in the shower, apply a lot of deodorant and too much perfume and rummage through my clothes for something to wear. Most of the clothes I have with me have been subjected to the Freda treatment by now and bear the scars accordingly, but I find a skirt I haven't worn yet, and a black sleeveless top that looks vaguely cool. There is no time to blow dry my hair, so it will dry into a frizz, but it will have to do.

They have had their tea and are ready to go when I get back downstairs, and they depart amid little cries of appreciation from Susan Forrester – *So kind! Really very kind!* I wave them off and wonder what to do next. For some reason, the most urgent thing seems to be the blow drying, so I do that, taking Freda with me and giving her my strings of beads to play with.

When I turn the hairdryer off, we hear the sound of a car on the gravel outside and then a voice issuing orders. 'No, keep it the right way up, Ben! It'll be wrecked if you carry it like that!' The tone would be unmistakeable, even we didn't recognise the voice. It has a particular brisk bossiness that is passed down in the female line in my family – on the mitochondrial DNA, I believe – and Freda is already showing signs of it. For the moment, though, she looks at me wonderingly. 'Mummy?' she asks.

We speed downstairs to a frenzy of hugs and kisses. Then Annie appears from nowhere and before long I am *de trop*; it is clear that she intends to give Ellie the narrative of the week's events and would rather not have editorial interventions from me.

'Well, I'll leave you to it,' I say, 'but if you want to know about my three-hour interrogation by the police, Ellie, I'll be happy to tell you some time. And Freda, do tell Mummy what we had for our picnic today.'

I wander off to consider the next few hours. I wonder where David intends to stay. He doesn't know that Ellie is here and I am released from Freda duty, so that should be a joyful surprise, shouldn't it? The cool, blue room at the Marienlyst begins to seem like less of a fantasy; Ellie and Ben and Freda can have the room here, can't they? And I can decamp with David. I find my laptop and get onto the hotel website to find the phone number. Then, because I have no phone, I go through the garden to the beach to see if I can find someone to borrow a phone from.

Most of the company are on the beach, but they are not the raucous crowd we encountered when we arrived five days ago. There are no ball games going on and no-one even seems to be swimming. They are sitting or lying around in groups, reading or talking quietly. If it weren't for the sand and sea setting, they would most resemble travellers who have encountered an unexpected hitch and been delayed on their journey. They look like people who are waiting for something, unable to enjoy the present moment, pleasant enough though it is, because the next stage is the important thing. I see Zada sitting on a rock like a siren, talking animatedly on her phone and I wait until she has finished before moving across to her. Her expression as she watches me approach is alarmed and defiant both at once, with defiance winning by the time I get close.

'It's all right,' I say. 'I haven't come to shout at you. You told the police what you knew, like we're supposed to. It led to my spending a day at the police station and having my phone confiscated, but don't worry about it.'

'I do feel a bit bad,' she says.

'Bad enough to lend me your phone for a quick call? It's local.'

'Feel free.' She hands it over. 'You chose a good day to be out. The police have been here looking for James's mobile and I have to tell you they treated my vintage Issey Miyake with total disrespect.'

'That's why my room's in chaos. I thought I'd been singled out.'

'Nope. We all got the treatment. Shall I move away?'

'You're fine. It's not personal,' I lie.

When I get through to a young woman in reception at the Marienlyst I ask if a Mr David Scott has a reservation for tonight and I'm told, as I feared I would be, that she cannot give out that sort of information. 'How awkward,' I say. 'The thing is, (giggles girlishly) he is my boyfriend.' There, I've said it. 'We're supposed to be meeting here for a few days' break but I've got a feeling that we may have got our wires crossed and we both think the other one has booked a room.' Silence. 'Of course,' I say, 'if you still have rooms available, it's not a problem. We can simply – do you have rooms available?'

'We have one or two,' she concedes warily.

'Well, look, I think the best thing is if I book one of those just to be on the safe side, and if it turns out that he has already booked then we can cancel one. Of course, that will be a bit annoying for you, having two rooms tied up and not available for anyone else, especially as he won't be arriving till quite late, but –'

'Did you say Scott?' she asks.

'Yes. David.'

'Mr Scott has already a reservation,' she says coldly.

'Oh fine, good. Excellent. They're not always as useless as you think they are, are they? Men, I mean.' I'm wondering now how I can find out whether he's booked a double room. 'I hope he's booked a really nice room,' I say. I try the girlish giggle again.

'Mr Scott has a reservation for a double room with a sea view,' she says. 'Is there anything else?'

There isn't and I hang up.

Zada has been listening to this with delight. 'Gina Gray,' she says, 'what are you up to?'

'Planning to have my wicked way with a policeman, Zada,' I say and return her phone. Then I run upstairs and pack some things into my hand luggage bag. The sight of my sweaty cotton pyjamas brings me up short, though, and I snatch up my purse and run crazily down the road to the little parade of shops where I spotted the underwear *butik* on that innocent day when we first arrived here. The wares here are pretty cheap and quite nasty, tending to slippery viscose in unconvincing colours, but I find a sky blue nightdress that will be all right when I've cut the large bow off the front of it, and is certainly an improvement on the sweaty pyjamas. I pay and run back, getting indoors just before David returns.

My plans for tonight's sleeping arrangements are, astonishingly, accepted without argument; Ellie and Ben may have an argument with Freda if they try to displace her from the big bed but I shan't be there so it doesn't matter. David has found a guest house for Susan Forrester near the hospital and freed himself from responsibilities there, so in the early evening we drive up to the Marienlyst Hotel's calm, wide, white stucco front for all the world like any normal couple away on a mini-break. A policeman and a murder suspect? Who knew?

Our room actually is cool and blue and we pour ourselves drinks from the mini-bar and sit out on the balcony watching the sea. When we're settled, though, and I try to get started on my theories about Conrad and Sophie, David absolutely refuses to listen. He's seeing Anders Mortensen tomorrow, he says, and he needs to go in with a completely open mind. He will happily discuss it all with me after that but for this evening the subject is off limits.

'Well, what are we going to talk about, then?' I demand truculently, and he says rather snappishly that I could ask him how his week has been, so I get sarcastic and we very nearly have our first row before we've even got as far as dinner. Then it starts to rain (really, the weather here is so like ours it's no wonder Hengist and Horsa felt so much at home in England) and we decide to go and eat. We find we have the choice of an American barbecue or an ultra-chic menu on which all the vegetables seem to have been reduced to heaps of pastel foam. We opt for this one and though we can't dine under the stars, as I had imagined, because of the rain, our shared amusement at the foams gets us into a better humour. And David tells me about the Viking ship museum in Roskilde, which he came to on a holiday with his parents, and it's such a relief just to sit and listen and not have to talk that I cheer up considerably and eat two puddings since the foams were not at all filling.

Back in the cool blue room, we don't open the windows wide to the song of the sea because of the rain and because the wind has got up sufficiently to blow small objects off the dressing table. When I put on the sky-blue nightie and get into the wide, soft bed, I feel a wonderful sense of relaxation and release from thought, as though my brain has been injected with a local anaesthetic, and as I drift off to sleep while David is in the bathroom cleaning his teeth, I think that there is something I'm supposed to be staying awake for but I can't remember what, and it probably doesn't matter anyway.

14

COLLABORATION

'You really will have to wake up now,' Scott said, 'or the coffee will be cold.' He watched as she struggled up from sleep.

'What?' she said. 'Where – who's – why are you wearing a suit?'

'Official business. I'm seeing Anders Mortensen at ten thirty. I left it as long as I could to order breakfast.

'Breakfast? Where?'

'Out on the balcony if you think it's warm enough.'

She climbed out of bed, took down his raincoat which was hanging behind the bedroom door, slipped her feet into his slippers and shuffled out onto the balcony. 'Lovely,' she said, putting a croissant on a plate and pouring coffee. She lapsed into silence though as she ate, her eyes preoccupied. She was looking slightly better for her night's sleep, he thought, but still oddly unlike herself. Wrapped in the oversized grey-brown coat, she looked sallow and small and almost vulnerable, if one could ever use that word about Gina.

Eventually she said, 'So you've told Mortensen you're a policeman?'

'Yes. *Happened to be in the area. Wondered if I could offer any help from the UK end.*'

'Did you mention me?'

'God, no. He won't talk to me if he thinks I've got a personal interest, will he?'

'I suppose not. So what's your cover story? Why are you *in the area*? Viking ships?'

He smiled, pleased with himself over this particular inspiration. 'Well, meeting Susan Forrester on the plane was a piece of luck. I was having trouble coming up with a convincing story but she's the perfect cover. I can say I'm an old friend and she's asked me to come along and give her some support at this difficult time. I've asked her and she's happy to go along with that if it means I can winkle information out of the police here.'

'Isn't that a personal interest?'

'Not the same,' he said. He looked at his watch, realised it was time to go and went inside to gather up wallet, keys, sunglasses and phone. 'Sophie's a victim,' he called. 'You're a suspect.'

'Well, thanks.'

He turned to look at her. She looked stricken. What had he said?

'What's the matter?' he asked, going out to her.

'Nothing's the matter. It's fine.' She had her face hidden in her coffee mug.

'When I said you're a suspect, I didn't mean that *I* think you're a suspect. I just meant – you know what I meant.'

'Do I?'

'Yes. And the aim is that by the end of my session with Mortensen you won't be a suspect any more.'

'Right.'

He looked at her. 'OK?'

She nodded. 'It's just –'

'Just what?'

'Just that this isn't how I imagined it would be.'

'How what would be?'

'Your being here.'

'You told me not to come, as I recall.'

'Yes.'

'But you imagined what, exactly?'

'Oh, you know, the knight in shining armour thing. Like you're doing for Susan Forrester.'

'Well,' he said, turning to go, 'I think you'll find this method will do the job better. The shining armour thing would just have got me booted down the station steps.'

'OK.'

'You look exhausted,' he said – unwisely, as he realised from the look on her face. 'Go back to bed. Rest. Don't think. I'll see you later.'

'See you,' she said, and turned to look out to sea.

Anders Mortensen greeted him civilly but not warmly, much as he himself would have greeted an officer from a foreign force who strayed onto his patch in the middle of a murder inquiry, Scott conceded. 'So, what brings you to Helsingør exactly?' Mortensen asked,

'I came with Susan Forrester, Sophie Forrester's mother. She's very upset, obviously. Her husband's dead and she was worried about coming here and coping with all this on her own so I offered to come with her.'

'And what is your relationship with her?'

'I don't have a rel – I'm an old friend. An old family friend.'

'I see.' They had arrived at Mortensen's office and he stopped at the door to give Scott a searching look. 'I'm sure you'll understand,' he said as he ushered him into the room, 'when I tell you that I made some background checks on you after you telephoned.'

'And what did you find?'

'That you are who you say you are.' Mortensen smiled briefly. 'You are a detective chief inspector in the Marlbury police force. What size city is Marlbury?'

'Not large. About 40,000 people.'

'There are two residents of Marlbury involved in this case. I wonder if you know them at all? Virginia and Marianne Gray?'

He was looking intently at Scott as he produced the names. Scott had expected that he would make the Marlbury connection but it still felt like an on the spot decision when he said, 'I have come across Virginia Gray, yes. She works in one of the universities.'

'So she does. But these are not her students.'

'No.'

'She is here at her daughter's request, I understand. She has prepared the costumes for their performance.'

'Really?'

'Really.' Again Scott got the intent gaze, then Mortensen seemed to relax. 'So,' he said, leaning back in his chair, 'you said you have been following reports of the case – or cases – in the newspapers. What do you know so far?'

Scott sketched in what he knew about Conrad's death, omitting circumstantial detail provided by Gina, and then said, 'About Sophie Forrester I know only that she appears to have fallen, jumped or been pushed from the battlements into the moat at the castle and that you are holding one of the students, James Asquith, in custody. I've not been to the castle yet but I've looked at some images on line. They're not battlements as one might imagine them are they? It's a grassed over area.'

'But it's a long fall.'

'Oh yes.'

Mortensen watched him. 'Mrs Forrester – Susan, did you say? – has not yet spoken to me –'

'No. She's most concerned with what the hospital can tell her. That's why she asked me to –'

'What has she told you about her daughter's condition?'

'That she has been kept in a medically induced coma but that the doctors are hoping to bring her out of that today.'

'Nothing more?'

'No.'

'No mention of a pregnancy?'

'No?'

'It may be that the hospital staff have not told her that. But Sophie was pregnant – only a few weeks – and she lost the child after her fall. James Asquith admits that he was the father of the child, and he admits that their relationship had broken up because he didn't want her to have the child.' He opened a file and handed a sheet of paper to Scott. 'A transcript of a text message we found on Sophie Forrester's phone. It was sent to her at 07.05 on the morning of her fall.'

Scott looked at the words on the page, scanned, it seemed, from the screen of a phone.

Police are releasing me this
morning. Want to start with
a clean slate. A chance for
you and I to put things right.
How about we meet and
rehearse our scene just the
two of us? Our secret. Then
we can knock their socks off
at rehearsal. Wear the white
dress to get us in the mood,
you look beautiful in it anyway.
Not sure about my timing.
9.30ish? On the battlements.
xxJ

Scott scanned the message and wondered what Gina would make of it.

'What does he say about this?' he asked.

'He denies that he sent it. He says he didn't have his phone with him when he was brought in.'

'And he wasn't searched?'

'He came voluntarily for questioning. He wasn't arrested.'

'What would his motive have been?'

'Sophie Forrester told someone that Conrad Wagner was blackmailing Asquith. It is possible that he wanted to silence her.'

'What was the blackmail about?'

'We don't know and we won't until Sophie is able to talk to us.'

'The person she told about the blackmail –'

'– Says that Sophie refused to say any more.'

'And you believe that?'

'I'm not sure. The person is Virginia Gray, as it happens.'

'Really?' Scott was thankful that he had not let Gina tell him this part of the story and didn't have to act surprise. 'But she thought it was worth telling you about it all the same.'

'In fact, she didn't. This information came to us from one of the other students who overheard the conversation.'

He digested this for a moment and then asked, 'What does Asquith say about the blackmail?'

'He absolutely denies it. He says that Sophie is a hysterical person. Virginia Gray is of the same opinion.'

'Is she? Right.'

Mortensen cleared his throat. 'We are,' he said, 'uncertain what part she played in Sophie's fall. She was at the castle at the time and offered no very convincing reason why.'

'What reason did she give?'

'That she took her granddaughter to the café at the castle for breakfast.'

'Sounds reasonable,' Scott said, aiming for casual detachment.

'But she came first here to the police station to collect Asquith, who we had just released.'

'Came to collect him?' Scott pictured Gina on her bike. 'In a cab?'

'No. The students have a van. She came with Asquith's

friend in the van. And then she invited them to come for breakfast. Isn't that strange, when she was taking her granddaughter to breakfast?'

Scott pondered for a moment the continuing mystery that was Gina. 'Perhaps she felt sorry for him,' he suggested lamely.

'Perhaps. And then the gatekeeper had trouble with her – a story about a missing key which was a lie. And she was heard having an argument with Sophie, which she doesn't explain well. Her account of her movements is full of inconsistencies.'

God, Gina, Scott thought, *what the hell have you been doing?*

He said, 'But, as I understand it, she had her granddaughter with her, so she can hardly –'

'Oh, we don't think she pushed the girl herself, but we did wonder if she was part of the trap. Now that we have this text message, though, that looks less likely. The trap, it seems, was set without any help. But her behaviour is still puzzling. And it has been all along. She seems to be very attached to Asquith.'

'Attached?' Scott asked evenly.

'Very ready to defend him. From the beginning, she argued that he was not responsible for Wagner's death.'

'What puts him in the frame for Wagner's death? Apart from the blackmail story?'

'He is the only person we can place near the car at the right time. We've been through the CCTV images and no-one approached the car in the course of that afternoon. Unfortunately, we don't have complete images of the car during the morning when Wagner and Asquith were working on it. A –' he sought for the word '– camping van with tall sides was parked next to it for a while and it obscured the picture.'

'Was Asquith alone with the car at any time?'

'He says not and the CCTV gives us no help on that. It may be that it was done under Wagner's nose, so to speak.'

'Not an easy thing to do.'

'No.'

Mortensen shifted in his chair and Scott took is as a signal that he had been given as much time as professional courtesy demanded. 'Just one last thing,' he said. 'Where did Asquith say he left his phone?'

'On a table at the house where the students are living. We have tried to locate it but it is switched off, naturally. We have questioned the other students and made a search. We have also made a search in the grounds of the castle.'

'How did Asquith arrange to be picked up from here that morning?'

'He used the pay phone.'

'Right.' Scott stood up but didn't move immediately to the door. 'Thank you for being so open with me. What strikes me – and I'm sure it has struck you too – is that if Asquith is guilty, and if his motive was to silence anyone who knew why he was being blackmailed, then anyone else who might know about the blackmail – Gi – Virginia Gray, particularly, and whoever it was who overheard her conversation with Sophie –'

'– An Armenian girl – Zada Petrosian.'

'Right. Well, if he's responsible then all the time he's in custody, they're safe. I take it you're intending to keep him until you've been able to talk to Sophie Forrester?'

'We are. But we have to play by the rules here, especially in this case. Asquith's father is a former ambassador. We have already had representatives from the British embassy on the phone. We will have to charge him or release him in the next twenty-four hours. Excuse me for a moment. I have just thought of something.'

He went out giving Scott the opportunity he had feared he wouldn't get of transcribing into his diary the words of the message to Sophie. *No gift*, he thought, *could thrill Gina more.*

Mortensen came back, apologising. 'Talking of playing by the rules made me think that we might be able to return to Mrs Gray her mobile phone, since all the traffic on it appears quite innocent. I thought you might be able to return it to her if you are going to the students' house at all, but it seems the laboratory is not quite finished with it yet. Tomorrow, perhaps.' He shook hands with Scott and ushered him out.

A visit to the castle to view the crime scenes was next on Scott's agenda. He parked in the car park and looked around it with interest, noting the positions of the CCTV cameras and how much of the area was visible from the gatehouse. He wondered whether the high-sided camper van had parked after Wagner had parked his car or whether he had chosen to park next to it, possibly at Asquith's suggestion. Then he took the sweeping path into the castle, pausing on the bridge to look up at the ramparts and the length of the drop into the moat, He walked on up to the ramparts and looked down into the grey water below, wondering how deep it was, whether Sophie Forrester could swim and who knew whether she could or not. She had hit her head, of course, so the question was academic to some extent.

Driving back to the hotel, he considered what to tell Gina. He had hardly ridden to her rescue as she so uncharacteristically wanted him to, but he had the text message, a *tomorrow perhaps* for the return of her phone and a *now that looks less likely* about her involvement. A pretty good haul, he would have said, but her face this morning had suggested that complete vindication or nothing was what she had in mind. It was only twelve-thirty and he half expected to find her back in bed or still sitting gazing out to sea, but he found the room cleaned and empty. He reached for his phone and remembered that would be no use, so he wrote her a note on a sheet of the hotel's crested paper – *Not a bad morning's work. Have a present for you. In the bar. Lunch?* – and left it on the bed.

The bar was in the interior of the hotel, without access to the brilliant light of sun on sea; it seemed to be furnished and lit for a moody evening ambience but he bought a pint of

Carlsberg and settled down on a leather sofa at the far end of the room with a view of the foyer and re-ran the morning's conversation in his head. What he came up with was a list of unasked questions, which he made a note of, wondering whether he could somehow claim a second session with Mortensen. Only if he had something to give in return, he thought, and that would depend on Gina.

He had finished his lager and was thinking of ordering lunch when Gina appeared. He watched her warily as she scanned the room; you just never knew with her what you were going to get. This morning he'd got wounded and tragic; now cats and cream came to mind. She had changed something about her appearance, he thought as she sashayed across to him, so this was a test – not just noticing the change but approving it in the right terms. It didn't do to refer to the mechanism of the change; women could say to one another *you've changed your hair colour* or *I like that lipstick*, but men were supposed to be impressed by the effect without knowing how it was achieved. And if you were dealing with Gina then you had the additional challenge of steering clear of anything banal as well.

'You look –' he said, and was momentarily blank as unusable clichés flooded his mind. '– dazzling,' he managed.

It was good enough. 'Good,' she said, kissing him. 'I aim to dazzle.'

'Lunch?' he asked.

'Absolutely.'

He watched her as she picked up the menu from the table and studied it. It was the hair mainly, he decided. Shorter, maybe blonder, definitely smoother. Very good, in fact. And she was wearing a dress he hadn't seen before, dark green and sleeveless, that looked good against her skin. And she had had her nails done. He saw a pink, polished forefinger running down the menu and almost laughed aloud. He had never before seen her with painted nails. What was going on?

'What are you drinking?' she asked. 'Carlsberg? I'll have a half then. And gravad lax with dill sauce, please.'

'Your present,' he said, handing over his copy of the text message to Sophie before he went to the bar to order.

When he came back with their drinks, she laid the sheet of paper on the table and tapped it with a pink nail. 'This,' she said, 'makes no sense at all.'

'Well Mortensen seems to think that it lets you off the hook so I wouldn't be too quick to rubbish it.'

'I can't help that. This text lets James off the hook too.'

'Why?'

'Because it's the wrong dress.'

'Wrong in what sense?'

'The text says, *wear the white dress to get us in the mood* – i.e. in the mood for rehearsing their big scene. Only that's not the dress Ophelia wears in that scene. The white dress is a beaten up wedding dress – a bit Miss Havisham. When Ophelia goes mad she is obsessed with sex and the faithlessness of men. One of her songs has the lines:

'Quoth she "Before you tumbled me
You promised me to wed."
"So would I ha' done by yonder sun
Hadst thou not come to my bed."'

'So I had the idea that she could be in a wedding dress – maybe her dead mother's – but it's too long for her, especially as she's got bare feet, and it's all muddy and bedraggled round the bottom and –'

'Could we come to the point, do you think?'

'That is the point. It's her mad scene dress and it's the last thing we see her wearing, so when the queen comes in later and describes how she drowned, and how her draperies spread out on the water and held her up for a while, that's what we imagine she was wearing. And it is what Sophie was wearing when she went into the moat, which made me think that she might have thrown herself in, turning herself into drowned Ophelia for dramatic effect.'

'Why would she?'

'She was depressed – more than depressed, distraught. She was pregnant and the baby's father not only didn't want the child but didn't want her either.'

'Quite a lot of women find themselves in that situation. They don't kill themselves.'

'I know they don't but you don't know Sophie. You've met Susan, though. You can see what she's like and Sophie's cut from the same cloth. She's used to being cosseted and doing what's expected of her. She's used to being a good girl, a nice girl, her mother's pride and joy. I don't think she would have any idea how to set about life as a single mother.'

'An abortion then.'

'Well, that's the thing. I don't think she could face that on her own either.' She fished in her pocket, brought out a square of card and laid it on the table. 'I found this among her things when I packed them up. You can see it's one of Conrad's pretentious cards and I wouldn't mind betting that it's the number of an abortion clinic in Copenhagen. I looked up *Ro i Sindet* and it means *peace of mind*.'

'You didn't try ringing the number to find out?'

'David!'

'You haven't got a phone.'

'Exactly. Anyway, I think Conrad was going to help her. Possibly pay for it. Certainly take her there. They went off together to hire the car and Sophie was transformed when they came back – on top of the world. I thought it was a ploy to make James jealous, but now I think Conrad was her rescuer and then suddenly he was dead.'

'It was a possibility,' Scott said as their food arrived, 'but this text rules out suicide, doesn't it?'

'It does in a way but it can't be from James,' she said,

dolloping dill sauce onto her salmon. 'James would never have suggested that she wore that dress to rehearse their scene. Her dress for their scene is a neat little thing, short but not too short – the kind of thing the Duchess of Cambridge used to wear when she was *waity Katy* – young but respectable enough for a girl who thinks she might be going to marry the heir to the throne. And she wears it with high heels. She rehearsed in it the other day because we needed to see how much James could throw her around in that scene without it becoming indecent, so James would never –'

Scott put down his sandwich and reached out a hand to stop her. 'I hate to say it,' he said, 'but you're losing the plot. If James was making an arrangement to kill her rather than rehearse with her, it didn't matter if she was wearing the wrong dress, did it?'

'But why tell her to put that dress on?'

'Maybe so people like you would draw the same conclusion that you did – that she put the dress on to drown herself in it.'

'All right. But there are other things wrong with that text. Stylistic things. I'll need more time on it, but I'll nail them.'

'Hunches won't do. It will need to be hard evidence.'

'It will be.' She picked up her knife and fork and addressed herself again to her lunch.

They ate in silence until she had finished and then she pushed her plate away, leaned back in her seat and said, 'The thing is, if James had sent that text, wouldn't he have known that the police would find it on Sophie's phone?'

'I'm not clear about where they found her phone. Maybe he expected she would have it with her and he could sling it in the moat, but she'd left it somewhere.'

'With her clothes in the wine cellar, probably.'

'Where?'

'The king's wine cellar – it's our wardrobe. And no-one except the police could have got it from there because I'd locked it. They ought to ask the gatekeeper whether anyone asked him to unlock it, though.'

'OK.'

She reached for her drink and drained the last of it. 'I need a break from this,' she said. 'I propose we devote the afternoon to pleasure – a walk along the beach and any other pleasures we can devise. Then I've got some stuff on my laptop to show you – useful background information. We can go through it with our pre-dinner drinks.'

'Perfect,' he said. 'Who needs peanuts?'

'Prosecco?' he asked soon after six that evening, looking into the minibar.

'Save that for when we've nailed this thing. What else is there?'

'More Carlsberg.'

'Fine.'

When he took the two bottles out onto the balcony she had her laptop open.

'What is this exactly that you've got to show me?' he asked.

'A slew of emails. Annie forwarded them to me as background info so I could get a purchase on the group when I started on the costumes. They cover the assembling of the cast and crew. A bit like the opening of *The Magnificent Seven* – getting the posse together. Though not so exciting, of course.'

'I imagine not,' he said, pulling a chair round to sit beside her.

'Annie sent them to me but most of them were forwarded to her by Adam. He seems to have sent her everything. *Keeping her in the loop* he calls it.' Her eyes were on the screen as she scrolled down. Then she turned to him. 'And who is Adam?' she quizzed him.

'Can't remember.'

'Yes, you can, David.'

'Yes, I can. He's the director. Why don't you assume that

since I read and digested your email summary and I listened to Mortensen this morning, I know who people are, unless I tell you otherwise?'

'OK. Just don't be too proud to ask.' She turned back to the screen. 'Here's my inbox. I've grouped the messages by sender so all Annie's messages are together.'

Scott looked at the screen and saw a collection of a dozen or so messages dated between 3rd and 12th May, all forwarding other messages. These were followed by six messages, all with the subject 'Hamlet', which appeared to be correspondence just between Annie and Gina.

'Start with that one,' she said, pointing. 'The earlier ones aren't important really, but you can look at them later if you like.'

He pulled the laptop towards him and edged his chair away in a vain attempt to suggest that he would like to do his reading unprompted and without commentary, but he started on the one she had pointed out.

– – – original message – – –
From: Adam Barrie
To Marianne Gray
Sent 5th May 2011 23. 28
Subject Fw; Another chance

Hi Gorgeous

It occurred to me that I ought to keep you in the loop with negotiations over cast and crew. After this week's auditions the wires will be buzzing and here, predictably, is the first. I'm about to email James and do whatever it takes. If I can't get him I'll have to think again but IT WILL NOT BE CONRAD. You were there at his audition, I don't have to tell you. More to come. Watch this space

Grateful beyond words for your support.
xxA

– – – original message – – –
From: Conrad Wagner
To: Adam Barrie
Sent: 3rd May 2011 20.32
Subject: Another chance

Hi Adam

I have the feeling that I didn't do myself justice this afternoon. Auditions are such deadly things, aren't they? Could you bear to hear me again, do you think? The truth is, I really feel that Hamlet is my part and I would put my heart and soul into it.

All right if I drop in tomorrow evening after dinner?

Thanks

Conrad

Scott moved on through the messages. He was not sure what he was supposed to be looking for or noticing and he thought Gina wasn't sure either, but he surfed on through.

'Then you get Adam desperate to recruit James before he gets backed into a corner by Conrad,' Gina prompted. 'There's a reply, so you have to scroll to the bottom for the original message.' Then she seemed to notice the expression on his face and added, 'Obviously.'

'Obviously,' he said.

– – – original message – – –
From: Adam Barrie
To: James Asquith
Sent: 5th May 2011 23.35
Subject: Playing the Prince

Hi James

Can't I persuade you to read for Hamlet? I heard several yesterday but none of them was really what I want. You would fit my conception exactly.

Would it make any difference to your decision if I told you that I'm planning to cast Sophie as Ophelia?

Yours

Adam

– – – original message – – –

From: James Asquith

To: Adam Barrie

Sent: 6th May 2011 07.45

Subject: re: Playing the Prince

Dear Adam,

I am most flattered that you should think me right for Hamlet. At any other time I would be delighted but the imminence of Finals is concentrating my mind wonderfully and I should like to keep it that way.

Yours,

James

After that came an exchange with Sophie Forrester.

– – – original message – – –

From: Adam Barrie

To: Sophie Forrester

Sent: 6th May 2011 23. 29

Subject: James

Sophie darling

I'm so delighted that you've agreed to play Ophelia. Now can you use your undoubted influence with James to get him to say he'll play Hamlet? Conrad is breathing down my neck and I'm getting desperate.

xxA

From: Sophie Forrester
To: Adam Barrie
Sent: 7th May 2011 10.17
Subject: re: James

Dear Adam

I'm so excited about doing Ophelia and I shall do my utmost to get James on board. Communication between him and me is a bit hit and miss at the moment as his head is somewhere in Arabia and it won't come out until the horrors of Finals are over. I think he will do it but you may not get an answer for a while. Can you bear to wait?

xSophie

Scott ran his eyes down the subjects of the remaining emails until he found another headed *re: Playing the Prince*. It was dated 10th May.

From: James Asquith
To: Adam Barrie
Sent: 10th May 2011 07.45
Subject: Re: Playing the Prince

Dear Adam,

I can see that there will be no peace between Sophie and me until I give you an answer about Hamlet. She is terrified that she might end up playing opposite Conrad and I can see that this is not a consummation to be wished. I will, therefore, say yes, I will do it as long as I am not required to think about it until after June 18th.

My apologies for sounding so ungracious but you will understand that I need a First or I fall at the first fence.

Yours,

James

Adam celebrated this news, Scott noticed, by emailing Conrad almost at once.

– – – original message – – –
From: Adam Barrie
To: Conrad Wagner
Sent: 10th May 2011 09.04
Subject: Hamlet

Hi Conrad

Sorry about the delay in letting you know about Hamlet. It's not easy juggling the parts and getting the right balance in the casting. In the end, I am afraid, after a lot of agonising, I decided to offer Hamlet to James Asquith. It's a matter of how the other characters fit around him, really. I know this will be a big disappointment to you, but this will be a great project to be involved in, I hope, and it will look good on a CV, so I'm wondering whether you would be prepared to play Rosencrantz for me. R and G are underrated characters, I think, as Stoppard made us realise, and I want really good actors in those roles. Marianne Gray, who is AD on the production, is going to play Guildenstern and I think it will be possible to work up an interesting relationship between the two of you.
Yours
Adam

– – – original message – – –
From: Conrad Wagner
To: Adam Barrie
Sent: 11th May 2011 00.16
Subject: re: Hamlet

Hi Adam

I am very disappointed at your decision and feel that you

may be making a serious mistake, but it's your production, of course, and I accept your decision. I am a team player and I'm willing to understudy. I'm ready to play Rosencrantz if that's what you feel the part needs.

Yours

Conrad

After that came a group of emails all headed 'A Royal Pair'.

– – – original message – – –

From: Zada Petrosian

To: Adam Barie

Sent: 8th May 2011 10.16

Subject: re: A Royal Pair

Darling Adam

Thank you so much for your email which lifted the gloom of this horrid term considerably. Of course we would LOVE to play Claudius and Gertrude at Elsinore – it would be marvellous. Sickeningly, though, there is a hitch. When I mentioned it to my parents, there was great rending of garments and tearing of hair because they were planning to take Jon and me on the yacht with them round the Greek islands – a post-Finals surprise! I've persuaded Daddy to try and change the date and he's going to have a go but it means cancelling complicated business meetings and such like, so I don't know how hard he'll try.

Sorry to be such a nuisance. PLEASE don't give the parts away yet. I'll let you know as soon as I can.

Lots of love

Z

– – – original message – – –
From: Jonathan McIntyre
To: Adam Barrie
Sent: 9th May 2011 08.15
Subject: re: A Royal Pair

Dear Adam,

I gather Zada has already written to you – rather precipitately from my point of view – so I thought I should make my own position clear. As far as I'm concerned, I'd rather miss the Second Coming than the chance to play Claudius, so whether Artos Petrosian reorganises the jaunt or not, please count me in.

Yours,

Jon

– – – original message – – –
From: Zada Petrosian
To: Adam Barrie
Sent: 11th May 2011 11.22
Subject: re: A Royal Pair

Adam, darling.

We can do it! All is rearranged and I am at your disposal!

I would love to talk to you about the part if you've got the time. Will you be in the library? I have sworn to go into the Bod to revise every day. If you come and take me out for coffee I shall be even more devoted to you than I am already.

xx Z

Below this in the inbox was a series of messages with the same arresting subject line.

From: Adam Barrie a.barrie@ox.ac.uk
To: m.gray@ox.ac.uk; k.mahon@ox.ac.uk; j.asquith@ox.ac.uk;
j.mcintyre@ox.ac.uk; z.petrosian@ox.ac.uk; s.forrester@ox.ac.uk;
d.underwood@ox.ac.uk; c.wagner@ox.ac.uk;
s.pienkowsky@ox.ac.uk; t.yeoman@ox.ac.uk
Sent: 11th May 2011 23.17
Subject: naked and in the dark

Hi Everyone

We have a company! And I'm sure we're going to make a fantastic team. It's a great cast and we have the beginnings of a good backstage team – Marianne Gray as AD, Tom Yeoman doing great stuff with the music and Kelly Mahon stage managing. HOWEVER you will be performing naked and in the dark unless I can find someone to take on costumes and lighting, where I've drawn a blank so far. If any of you have any ideas for filling those roles please let me know asap.

I'm going into purdah now, re-emerging after June 18th, and I'm sure you're all doing the same.

Break a leg, all of you!

Adam

– – – original message – – –
From: James Asquith
To: Adam Barrie
Sent: 12th May 2013 08.30
Subject: re: naked and in the dark

Dear Adam,

I know a chap who might be able to do lighting, I have forwarded your message to him so he has your email and will be in touch.

Yours,

James

– – – original message – – –
From: Raymond Porter
To: Adam Barrie
Sent: 12ᵗʰ May 2011 10.12
Subject: in the dark

Hi Adam

Jim Asquith tells me you need someone to do lighting for your play, I can't pretend I'm an expert but I did a bit of stage lighting at school and I know what I'm doing around electrical stuff so I'm willing to have a go.

We should meet and talk when your exams are done, maybe you can meet James and I for a drink some time.

Ray Porter

– – – original message – – –
From: Marianne Gray
To: Adam Barrie
Sent: 12ᵗʰ May 2011 10.32
Subject: re: naked and in the dark

Hi Adam

I think I could persuade my mother to do costumes. She did them for a production my sister directed and they were pretty good. I'll tell her it's only fair she does them for me!

Leave it to me.

xx M

Scott leaned back in his chair assembling his thoughts. He would have liked some time for silent contemplation but if he didn't start talking Gina would be doing it for him, telling him what he was supposed to think. 'Well,' he said, 'Adam is quite an operator, isn't he? He obviously regards women as a soft touch. You have to admire the way he deals with

Conrad, don't you – bigging up Rosencrantz as a really important part.'

'Aren't you glad now,' she said, 'that I made you watch the Branagh film the other day? Now you know who all the characters are.'

'Absolutely,' he said. 'And it would have been nothing without your informative running commentary. I do like my films to come with additional features for the hard of understanding.'

She ignored him. 'That bit about building up his relationship with Annie as Guildenstern sounds a bit dodgy,' she said. 'It's almost pimping.'

'Apart from that,' he said, 'you can see the strains in the two relationships – James and Sophie, and Jon and Zada. It's not surprising that they'd fallen apart by the time they got here. And Zada is with Adam now, did you say? Well that was on the cards. Sophie sounds quite cheerful, doesn't she, in spite of James having his head in Arabia? Presumably she didn't know she was pregnant then.'

'Presumably. But that's character and situation. What about language? Not what they say but how they say it? What did you notice there?'

And here we are back in the seminar room, he thought, *except I'm a class of one.*

'It could be the stuff of nightmares,' he said, 'being your only pupil.'

'What?'

'Never mind. What did I notice? I noticed that James sounds like a stuffed shirt. You'd think he was a middle-aged academic already.'

'Exactly! That's what I mean about that text message to Sophie. Now there's a difference between emails and texts for some people, I know – they think of an email as a kind of letter and a text as written speech, but I don't believe that anyone who writes an email like that, with the commas after *Dear Adam* and *yours* and no short forms – no *I'm*s or *you're*s – would ever have written something so slapdash and ungrammatical in a text.'

'So does your textual analysis of these messages tell you whose style it is?'

'Not really. I've got a sort of idea but I can't make sense of it yet. There are two more people I need to tell you about, though – nothing to do with the emails.' She pulled the laptop across to her and closed the lid. 'Karin and Jonas Møller. I'll tell you about them over dinner. I'm hungry now.'

'Do you think we should try the American barbecue?' he asked. 'I think the foams might have lost their entertainment value.'

'OK but it's not good for you, all that chargrilling,' she said as they left the room. 'Still, we can have blueberry pie for pudding to make up. Blueberries are superfoods, you know.'

'Well, that's a relief,' he said.

15

DAY EIGHT

Oh villain, villain, smiling, damnéd villain. 1.5

It is quite wrong to be feeling so cheerful while the young are laid waste all about me – one dead, one comatose, one in hospital and one in a police cell – but I can't help it. I suppose it has to do mostly with the wide bed and the blue room and the windows open to the song of the sea. I've had a song running through my head since yesterday, when they were playing it in the *butik* where I bought my dress. The lyrics are mostly terrible and the tune banal but I was grabbed by the second verse and asked the girl in the shop whether they could play it again:

I close my eyes for a second and pretend it's me you want,
Meanwhile I try to act so nonchalant.
I see a summer's night with a magic moon
Every time that you walk in the room.

Nonchalant! Do you know another pop song that manages to fit *nonchalant* into its lyrics? Well, I'm making that my justification for enjoying the soppiness and sloppiness of the rest of it. I googled it later and found out that it was sung by The Searchers, one of those sixties groups that keeps going, like the Stones, and the CD I was hearing was recorded live a few weeks ago at a concert in Sweden. Hence its appearance in a Danish clothes shop, I suppose. Yes, I know it's a song for adolescents and that Searchers' concerts these days are attended by sixty-somethings and it's all incredibly naff, but there you are – you can't help an ear worm, can you?

Anyway, it suits my mood. I am pleased in general with yesterday's shopping and grooming expedition. I am pleased with myself for not spending the day sulking about David's attentions to Susan Forrester and for resorting instead to the classic makeover. I'm delighted with my hair and I've got the new dress on again today. Getting a manicure may have been a step too far, though; I'm really not the polished type.

This morning, in my new persona of svelte woman in her prime, I go to the station after breakfast to wave goodbye to my family. Ellie, Freda and Ben are getting the train down to Copenhagen and flying home this afternoon. I'm glad they are taking Freda home. I've heard nothing more from Anders Mortensen about questioning her as to my movements on the day of Sophie's fall, but I shall be happier when she's safely back in the UK. David drops me at the station and goes off on some mysterious errand. Annie has come down to see them off too, and when we have bought provisions for the journey, taken Freda to the loo, hugged, kissed, waved and watched them disappear, she says, 'Come back to the house for a bit, will you? All the parents turned up this morning and we don't know what to do with them.'

The new me feels that it's beneath her to slum it on the bus, so we get a taxi to the villa, and I take the opportunity during the journey to borrow Annie's complicated phone and ring my mother; one of the nagging worries about having my phone impounded is that she might be trying to contact me. She very rarely rings me, in fact, but if she did it would be because something was wrong. Nothing is wrong, though, except that a mini heatwave is playing havoc with her garden. She has given up watching the TV news and rarely reads a newspaper so the carnage here, though it has been of interest to the British media, has passed her by. Her world has become a very small place, I realise, since she returned home from her stay at my house. She asks how Freda is and I tell her she's on her way home, and then we run out of things to say.

'Well, take care of yourself,' I say, lamely.

'And you,' she says. And that's it.

It's thirty-six hours since I was last in the villa and it feels changed. An air of desolation hangs about it and its untidiness is no longer the vigorous clutter of young people too busy to pick things up but the listless mess of the dispirited and displaced. And they do seem literally to have been displaced; the verandah, always the hub of the house, has been taken over by grown-ups. I see what Annie means. There are eight of them, sitting in two groups, in hailing distance but ignoring one another. The groups are not hard to work out. With Susan Forrester are a couple who can only be the McIntyres, he bald with a bristly gingery moustache and she with fading fair hair and quiet blue eyes behind steel-rimmed glasses. Their clothes are unmistakeably British, his grey flannels and white shirt worn with no jacket but with a tie, hers a white blouse tucked into a neat pale blue linen skirt. Also sitting with them, I see, is a surprise guest – the kind you wish you hadn't opened the door to – my ex-husband, Andrew. *All the parents turned up,* Annie said. She couldn't have been more specific?

The other group are on sofas, facing each other across a coffee table: two tanned, fleshy, successful looking middle-aged men and two younger, blonde, decorative women. It's not hard to tell who's who though. Even if he didn't have a protective/possessive arm round Zada, I could have identified Artos Petrosian simply from Zada's account of him. He is an enormous man with a heavy, mournful, dark face and a head of suspiciously black hair. He has the huge shoulders and deep chest that can only, surely, be acquired from hours spent in a private gym, and he is gesticulating with a heavy, hairy arm that glints with gold as he speaks. The other man, by contrast, looks deskbound. He may have decided that Florida beach wear was appropriate for the north Danish coast – floral short-sleeved shirt and sandals, but he has an indoor pallor and serious spectacles. Edith Wharton describes one of her minor characters as *'a man with a business face and leisure clothes'*; well, that's Jacob Wagner. Nor could the two stepmothers be confused with one another: the third or fourth Mrs Wagner may or may not be an actress, since I imagine everyone who lives in Hollywood looks like an actress. She too has adopted the beach wear option and is wearing a halter top and Capri pants, teamed with impeccably tanned legs, an ankle chain, tiny sandals and toenails like rubies. The Honourable Alicia Petrosian, on the other hand, has opted for something with more of a yachting motif – classily cut navy trousers, leather deck shoes, white cotton sweater gleaming with just a touch of silk, discreet jewellery and hair caught back with tortoiseshell slides.

I watch them from the doorway. Artos Petrosian is doing the talking in his group, with the three women smiling and nodding, for all the world like his backing group. Jacob Wagner has gone into some sort of internal exile, intent, it would seem, on the boats out in the Sound. Adam is sitting next to him, perhaps because he feels it's his duty, perhaps because he hopes to get noticed. He's an ambitious lad is Adam, but he doesn't seem to be doing that well. As I hover, lacking an entrée to this group but unwilling to face the unwelcome surprise in the other one, Zada spots me and leaps up.

'Gina! You must come and meet my papa,' she cries, propelling me towards him. He clasps my hand in a fearsome grip and looks me intently in the eye. 'Thank you for being kind to my girl,' he says, his voice a seismic rumble of emotion.

'Oh, really, I – nothing, really,' I burble helplessly, and then turn to the Wagners. 'I am so sorry for your loss,' I say, attempting to catch his eye but failing. Mrs Wagner III or IV takes my hand. 'Thank you so much,' she breathes huskily. 'My husband appreciates it.'

After that, there seems to be nothing more to say so I make my excuses – 'Well, I must just er –' and go to join Annie in the other group. 'You didn't tell me your father was here,' I say with dangerous brightness to Annie. 'What a surprise.'

'Annie felt that I should be here,' he says with that note of sonorous self-righteousness that I have always found particularly annoying. As I sit down, he bends forward to give me, for PR purposes, a kiss on the cheek but I bend my head to pay sudden attention to the strap of a sandal and manage to hit him a glancing blow on the nose with my head. Then I determine to behave well. The McIntyres look like people with whom one would like to behave well – gentle, civilised, restrained. Spurts of malice and fury would leave them puzzled and disappointed, one feels. They are doing most of the talking here, quietly and politely keeping the conversation afloat with nice, neutral topics. Ray is with them too, helping things along, though I see Susan flinch once or twice as his breezy tone gets too much for her. She is tense and silent, her face set in an unwavering social smile, her head somewhere else.

I do a quick assessment of Andrew as he does travel talk with the others. He is still a very good-looking man, which is infuriating. (I sometimes think that I divorced him not only because he was a hopeless husband but because I resented the fact that he was better looking than me.) He still has a head of thick, dark blond hair, only mildly grey at the temples and still with a boyish lock flopping over one eye, which is, actually, ridiculous at his age. He is as well dressed as ever, in a linen jacket of an expensive caramel colour that complements his tan. Like Tony Blair, Andrew always has a tan. It's a perk of the international lawyer's life, as it is of the roving ambassador's – or whatever it is that Blair does nowadays besides after-dinner speeches, which don't get you a tan. For reasons I've never really thought about, tyranny and corruption seem to flourish in the sunnier parts of the world and where they are, there is Andrew – hence the permatan.

Looking at Annie sitting there with Andrew and the McIntyres, it strikes me that I don't really know what the situation is between Annie and Jon. Who knows what kind of understanding has developed in the four days since I last saw them together in the hospital? Annie had a proprietorial look about her even then, and he can hardly run away, can he? From the way she introduces his parents as Gordon and Jean and the way Jean calls her *my dear*, I judge that she has been accorded some kind of girlfriend status, at least by them, which puts me behind the curve.

Susan's phone rings and she reacts as people do who don't really use their mobiles, rummaging in her bag, peering at the display, fumbling to open it. Once she is connected, she listens, says, 'Oh, that's wonderful,' and starts to cry. 'She's awake,' she says, turning to me, 'and she's asking for me.'

She looks around her helplessly. 'I'd like –' she says.

'To go to the hospital,' I say. 'Would you like me to come with you?'

She would and we get up to go. Gordon McIntyre gets to his feet too, suggesting that he could take her and talk to the doctors, and Ray brandishes his keys and offers to drive her in the van. Andrew is vaguely offering something too, I think, but I'm not sure what. And now the other group is involved. Zada comes over to give Susan a hug and Adam is chipping in too. Everyone wants to be in on the drama, volunteering company and support. Susan stands, bewildered by this superfluity of kindness, not knowing whom to offend. Well, I offered first and she'll be more comfortable crying all over me than she will over either of the men, and if Sophie is going to say anything about what happened to her, aren't I the person to be there to hear it? 'We shall be fine,' I say rather loudly, and then, to soften it, I add, 'It's a mother thing, you know,' and I start to guide her through the house. Ray is following us, still rattling his keys but I can see that he's too much for her at the moment. I stop and look him firmly in the eye. 'Thanks, Ray, but we'll get a taxi. I've got a card from the cab that brought us here just now. We don't need looking after, you know. We'll be fine.'

Susan is not disposed to chat during the ride in the taxi and this gives me some thinking time – my last chance to work out who attacked Sophie before she opens her eyes and tells us. I am nearly there. That text message is the key: it's not just the slackness of *How about we meet*, nor the commas where the laws of syntax require full stops. It's that *A chance for you and I to put things right*. It's a common enough mistake – *I* instead of *me* after a preposition when it's coupled with a noun or another pronoun. No-one would say *A chance for I*, but they will say *A chance for you and I*. It's very odd but remarkably widespread. I remember John Major got laughed at for getting it wrong in the House of Commons – *Put your questions to my honourable friend and I* – and I hear it in TV dramas all the time, from scriptwriters who ought to know better – or perhaps it's the actors who change it. It's not one of the grammar things I care about deeply and it really doesn't matter but I'm quite certain that it's not a mistake James would make even if he was being hasty and careless. Being educated at Eton doesn't guarantee getting it right, I'm sure, but the thing about James is he's a linguist; he started out as a classicist and then took up Arabic so grammar must mean as much to him as it does to me. That only takes me so far, though; the other bit I'm groping for is where I saw that error just recently. It must have been in the emails I showed to David last night and I can find it again when I get back to the hotel, but I want to nail it now. And, just as the taxi draws to a stop outside the hospital, I do.

There is a policewoman stationed outside Sophie's room, which freaks Susan a bit and makes me wonder just how certain Mortensen feels about James being her would-be killer. The security is serious: Susan is made to prove her identity, which she does by brandishing her passport, and I, to my fury, am denied admittance, identification or no. 'Close family only,' the policewoman repeats stolidly in the face of my bluster and blandishments, and I am forced to retreat. Still, I've got plenty to reflect on and I find my way to the cafeteria for a cup of coffee and some thinking time. I am buzzing with the conviction that I'm right about *who* – though one grammar error is hardly solid evidence – and *how* isn't difficult to guess at, but I haven't yet worked out *why*. I can only conclude that whatever James was being blackmailed about involved my suspect too, and that Sophie was getting out of control and loose-tongued and had to be shut up. I sip my coffee and think about this and then, suddenly, my stomach plunges as violently as if I'd just stepped off a stair into empty space. Wasn't my suspect there when Susan got the message from the hospital *Sophie's awake and she's asking for me*? What to do then, when very soon Susan would be at Sophie's bedside hearing the story from her? Well, plan A was obviously to accompany her to the hospital. And then do what? Abduct her? Tie her up and leave her somewhere before coming here and dealing with Sophie? If you watch enough TV dramas you can come to believe that it's remarkably easy for a determined murderer with no previous medical knowledge to approach a hospital bedside and, with lightning speed, detach a crucial drip, lethally twiddle the dials on a hi-tech machine or administer a fatal injection and slip away unnoticed. And since Susan turned down all offers except mine, plan B must have been to get here before us. There was a car parked outside the villa when Annie and I arrived this morning. I didn't think about it but I'll bet it was Andrew's; he's never comfortable unless he's got a snazzy car at his disposal. He'd have given anyone a lift without asking questions. And then there was the van, with Ray dangling his keys so invitingly. Susan and I waited at least fifteen minutes for our taxi, and we were in the house during that time while Susan went through Sophie's suitcase, looking in vain for clean pyjamas and exclaiming in horror at the state of her brush and comb. Plenty of time then for anyone to pre-empt us, with no need for any abduction or tying up.

I abandon my coffee and head back to Sophie's room as fast as I can go without actually running and risking getting thrown out of the hospital. I pant to a stop in front of my friend the policewoman on the door. Everything looks calm – no sign that Susan went in and found Sophie undripped or lethally injected. 'Is she all right?' I demand. 'Is her mother with her?'

'She is,' she says, stirring herself for another battle with me.

'Was there anyone here earlier?' I ask. 'Young? Student age?'

'Close family only,' she says.

'But someone was here?'

'Only the mother,' she says.

'Only her mother has gone in, yes. But did someone try to go in before that?'

She shrugs. 'You did,' she says.

'I know that!' The desire to slap her is almost overwhelming. 'Was there anyone else? This is important. You're supposed to be protecting her.'

'Like to you, I said close family only.'

'So you didn't let them in?'

She gives a self-satisfied little smile.

'No,' she says.

'Brilliant!' I say, giving her a dazzling grin in return. 'Well done. Excellent job.' And I leave her looking astonished.

This, however, is all very well but it doesn't solve my problem. Sophie and Susan are safe enough behind their police guard, but I am shut out of Eden. I am doomed to wander these corridors, a prey to attack. My stalker doesn't know that I was denied entry, will assume that I know everything and will be determined that I shan't get away from here to spread the word. I am probably being stalked at this very moment, in fact. I consider my options.

What I would like to do is to go back and beg to be allowed to sit with the policewoman in her reassuring uniform and put myself under her protection, but I know I can't do that.

What I should stop doing is walking towards the hospital exit because that is the logical place for my stalker to lie in wait for me.

What I need to do is to summon help but the police have got my bloody phone.

What I actually do is to sprint to a pay phone which I see at the end of the corridor, nearly knocking over a man who might possibly get there before me. I make two failed attempts because the instructions are in Danish and my hands are trembling, but eventually I connect.

'David,' I say. 'Are you busy?'

16

MISSION

Karin and Jonas Møller, Scott thought, when he had dropped Gina at the station and was fighting his way through the town centre traffic towards the castle, deserved some attention. Gina had produced them over dinner the previous evening as though they were a particularly delicious and exotic side dish but he had to admit they were intriguing all the same. And they were completely off Mortensen's radar, which made them even more appealing. Mentally, he listed their points of interest:

Karin Møller, known to both Conrad Wagner and James Asquith. How?

Karin Møller seen approaching the police station and turning back on seeing Asquith. Why?

Karin Møller's face injured after she is hit by a car. Who?

Jonas Møller loaned the car to Wagner. Brakes already damaged? Why?

Jonas Møller played down Karin's injuries. Why?

Spotting *Kronborg Garage* to his right, he swung in and drove past the petrol pumps to an office behind them. It was a low, wooden building with posters of fast cars pasted to its walls. There was no-one at the reception desk but at the far end of the room with its back to him was an undoubtedly female figure in dungarees, kneeling down, busy opening a large package. Hearing him, she jumped up and came towards him. She was tall, had a good figure even in the dungarees and would have been more attractive if her expression had been less guarded and her face not disfigured by yellowing bruises and an angry graze.

'*Hej,*' she said.

'*Hej,*' he said, trying a big smile. 'I wonder if you can help me.'

'I'll do my best.'

'I hired a car in Copenhagen and it's not running that well. I wondered if someone could give it the once over.'

'Yeah, I can look it over. Where is it?'

'Just outside.'

'OK. Let's take a look.'

She circled the car and then knelt down to look at the near front tyre. 'Well, this tyre's dodgy for a start. When did you pick the car up?'

'Day before yesterday.'

She looked at the hire company's logo on the back windscreen. 'I don't know this company,' she said. 'Where did you find them?'

'They have a place near the airport.'

'Huh!' she laughed. 'You want to watch out with those places. A lot of cowboys there ready to rip you off.'

Phrasal verbs, he thought. That's what Gina called them: *look it over, pick it up, watch out, rip you off*. When someone could get those right then they could really speak English, that was what she said.

'You speak very good English,' he said. 'Very colloquial.'

'Thanks. She put out a hand for the keys. 'I worked for an English family for a year. Au pair.'

'Really? Whereabouts in England were you?'

She was turning the engine over. 'I was only in England for three months, actually – West London,' she said, listening to the engine. 'Then we went abroad. Cairo.'

188

'Interesting.'

'Yes.'

She turned the engine off and got out. 'If you want to leave it with us we can check it over,' she said.

'All right if I bring it back this afternoon?'

'Fine. Come with me and I'll book it in.'

As he followed her back into the office, he said, 'I suppose you get a lot of British tourists here, do you? Because of the Hamlet connection?'

'Quite a lot,' she said, opening up a large, dog-eared ledger on the desk.

'There's that group of students doing *Hamlet* at the Castle, of course,' he said. 'Have you come across any of them?'

'Don't think so,' she said, her head down, bending over the desk, apparently intent on date and time, but he saw colour flood her face.

'But you must have heard about the car accident, of course,' he said.

'What car accident?' she asked, still not looking at him, and then, without waiting for an answer, 'What time do you want to bring it in?'

'I don't know,' he said. 'That depends on how long we're going to spend at the police station.'

She slammed the book shut and glared at him. 'What are you talking about – police station?'

'Detective Chief Inspector David Scott,' he said pulling out his ID, and added, only moderately untruthfully, 'I'm working on the investigation into the death of Conrad Wagner, the fall of Sophie Forrester into the castle moat and, quite possibly, the incident in which you were knocked off your bike.'

'I don't know what –'

'Of course you do. Wagner hired the car from this garage. You've had the police all over here. You know all about it.'

'I just didn't want to talk about it because it's bad for bus –'

'We have a witness who tells us that you knew Conrad Wagner and you know James Asquith, who's being held by the police at the moment on suspicion of killing Wagner. They'll be very interested in anything you have to tell them.'

'I haven't got –'

'Who knocked you off your bike, Karin?'

'I don't know. I didn't see. He just reversed away and made off while I was still picking myself up.'

'And you aren't worried that he'll have another go?'

'What do you mean?'

'I think you know what I mean. The safest thing, Karin, is to tell the police what you know. Then there will be no point in trying to shut you up. I can send someone to arrest you or I can drive you to the station myself. It's up to you.'

She looked at him for a long moment.

'You'd better go slow on that dodgy tyre then,' she said.

She was silent in the car but once installed in Mortensen's office with a cup of coffee she was surprisingly composed. In the jeans and sleeveless top she had changed into before they left, she looked younger and less wary. She and Mortensen agreed to speak English for Scott's benefit and she even made a joke about doing it in Danish but with subtitles.

'To start off with,' she said, looking them both in the eye, 'I've done nothing wrong – nothing. If anything, I'm a victim – let's get that clear.'

'Fine,' Mortensen said. 'We may have some questions about that but why don't you tell us your story and we'll see.'

'OK.' She took a swig of coffee, leaned back in her chair and pushed her hair off her face. 'When I was seventeen I got a job as an au pair with a British family. He was the UK ambassador in Cairo and they had two young children – five-year-old twins – as well as their older son. He was at a boarding school in England but he was at home for the holidays.'

'And this was the Asquith family?' Scott asked. 'Sir Bruce Asquith?'

'He wasn't Sir Bruce then. That came later.'

'And the older son was James Asquith?'

'Yes. So –'

'Just one more thing,' Mortensen said. 'How did you get the job? Seventeen is young for such a job, isn't it?'

'I signed up with an agency. I was surprised to be offered a job with a family like that but the agency said not many girls wanted to go to somewhere like Cairo – they wanted a year in England. And I had some experience. My mum worked as a child minder and I used to help her in the school holidays.'

'And you didn't mind going to Cairo?'

'I didn't care where I went.'

'Why was that?'

'My mum had just died. I just wanted to get away.'

'So you went with the family to Cairo and you got to know James. How old was he then?'

'Fifteen, I think. In the summer holidays he brought his friend with him – Conrad. That's how I knew him. We all got on well. They were only a bit younger than me and we had fun.' She paused for more coffee. 'Then, at the end of the summer, I realised I was pregnant. Katharine – Mrs Asquith – found out and ha!' She gave a little bark of laughter. 'My feet didn't touch the ground. Before I knew it I was on a plane with a month's wages and enough money for an abortion in a private clinic. Very considerate of them, wasn't it? Though it would have been nice if they'd given me a chance to say goodbye to the twins.'

'Which of the boys was the father of your child?'

This time she laughed genuinely. 'Neither of them. It wasn't like that between us. But I did tell them I was pregnant and Conrad thought they'd treated me badly. He kept in touch, phoned me sometimes to see if I was all right.'

'But not James? He didn't keep in touch?'

'No. It was more complicated for him.'

'Why?'

'Because of Bruce being the father. That's hard to deal with when you're fifteen.'

'You and Bruce Asquith – '

'– were having sex, yes. I don't think you could say we were *in a relationship* – we just had sex sometimes.' She leaned forward and drained her coffee. 'This is the difficult bit,' she said. 'When I look back on it now I suppose you could say I was abused. I was only seventeen – a child, really – I'd just lost my mother, I was in a foreign country and he was my boss, but at the time I thought I was choosing it. I wasn't a whore but I wasn't a virgin either – I'd had a couple of boyfriends. I was never in love with him or anything but it was flattering, I suppose. It started soon after I arrived and just carried on. He just came to my room sometimes. It was quite exciting at first and then it was boring really. In the end it just seemed like part of my job.'

'Until you got pregnant?'

'Yes. I told Bruce, he told Katharine, there was a huge row and whoosh! I was out of there.'

'What did you do when you got home?'

'I looked in a phone directory at Copenhagen airport for the name of a clinic, took a taxi there, had the abortion and then told my brother. My father left us years ago so Jonas was the only person I had. He was just starting up the garage here and I came and joined him.' She leaned back again. 'As you see, I'm fine. My life wasn't ruined. I'm a very good mechanic, I have boyfriends, I have a life.'

'The clinic you went to,' Scott asked, 'did you give the name of it to Conrad?'

'He rang me about two weeks ago. He said a friend of his was coming over here and needed an abortion and he asked me for the phone number of the clinic I went to. I didn't have it but I said I'd find it. A few days ago he called in and got it from me.'

'And was that when he suggested the idea of blackmailing James?'

'No. He'd already talked about that on the phone. And look, I said absolutely not. I wasn't going along with anything like that.'

'That's fine,' Mortensen said. 'Just tell us what it was he wanted you to do.'

'To be honest, I never quite knew what it was he was after. It was something to do with this play they were doing at the castle but I couldn't see how a play could be such a big deal. He told me a long rigmarole about Bruce starting a new political party and if it got out about our affair and my abortion it would ruin his chances because all his voters are Muslims. He wanted me to threaten James that I'd go to a newspaper with the story. I thought it was a load of nonsense. Conrad could be like that sometimes – a bit mad. He was like it when he was fifteen and he didn't really change.'

'How did he react when you said no?' Scott asked.

'He tried asking Jonas – my brother – instead.'

'And what did he say?'

For the first time she looked discomposed. She covered it with a shrug but Scott noticed it. 'I don't know,' she said.

'But he loaned a car to Conrad?'

'Yes. And there was nothing the matter with the brakes of that car. I checked it over myself and I can tell you for su –'

'That's all right,' Mortensen said. 'Wagner checked the car himself and didn't find anything wrong. We are told that he knew a lot about cars. Is that true?'

'He always loved them. He used to ring me or text me two or three times a year and it was usually something about a car. There was a weird moment, actually, when he came to pick up the car. He stood on our forecourt looking round and he said, *Perhaps I'll pack it all in and come and work here. Would you have me?* We joked and said he was welcome any time and that was the last time we saw him.'

'What did you think,' Scott asked, 'when you heard about the accident?'

'Well first I was sad. I was fond of Conrad. He was a bit mad but he was a kind boy. I liked him. Then, of course, we were worried with the police coming round and all the questions. Jonas was afraid we'd be charged with negligence but I kept telling him that I'd done a full check of the car and entered everything in the log book. But even when the police left us alone we were worried about the publicity and the effect on the business.'

'You never thought that someone might have wanted to kill Conrad?'

'No.'

'Not even when you started getting threats?'

She looked at him sharply. 'How did you know?'

'Just a guess. You were seen outside the police station but you turned away when you saw James Asquith. You were knocked off your bike by a hit-and-run driver but your brother didn't want you to go to the police about it.'

'Have you had someone following me?'

'Just an observant witness. Tell us about the threats.'

'The day after Conrad was killed Jonas had a visit from someone. I didn't see who it was but Jonas was scared. I think –' she hesitated, '– I think when Conrad first talked about the blackmail business Jonas may have got some money out of James – got paid off – and then he got warned that if we ever went near James again we'd be dead. Those were the words – we'd be dead. And then I started getting threatening texts on my phone. I didn't like it and I hadn't done anything to deserve it. I arranged to meet James the day he got here and I told him I wasn't going to say anything to harm his family. So I was for going to the police about it because whoever it was who was threatening us had to be one of those students and it shouldn't be too difficult to find out which one. But Jonas wouldn't go to the police because he'd taken the money from James. He paid it back when he got threatened but he was still worried about it.'

'So you decided to go to the police yourself?'

'Yes. I woke up one morning and found another of those text messages on my phone and I decided I'd had enough. Only just as I was going into the police station I saw James coming out and I was scared. I'd been threatened not to go near him, so I walked away.'

'And later that day you were knocked down by a hit-and-run driver.'

'Yes.'

'And you really can't tell us anything about the driver or the vehicle?'

'No. I was cycling home from work and something came at me from my right. It was just before I needed to make a left turn, so I was looking ahead to get onto the crown of the road to make my turn. The next thing I knew I was on the ground under my bike and I just heard the scream of tyres as something reversed back down the road to my right. I was lucky that I was going home early and the road was quiet. As it is, these –' she touched her face '– are just the visible injuries. I'm actually grazed all down my left side.'

Scott's phone rang. The display showed *no number* but he decided to answer it. He would be able to terrify himself in the years to come with the thought of what would have happened if he had chosen to ignore it. Outside, he walked down to the blind end of the corridor. 'David Scott,' he said. There was a great deal of background noise and he almost switched off, assuming that he was through to a call centre, but then a small voice came through. 'David,' it said, 'are you busy?'

Back in Mortensen's office he found, to his relief, that Karin Møller was gone. 'Raymond Porter,' he said to Mortensen. 'What do we know about him?'

Mortensen scrutinised his face. 'What was your call?' he asked.

'Gina Gray.'

'Gina Gray has your cell phone number?'

'Yes. I – I probably should have made it clear that I know her quite well.'

'How well?'

'Look, could we discuss this later? The point is that she's at the hospital, and so is Raymond Porter, and she believes he's the man we're after. Her reasoning is complicated and it has a lot to do with English grammar but I've never known her to be wrong about that so I think we have to take her seriously. What do we know about him?'

Mortensen's body language made it clear that he had noted Scott's agitation but that he was not prepared to be rushed. Slowly, he swivelled his chair to face his computer and put on his glasses. He clicked the mouse several times and then said, 'Ah yes. Interesting but we didn't see any link with the case. Raymond Porter is not a student. He is twenty-three years old and spent four years in the British Army. He left the army a year ago. The circumstances under which he left are not clear.'

'What's he been doing since then?'

'Private security, so he told us. We have no verification of that.'

'He didn't say who he's been working for?'

'No. But we know Conrad Wagner's father was concerned about his security. Maybe –'

'No. He'd use Americans. A man like that wouldn't trust anyone else's security firms. Porter was recruited to work on this play by James Asquith. I've seen emails to that effect. What did he say to you about how he got involved with the play when he's not a student?'

'He used to drink with Asquith in a pub, he said. Asquith told him they needed someone to manage the technical aspects of the play and he was without a job at that time so he volunteered.'

'Much more likely he was sent here as Asquith's minder. Especially if Wagner was already threatening exposure about the Møller affair. My guess is that Porter was already working for Sir Bruce and when James Asquith started getting pressure from Wagner, Porter was sent to sort it out. And his method of sorting it out pays tribute to his army training – wipe out anyone who knew about the Møller affair and might cause trouble – Conrad Wagner, Sophie Forrester, Karin Møller, and now he knows that Sophie Forrester is conscious, he'll be after her again – and anyone else she might have talked to, including Gina Gray.' Scott was pacing the small office, trying to inject the inert Mortensen with his own sense of urgency.

'Forgive me,' Mortensen said. 'I sense that you feel we are at a crisis but tell me something. Wagner was trying to blackmail Asquith but for what? What did he hope to gain? Not money, surely, since his father is far richer than Asquith's father, I imagine. So, for what? What did he want?'

'He wanted to play Hamlet!' Scott almost shouted. 'He was desperate to play the part of Hamlet but Asquith was playing it. He thought he could get him to give up the part.'

Mortensen took off his spectacles and stared at him. 'You are telling me,' he said, 'that all this – a murder, and maybe two attempted murders, as well as the injuries to the boy who was driving the car – this is all about a play?'

'Yes. No. Yes and no. That's what the blackmail was for but the crimes – they're all about the Harmony Party and keeping the Møller business quiet. Not even about that, actually, I would guess. I'd be surprised if Sir Bruce Asquith was issuing orders about disposing of the people who posed a threat. That's not how these things are done. He'll have told Porter to deal with it and Porter is as obsessive as Wagner, only more dangerously. Look at him – he's a failed soldier bumming around with a taste for killing and nowhere to go with it. Suddenly, he's given carte blanche: *Sort it out. Save the Harmony Party.*'

Scott was still pacing but now he stopped and stood over Mortensen. 'And now I hate to hurry you but it is very likely that Porter is at the hospital and Sophie Forrester and her mother, and Gina Gray, are all at risk. This is a man who is out of control.'

'Well,' Mortensen said with infuriating slowness, 'there is no danger, I think, to anyone who is with Sophie Forrester. We have a guard on the door and I have just sent another officer to be ready to take a statement from her when she is able to give one. My latest information from the hospital is that she is awake but not yet able to –'

'Gina Gray is not in Sophie Forrester's room,' Scott growled. 'She was not allowed in by your police guard. There are two reasons for going to the hospital now: one is to find her and the other is to arrest Porter before he kills anyone else. I'm going now to find Gina Gray but if you want an arrest made you'll have to do it yourself.'

'You have to understand that we have no evidence,' Mortensen protested. 'This is all supposi –'

But Scott had slammed out of the room.

17

PIECES OF EIGHT

What do you call the play?
The Mousetrap 3.2

When I put the receiver down I feel like I imagine a climber might feel if they'd just had their rope cut. Actually, I have no idea how climbers feel, never having done anything more challenging than fall over on the nursery slopes while trying to learn to ski, but I feel I've lost my lifeline and I'm having to work very hard not to panic. *Stay where there are plenty of people around*, David said. *Don't try to leave the hospital – he'll be expecting that. But keep near the entrance so we can find you.* This is all very well as advice goes but near the entrance is where he'll be waiting for me, won't it?

I walk cautiously in the direction indicated by the UDGANG notices. I must look like a large bird, the way my head swivels nervously as I go and my beady eyes peer out for danger. I find a kind of outpatient reception area that looks promising. Large numbers of people are lined up in chairs and nurses appear from various directions calling out names, summoning patients to different clinics, I assume. You could sit here for quite a while without anyone noticing that you're not progressing to the next stage, I think, so I find myself a chair between two other people and hope, meanly, that they're in for a long wait and won't be leaving an empty chair next to me for a while. I look at my watch. Is it five minutes since I phoned David? What is he doing now? He's not going to come dashing straight up here, is he? *So we can find you,* he said. He's being a policeman, not my boyfriend/lover/partner/significant other. How long will it take him to tell Mortensen my story and how likely is it that he will believe him? And then how long will it take them to get here?

Two things happen almost simultaneously: the woman next to me hears her name called, stands up and moves away, and a man sitting with his back to me some distance away stands up, turns round and reveals himself to be Ray. He comes towards me, beaming, and just for a moment I wonder whether I am completely wrong about all this, but when he gets closer I can see the sweat on his face. I may be scared, but he is desperate.

'So,' he says, sitting down in the empty chair, 'how's Sophie?'

'Oh, I didn't see her,' I say, and though this is completely true, my face goes hot with panic. 'Close family only allowed in so I left Susan there – well, you can understand it,' I burble, 'it's not even visiting time, after all, and she must be very weak, and there's this big police guard on the door, so – you know…'

I trail off and avoid looking at his face. How to tell the truth and sound as though you're lying through your teeth in one easy lesson. He won't be smiling now, that's for sure. I couldn't have made it plainer that I know he's a killer and I'm terrified of him.

'So what are you doing sitting here?' he asks.

'Oh – just waiting, you know, for Susan. And you?'

'The same.'

'Right.'

There is a long, long silence which I have no intention of breaking.

'So how about I run you home?' he says quietly in my ear.

'Oh no,' I squeak. 'I really should wait for Susan.'

'I can come back for Susan. I think I'll take you now.'

'No really –'

'Yes, really.'

And with that he has me on my feet. He is amazingly strong – all that bloody body-building. He has an arm across my back and a hand clamped round my upper arm and he is walking me towards the exit. A few people look up and watch us, but without interest. I have an out of body experience where I see myself being walked and see how it must look as though I'm being supported. I feel smothered by his bulk and stifled by the smell of his sweat, and my legs feel so weak that he probably is actually holding me up. Then a memory comes to me. When I was twelve, I was waiting for a bus one evening outside the church hall where I went to a weekly drama group. Everyone else had gone home – picked up by car – but my mother was a GP and she had a late night surgery on Thursdays so I took the bus home. That night the bus was late and it was dark and wet and silent in the quiet residential road. A car drew up and the driver rolled down the window and offered me a lift. I said, *No thank you* like the well brought up child I was and he leant across and pushed the passenger door open. *Come on*, he said. *It's a nasty night*. And then I screamed. It was a puny little scream I expect, but it did the trick and he drove away. And I stood there worrying that maybe he was a neighbour of ours I hadn't recognised in the dark and I'd be in trouble for being rude. That's one of the reasons why children and women are so easy to abuse – they're too bloody polite. So today I'm not about to die of politeness. I'm sorry to disturb the calm efficiency going on around me but I open my mouth and I scream. This isn't a puny scream – it's a rip-roaring blood-chiller and it startles Ray enough to make him loosen his grip. I duck under his arm, he stumbles over a low

201

table with magazines on it and I'm away, running down the nearest corridor. I see a *toilet* sign and dash inside. Then I stand, bemused. There's something the matter with these toilets and for a minute I can't work out what the problem is. And then I see it: I am not in the safety of the ladies' – I'm in the men's loos and there's no time to remedy my mistake because Ray must have been right behind me. There are a couple of cubicles in here besides those odd urinals and I dash into one and drive the bolt home. The door has a gap of at least a foot at the bottom, so I put the lid down on the loo and sit on it, pulling my feet up in the vain hope that he won't know I'm here if he can't see my little female feet in their pretty sandals.

No-one comes in and I start to wonder if the ladies' loos are next door and if he might think that I'm in there. He can't go in there, can he? So he'll hang around outside, waiting for me, which means that he'll see me if I come out of here too, so all I can do is stay here and hope that the police arrive eventually and pick him up. If only, I reflect bitterly, I had my phone, it would all be so simple, and I hate Anders Mortensen, at this moment, more than I've ever hated anyone in my life. These speculations don't last long, however. If Ray made an error, he soon realised it because now I hear him slam in through the door and bang a hard fist on my cubicle.

'What the hell do you think you're playing at, Gina?' he shouts and I hold my breath, which is a good thing to do anyway because the air in here is fairly unpleasant and some of that is my sweat, which I can feel trickling down my back and under my arms. I allow myself a brief pang of regret for my nice new green linen dress which, should I survive this episode, may never be wearable again. Ray bangs again and I see the door shake, It's very flimsy this little cubicle of mine, and the bolt is feeble. It won't take more than one good shove for Ray to be in here. I brace myself, but then I hear voices. Others have come in to use the facilities. I see Ray's feet move away. I crouch in my uncomfortable posture, listening. *Only you, Gina,* I think. *Only you could end up being in danger of your life in a men's lavatory.* If I survive, this is a story I feel I shall not want to tell.

The other men leave – I see their feet go by me – and then Ray follows them out. What is he playing at now? I don't have long to think about it. It's not more than five minutes before the door swings open and I see two pairs of official feet come to a rest outside my hutch. Chunky black lace-ups they are, regulation footwear designed to accessorise the uniforms of officialdom. My heart lifts. Policemen. They've come for me.

'Hello?' I call, sounding ridiculous. 'Are you the police?'

An answer of sorts comes back but it's in Danish and is accompanied by a fairly unfriendly bashing at the door.

'Do you speak English?' I call and there is further bashing at the door. I see it strain at its bolt and thinking that if it's sent crashing in and is followed by a large policeman I can hardly escape serious injury, I unbolt it and step outside.

They are not policemen. They are, I see, security staff, and from the aggressive way one of them takes hold of my arm and from the expression on Ray's face when I am led out into the corridor, I deduce that he has summoned them to remove me from this place where I don't belong and to escort me from the building. A clever ruse, I have to grant him that. Puzzlingly, though, we set off at a brisk pace in the opposite direction from the *UDGANG* signs. I attempt an explanation of my situation to my captors in the hope that I might yet get help from them, but I am breathless with panic and the speed at which we're moving and anyway they don't seem to understand a word I'm saying. Stonily silent, they march me deeper into the bowels of the hospital and it dawns on me that it would be bad PR for people to be seen being thrown out of the hospital's front doors, so I'm to be evicted via the back exit, where I shall be dumped among the bins and surgical detritus and where

Ray, doggedly pursuing us, will be free do whatever he likes with me unobserved. I redouble my efforts to get the security men to consider my security but it's too late. We're outside, they're letting go of me and they're back inside ready to harass someone else. And here comes Ray. I can think of nothing I can do. It would be useless to run even if my legs were up to it. I just stand and wait.

Since there's no-one else around, the coercion doesn't have to be covert this time. He takes my arm and twists it up my back in a way that makes me scream without having to think about it. He claps a hand over my mouth and I bite it, wondering stupidly, as I taste blood, if I might have infected myself with HIV. He responds to the bite by twisting my arm even further, I scream again and we seem set to go on like this except that suddenly something hits him violently from behind and he keels over, dragging me down with him. I hit my head and lie with my eyes closed, unable to move. I can hear sounds of a struggle, though, and a lot of swearing and the clink of something metallic. A constrained voice, the voice of someone still engaged in a struggle, calls out, 'Are you all right, Gina?' and I open my eyes and raise myself a bit with my good arm to look about me.

Ray is lying face down on the ground, still thrashing about with his feet, and David is on top of him with a knee in the small of his back, snapping handcuffs on him in a terribly efficient manner.

'Well, shining armour after all,' I say as a police car comes screaming round the corner.

18

INTERROGATION

'What I don't understand,' Gina said as Scott drove her to the police station, 'is how you knew I would be there – out at the back, I mean.' She turned to look at him. 'Why are you laughing?'

'Because,' he said, 'you know absolutely nothing about police procedure and you never bother to find out. You think we just bumble along, don't you? It doesn't occur to you that we have protocols.'

'*Protocols*,' she said. 'Lovely word. What sort of protocols?'

'For example, we always cover the front and the back of a building.'

'OK.' She looked out of the window. 'So it was just chance that it was you who came round the back? It could just as easily have been Anders Mortensen who saved me?'

'Absolutely.'

She was quiet and he glanced at her. Her face was dirty and grazed, bruising was starting to show on her bare arm, and her smart new dress was crumpled and stained with patches of sweat. 'He wouldn't have done it so well, though,' he said.

'Why not?'

'Because he's older than me and he doesn't work out, and he doesn't love you.'

She looked at him for a moment then turned back to the window. 'Bugger you,' she said. 'You've made me cry.'

'It'll do you good,' he said. 'Release of tension.'

She was quiet again. Then she looked back at him. 'Anyway,' she said, 'how do you know he doesn't love me?'

'Just guessing,' he said.

At the police station, she was cleaned up, given a cup of tea, checked over and advised to get the bump on her head seen at the hospital – advice which sent her into slightly hysterical laughter. Mortensen asked her for a detailed account of events at the hospital but declined to discuss her insights regarding Ray Porter. Scott drove her back to the Marienlyst, ordered room service sandwiches and, without consulting her, called Annie. When Annie arrived, he returned to the police station, where Mortensen had considerately waited for him before interviewing Ray Porter.

He had, instead, questioned James Asquith again. Asquith, he said, had acknowledged that Porter was employed by his father. *My minder*, he had said. Why had he not mentioned this before? Because he had never been asked, he said. His father, he elaborated, had been worried about his spending time in Denmark and possibly getting some publicity as he was playing Hamlet. Since the emergence of the Harmony Party, Bruce Asquith had been receiving regular anti-Islamic hate mail and the furore over the Danish Muhammad cartoons had unnerved him as far as his son's trip to Elsinore was concerned. Ray was picked because he was young enough to pass as a student. Obviously, they didn't want the others to know why he was there so James had suggested that he did the lighting for the show. He was good at that practical stuff and Adam had been desperate. He had never actually pretended to be a student – their story, if asked, was that they'd met in a pub but, as far as he knew, nobody had asked.

Questioned about Conrad's attempts at blackmail, he had shrugged them off. Conrad, he said, was crazy about playing Hamlet and had gone over the top with his threats about revealing what had happened to Karin, but Karin had been very grown-up about it and assured him that she had no intention of stirring things up. Yes, her brother had been more awkward and Bruce Asquith had provided the money to pay him off. Personally, he didn't grudge him the money: Karin had been badly treated and her brother had looked after her. And if some of the money went Karin's way that would be even better. Told that Jonas Møller had returned the money after Conrad's death, he had looked surprised. 'Well,' he said, 'Ray acted as go-between with Jonas. He must have dealt with it.'

When Mortensen asked him if he had ever wondered if Porter might have been responsible for Conrad's death and for the attack on Sophie, he had laughed it off. What motive could he have any more than he, James, had? Conrad was no threat because Karin was no threat, and as for Sophie, what harm could she do? Asked if Ray Porter had as sanguine a view of the threat from Conrad as he did, he had admitted that he had been more wound up about it but that seemed to be a lot about making the minding job more exciting; just spending time with a bunch of students putting on a play didn't feel macho enough for him.

'And your father?' Mortensen had asked. 'How worried was he about it?' Asquith had looked away from him then. 'I really don't know,' he had said. 'I didn't speak to him. Ray did all the reporting in. I don't have a phone chat relationship with my father.'

'Well,' Scott said, when Mortensen relayed this, 'you're going to have to have a talk with Sir Bruce, aren't you, even if his son doesn't? Though it may be hard to make anything stick on him. *'Always thought that I require a clearness'.'*

207

'What's that?' Mortensen asked.

'Shakespeare's *Macbeth*. Macbeth orders two murderers to kill a man he thinks is a threat to him. *'But some way from the palace,'* he says, *'always thought that I require a clearness.'*

'You are fond of Shakespeare?' Mortensen asked.

'I studied *Macbeth* for an Advanced Level English exam. Taught by Gina Gray, as a matter of fact.'

Mortensen gave him a long look. 'OK,' he said. 'Well, let's get to work on Porter.'

As they walked down corridors towards the interview room, Scott asked, 'What do you think of Asquith's story?'

'I think if he knew Porter was guilty he would have told us so from the start. He wasn't likely to sit in a cell here in order to protect the man who was supposed to be protecting him, was he?'

'Equally, how come Porter was willing to let Asquith get arrested? That can't have gone down well with Bruce Asquith, can it?'

'Well, I've thought about that. If Porter knew he was the guilty one, he'd know too that we would find no real evidence against Asquith and we'd have to let him go. I am surprised, though, that Bruce Asquith hasn't been more active on his son's behalf.'

'Someone from the embassy came, didn't they?'

'One phone call. No-one came. And no lawyer. No personal approach.'

''A clearness',' Scott said.

They found Ray Porter in a surprisingly bullish mood for a man who had been charged with murder and attempted murder and had been arrested in the course of assaulting a witness. He leaned back on two legs of his chair, arms clasped behind his head, challenging them to do their worst. Offered the presence of a lawyer, he refused. 'If you prosecute me,' he said, 'you'd better be sure of your evidence because I shall have the best legal team in the UK on my case and they'll make mincemeat of you.'

'Well,' Mortensen said amiably, 'we shall see.'

He settled himself comfortably in his chair and opened a file in front of him. 'Karin Møller,' he said, 'has been to see us. She told us the whole story – her relationship with Bruce Asquith, the blackmail attempt by Conrad Wagner, the threats made against her and the incident in which a white van deliberately knocked her off her bike.'

He paused and Scott looked at him. Karin Møller had been able to tell them nothing about the vehicle that hit her. Was Mortensen's claim about the white van just a bluff or did he have information unknown to Scott?

Mortensen tapped his file. 'So, we have a scenario: Conrad Wagner, Sophie Forrester and Karin Møller all knew the story – a story that discredits Bruce Asquith at a very sensitive time – and all had to be silenced. Am I right?'

'You tell me. Show me your evidence. I'm not doing your bloody job for you.'

'OK. Let us,' Mortensen suggested, 'set aside the question of Conrad Wagner's death for the present.'

Ray laughed. 'Yes, why don't you? You won't pin that on me and you know it. Because I didn't do it. I was nowhere near that car and didn't touch the brakes. If you had anything on me for that, I'd be the one you'd have had in a cell here the past three days, not Jim Asquith, so don't give me any blather over that.'

'As I say, we will set that aside for the moment and consider Sophie Forrester, who is conscious now and has made a statement to one of my officers in which she states quite clearly that it was you who pushed her into the castle moat. Strong evidence, wouldn't you say?'

'Oooh.' Ray pursed his lips in exaggerated concern. 'She

had a nasty knock on the head, didn't she? Out cold for three days. Can't tell facts from dreams, I wouldn't wonder. My lawyers would soon dispose of that. Sorry. Not good enough.'

'Are you denying that you pushed her or just questioning the evidence?' Mortensen asked.

'Absolutely no bloody comment.'

'Actually,' Mortensen said, 'we do have independent evidence. Given a photograph of you to jog his memory, the castle gatekeeper remembers a man very much like you asking for the key of the wine cellar shortly after the fall, and we have found your fingerprints on Sophie's phone, which she left with her clothes in the wine cellar. What did you want that phone for, I wonder?'

'You tell me.'

'You needed to delete the text message you sent her, didn't you? The one that was supposed to have come from Asquith? You didn't want to incriminate Asquith – that was the last thing you wanted. I should imagine your employer is very annoyed with you about that. You look surprised. Oh yes, we know all about your role as protection for Asquith. A poor job you made of it, I'm afraid.'

'A pity for you you didn't throw the phone away,' Scott chipped in, 'like the one you used to send the text. Didn't you know that a deleted message can be retrieved from a SIM card? You don't have be in a police lab to do it – anyone can. I'm surprised you didn't know that.'

Porter shot him a look of pure hate, and then turned to Mortensen. 'I really hope you do prosecute, you know. It'll be a pleasure to see my legal team get to work on you.'

The door of the interview room opened and a uniformed policewoman came in with a message. Mortensen looked at it.

'Well,' he said, 'we have found the garage that repaired your van.'

'Really?'

'And it turns out you were unlucky.' He passed the message across to Scott. 'We don't generally find that the public go out of their way to help us but you took the van to one garage where the owner used his brain and wanted to be helpful. You made him suspicious, it seems, with your story about how the van got damaged and why you weren't claiming on insurance. He replaced the damaged panel but he kept the old one, and the paint on it matches exactly the paint of Karin Møller's bike.'

Porter stopped swinging his chair and sat up straight. 'I reckon it's time I had my one phone call,' he said. 'You do have that here, do you – the right to make one phone call?'

'Be my guest,' Mortensen said, indicating the phone clamped to the wall.

'Do I get any privacy?'

'I'm afraid not.'

Porter patted the pocket of his jeans. 'I'll need my phone. The number I need's on there.'

'Well, your phone is in the lab now,' Mortensen said, 'but if you tell me who you wish to phone we can find the number for you.'

Porter laughed. 'Not this one you can't,' he said. 'This is Sir Bruce Asquith's private number I want. You won't find that anywhere.'

'Then we'll get you his office number. I suppose the Harmony Party has an office?' Mortensen walked to the phone on the wall, spoke briefly and sat down again. They waited in silence, Porter fidgeting in his chair, tapping a foot and whistling under his breath. When the phone rang, Mortensen answered it, made a note of the number and handed it over. 'You are welcome' he said urbanely, indicating again the instrument on the wall. Porter got up, went to it, dialled and stood with his back to them, facing the wall.

'Hello?' he said. 'Anya? It's Ray Porter here. Can you let

me have the boss's number? I haven't got access to my phone and I need to speak to him urg – what do you mean, can't talk to me? He's got to hear what I've got to say. Where is he? No, don't give me in a meeting. Get him out of the meeting then. Look, I've been arrested. You've got to tell him this is a mayday situation.'

There was a pause as he listened, his face growing scarlet. 'What do you mean doesn't want to talk to me? He can't decide that. He can't just leave me out to dry here. I need lawyers. You tell him, he leaves me here and I tell everything. Right? You just tell him. Hello? Hello?' he looked at the receiver in bewilderment for a moment, then hurled it against the wall. He stood looking at it as it dangled from its flex, visibly getting himself under control. 'Sorry about that,' he said. 'Bill me for any damage.' Then he dropped back into his chair. 'OK,' he said. 'New ball game. You got questions, I got answers. Shoot.' And he opened his arms wide, presenting a target.

In the event, there was little need for questions; Ray Porter in this mood was a self-starter. He leaned forward, his elbows on the table, hands clasped in front of him, and he talked, rapidly and intensely. Yes, Sir Bruce Asquith had taken him on as security for his son. He'd registered with an agency after he came out of the army and done various bits of security work, and then three months ago he had landed this job. It was supposed to be a standard minding job. Bruce Asquith said he was worried about the hate mail he'd been getting and didn't like the idea of his son being off in Denmark without someone to keep an eye on him, but now he thought about it – and here Porter unclasped his hands and rapped his knuckles against his head – now he thought about it, he realised that he'd been stupid. This job had been about the blackmail all along. Conrad had started his threats to Jim and his dad had taken him on to sort it out. That had been his job and he'd done it. 'Following orders,' he said. 'Just following orders.'

'You're talking,' Scott said, 'as though you were still in the army. Following orders is no defence in a civil court.'

Porter slapped his hand on the table. 'As far as I was concerned,' he said, 'I had a mission and it was my job to complete it. *Just deal with it* were my orders and that's what I did. Whatever it took.' He leaned back, momentarily sated.

'And whatever it took was three – maybe four – deaths?' Scott asked.

'Bollocks to that.' He leaned back. 'Deaths? I didn't kill anybody and didn't intend to. Let me tell you, if I'd wanted them dead they'd be dead. Three years in the army, I know how to kill.'

'What about Conrad?'

'I've told you – ' he was making a stabbing motion at Scott as he spoke '– I had nothing to do with that. That was when the trouble started. We'd sorted him. The woman – Karin – wasn't playing ball and there was nothing he could do. We paid off the brother to be on the safe side and that was that. Conrad was a pain in the arse and driving Jim mad but that wasn't my problem. Then he got himself killed and the girl – Sophie – went out of control, started blabbing about the blackmail story. I didn't know Jim had told her the whole thing. So she needed a lesson, a warning. Whatever it took to shut her up.'

'You don't think you misjudged your warning? You must have known there was a good chance you'd kill her.'

'It wasn't supposed to go like that. She struggled and it went wrong.'

'Excessive force. Was that what got you thrown out of the army?'

'No comment.'

Porter sat back, arms crossed against his chest. His eyes looked smaller, his face slack and puffy.

'And Karin Møller? What was the trouble with her,'

Mortensen asked, 'if she had said she was not going to tell her story?'

'She couldn't be trusted, silly bitch.' He was sullen now, his earlier excitement drained away. 'I saw her coming here. She ran off when she saw me but I knew she'd be back. She needed a lesson.'

'The irony is,' Scott commented, 'that if you'd left her alone she would have caused no trouble. It was your threats that made her decide to go to the police.'

Porter turned furious, piggy eyes on him. 'Bollocks,' he said.

'And Gina Gray. You got that wrong too. She hadn't been in Sophie's room at the hospital.'

Porter stared at him. 'Then why was she acting scared?'

'She'd guessed.'

'How?'

Mortensen intervened. 'It relates to deficiencies in your English grammar. Your text message to Sophie.'

'Well, bully for her. She'd be no loss anyway. Patronising old bitch.'

'You had a difficulty by then, didn't you?' Mortensen enquired gently. 'There were three of them – Sophie, ready to talk, her mother, ready to listen, and Gina Gray, not to mention the police. It was running out of your control. How were you going to silence them all?'

Sweat was breaking out on Porter's forehead and he wiped it off with the back of his forearm. 'One target at a time,' he said. 'That's operational procedure. One target at a time.'

'And Gina Gray was your first target because she was the one you could get at,' Scott said. 'As a matter of interest, what were you planning to do with her? Was she someone else who just needed a lesson or was she to be eliminated?'

'I hadn't decided.' He wiped his brow again. 'The priority was to take her out of circulation so I could deal with the others.'

'Were you planning to phone Bruce Asquith for your orders?'

'It wasn't like that.' Porter thumped the table. 'I made the decisions. It was my mission.'

'So what happened to *just following orders?*'

'You don't understand. I was given a mission. *Whatever it takes.*'

'And if it took killing Gina Gray?'

'Then I'd have done it. And I won't say I wouldn't have enjoyed it.'

Later, James Asquith was released and Scott was disconcerted to recognise the good-looking, middle-aged man who came to pick him up as Andrew Gray. How long had he been here? Why had Gina not told him he was here? Why was he making himself useful? Andrew Gray looked equally surprised to see Scott and the two of them nodded brusquely at one another.

'Gina Gray's ex-husband,' he said to Mortensen as they watched them leave.

'Really?' Mortensen looked at him speculatively and then consulted his watch. 'I don't know about you, but I had no lunch. Would you like to join me for an early supper in the town? There is a place nearby that does excellent *frikadeller* – meatballs.'

'Just let me make a phone call,' Scott said.

Gina's voice, as she answered the phone in her room at the hotel, had a slightly dangerous note of excitement in it. 'Did you get him bang to rights?' she asked.

'Pretty much.'

'Good. Well it's party time tonight. Passports have been returned and a lot of people are going home. And James is out – but you probably know that.'

'I do. But it was quite a surprise to find your ex-husband

picking him up. When were you going to tell me that he was here?'

'I discovered him at the villa this morning. The events of the day quite knocked him out of my head.'

'But you asked him to come, presumably, when you thought you might need a lawyer, two knights being better than one?'

'Oh piss off, David,' she said.

The meatballs were excellent, as promised, and they ate them sitting outside a small restaurant just off the town square. They came, fragrant and steaming, with a large dish of new potatoes and a heap of sweet and sour cabbage. They were washed down with several glasses of beer and were followed by a buttery apple cake. Scott determined to banish the Gray family from his mind and focus on the food. Mortensen was a good companion, ready to eat in silence for some time but then gently leading him into conversation. They talked about their careers but steered away, for the most part, from the personal. After they had finished their coffee, Mortensen suggested a walk round the town and they took a long, winding, leisurely stroll, which brought them back eventually, with the mild darkening of the sky that saw in the northern summer night, to the police station, where their cars were parked.

'Can you wait a moment,' Mortensen asked, 'while I fetch something?'

He went inside and came back with a small object in a brown envelope. 'Gina Gray's phone,' he said. 'I thought you might be able to give it to her.'

Back at the Marienlyst, Gina was in bed and the light was off. He put her phone down on the bedside table and she stirred. 'Did you get a confession?' she asked.

'More or less. He insists that he wasn't responsible for Conrad's death, though.'

'That's because he wasn't,' she mumbled and nestled further into her pillow. 'Tell you in the morning.'

19

MORE PIECES OF EIGHT

Not where he eats but where he is eaten. 4.3

I do wish David hadn't summoned Annie to look after me. I really don't need looking after. All I need is a bath and a hair wash and some clean clothes – and then some peace and quiet, which I won't get from Annie. So, we start off all right: I shut myself in the bathroom for a long soak and a hair wash and then wrap myself in the soft, white dressing gown provided by the hotel while Annie blow dries my hair for me, which is nice. When I'm done, she takes my poor little green dress down to reception to see if they can get it laundered for me, and it's when she comes back that things start to go wrong. I'm curled up quite happily in a chair in my cosy dressing gown but she reckons I've had enough recovery time and wants to pump me for details about what exactly happened at the hospital. I am both too tired to go over it all again and cautious about saying too much until I know that Ray has officially been charged, so I am evasive and she is cross. I propose that we watch television. Somewhere, I suggest, on one of the myriad channels offered, there will be a British or American film with Danish subtitles. We can enjoy the film and learn Danish at the same time.

'We can't possibly enjoy the film,' she says, 'because you'll spoil it by constantly pointing out fascinating things about Danish grammar and vocabulary.'

'How could that possibly spoil it?' I ask, reaching for the remote. 'Well, what do you know? *Gone with the Wind* has just started. Wonderful,' I say. 'I think you'll find on the table over there a little box of complimentary chocolates, which I've resisted so far. Now's the time for them.'

So, I enjoy myself anyway, though Annie huffs and puffs a lot, and rolls her eyes when I practice saying, *jeg vil aldrig være sulten igen*, which is of course *I will never be hungry again*. Before we get to *Helt ærligt min kære, jeg kerer ikke en døjt*, which is the one about giving a damn, Annie's phone rings and she has a long conversation out on the balcony, returning in high excitement to say that James has been released, Jon is out of hospital and they have all been told they can retrieve their passports. There is a move afoot to celebrate all this with a farewell dinner this very evening and here at the Marienlyst seems to be the best place, since the Petrosians and the McIntyres are staying here. As she is on the spot, she has put herself in charge and she heads off downstairs to harass people other than me. She returns briefly to say that it's all organised, that she's going back to the villa to change and that she hopes I've got something decent to wear. Then she's gone and I'm left to enjoy the death of Melanie in peace. After that I shall have to worry about what to wear.

It is a bit of an issue, actually, because the green dress is *hors de combat* and I'm not sure I have anything else that's even clean, let alone smart. I find, though, when I rummage in the wardrobe, that I have an outfit, prudently included for just such an occasion. I had a first or last night party in mind, and not this sort of last night, but it will do fine – some wide-leg silk trousers that I hesitate to call *palazzo pants*, since that seems to be laying claim to a level of glamour beyond my reach, and a fetching black top with a plunge neckline that Annie won't like. Excellent, then.

219

I start getting ready in great good humour: Annie has done my hair well, I have an outfit, I am a heroine of sorts, and I shall be going down to dinner with David by my side, which will be one in the eye for Andrew. Then David rings and is ridiculous about Andrew being here and I refuse to defend myself and he hangs up on me so now, I suppose, I shall not be going down to dinner with David by my side and the whole evening loses its savour. I could ring David and apologise, I know, but I'm a stupid, stubborn woman so I don't.

Because I'm not looking forward to the evening any more, I manage to be late going down and I arrive to find that of the two large tables commandeered by our group, one has all the adults on it. The other one, where things look a lot jollier, has no spaces so I take my place meekly among the old. That place, unnervingly, is between Artos Petrosian and Jacob Wagner. It never occurred to me that the Wagners would be here. It's hard to define exactly what sort of occasion this is, but whatever it is it hardly seems the place for them. It's not a celebration exactly, I know, but there's a lot of hilarity already on the other table: they've been released, they're going home. How can Conrad's father bear to be here? And how can it be, after all I've gone through today, that I'm the person who is going to have to negotiate a conversation with him? How come Andrew, the spectacularly absentee parent, is sitting in the parental role next to Annie, hobnobbing cheerfully with the McIntyres, while I am down the other end of the table, hemmed in by a couple of oversized multimillionaires?

I have a dangerous urge to stand up and 'out' Andrew. *This man is an impostor*, I want to declare in full prosecutorial style. *He is a fraud, an impersonator masquerading as a father when he has never done the job, not the first time round, nor the second time round, from the evidence we see before us. This man has a wife and baby back in England, Ladies and Gentlemen. A pregnant young wife and a year-old baby. What is he doing here?*

I don't, of course. Instead, I turn to Jacob Wagner and say in my best, empathetic voice, 'I'm afraid this must be very difficult for you.' I don't actually feel very empathetic. I hold him a lot to blame for the events of the last week or so, as a matter of fact, but I can be an impostor too, and this evening I've decided on quiet, smiling and sympathetic as my masquerade because it's quite restful and I haven't the energy for anything else. It turns out, though, that Mr Wagner can impersonate too; he can do the fatherhood thing just as well as Andrew can. Before I have even had time to butter a bread roll, he has launched onto a series of anecdotes designed to demonstrate what a great dad he has always been to his eldest son. The tales have some plausibility, it must be admitted. He doesn't try to convince me that he and Conrad barbecued or fished or sailed or hiked together like a happy father-son duo from one of his own movies. He tells me how the infant Conrad loved to get walk-ons in his movies (*first time on set, six days old!*), how he delighted in going to premieres dressed in a tiny tuxedo, how he was the most popular boy at school because he would invite friends home to watch cartoons in their home movie theatre. They have a ring of truth about them, these stories, but they're all about a time before Conrad was seven years old, and after a bit this seems to occur to Jacob Wagner as well. He has eaten hardly anything but he has had a bottle of whisky brought to the table and is going through it at an alarming rate when, quite suddenly, he hits the maudlin stage. His eyes fill with tears and he moves abruptly into lachrymose self-pity and incoherent self-reproach. I can't help him with this. I eat my dinner.

I am not left in peace for long, though. Seeing me disengaged, Artos Petrosian turns the full beam of his alarming energy on me. He too has been doing some serious drinking, to judge by the look of him, and I fear that he may weep over me as well. Zada is sitting on the other side of him and he throws a hairy arm round her from time to time as he is talking to me. Since his talk is all about her, he seems to be presenting her as a sort of visual aid. He is very free with his arm on my side, too, hugging me frequently, which I would rather he didn't, and which is embarrassing with his wife sitting not far from me.

The Hon Alicia, however, is being charmed by Andrew, always a sucker for the gentry. Next to him, Annie is being possibly over-solicitous to Jon, who doesn't seem to mind, while his mother watches him anxiously on his other side. Dr McIntyre, I see, is being delightfully schmoozed by Zada, who seems unruffled by her father's attentions. She is, presumably, used to them.

I have done my best but by the time the main course is being cleared away I feel smothered by Artos Petrosian to the point where I'm almost unable to breathe. When I look down the table to Annie for help, all I get is a frown and a little tugging motion at the front of her dress which tells me to adjust my top so as not to frighten my fellow diners with an unsightly display of my superannuated breasts.

When desserts are being ordered, I manage to break free and go out onto the terrace for a breath of air, but I've been there no time before Annie arrives. 'What are you doing?' she demands. 'Why are you out here? Everyone's wondering where you are.'

'I'm sure they're not. I just wanted some air. It's like a pressure cooker in there.'

'What do you mean?'

'All that parental pressure. All those expectations. Don't you feel it? Poor Zada, who can't call her life her own; Jon, who had to be a doctor because his father is; you doing law at Andrew's college just to please him. And then there's Sophie, who couldn't tell her mother she was pregnant, and Conrad – well more of Conrad another time. And James has had his life screwed up by his father, too – though at least his father's ambition is for himself, not by proxy.'

We have been standing side by side, looking out towards the sea but Annie gets hold of my arm and swings me round to look at her. 'What do you think I should be doing?' she demands.

'Whatever you want to do,' I say. 'That's the point. Whatever *you* want. Whatever will make you happy.'

'That's what you've always said. It's the way you've tried to stop me from doing anything demanding or ambitious. *Are you sure you want to go to Lady Margaret's, Annie? It's very academic and the teachers will be making comparisons between you and Ellie all the time, you know. I'm not sure you'll be happy.* Latin: *I wouldn't do Latin if I were you, Annie. You need an analytical mind for Latin. You'd be happier doing Spanish.* Law: *You'll find it very dry, Annie. You love Drama. Why not do Drama?* Oxford: *Terribly competitive. Such a lot of pressure, Even if you got in you wouldn't be happy.* Even my name you had to change. I like *Marianne* – it's got some dignity to it, but you've never called me by it. I had to be *Annie* – as in *Little Orphan* or a parlour maid. Low aspirations, that's what you had for me. You're a teacher, you know what low parental aspirations do to children. Why did you will me to fail?'

'I didn't. I was just responding to you. You didn't enjoy academic work. You got bored.'

'I got bored because I didn't think I could be the best so I didn't bother trying.'

'Well, I'm sorry. I apologise for not recognising your thwarted genius and for nearly condemning you to a life of mediocrity.'

'Yes, well, you're not sorry, of course, because you think you're perfect, don't you? Thank God for Dad, is all I can say. At least he believes in me.'

'And you're happy, are you?' I demand. 'You're enjoying life as an academic high flyer? Because you don't look happy to me. You look thin and pale and your hair's lank and I've barely seen you smile during this last year.'

'There are more important things than being happy. There's achievement and success. If I get those, then I'll be happy.'

'No, you won't! You'll –'

'I will. I will!'

Suddenly tears are streaming down her face and she stumbles off towards the beach. There is no point in following her, so I turn to go indoors, but Zada is coming out.

She peers at me. 'Are you all right?' she asks.

'Sort of.' I attempt a cheery smile.

'Nobody's quite sure what happened today. I know Ray's been arrested. Someone said he attacked you. Is that true?'

'It is but I'm over that. I'm just recovering from a wound to the heart – or maybe just the pride.'

She looks out towards the beach, where Annie is sitting on a rock looking out to sea. 'You two had a row?'

'I tried to ruin her life, apparently.'

'You know what Oscar Wilde says.'

'*Children begin by loving their parents* –'

'– *As they get older they judge them. Sometimes they forgive them.*'

'Yes, thank you for that. I think there's a further stage, actually. Forgiven or not, there's a point where your parents become just irrelevant. My mother has. What she did or didn't do really doesn't matter any more. We're probably not truly grown up until we get to the point of feeling that about our parents.'

'I can't imagine feeling that.'

'No? Well, if Annie can't forgive me then irrelevance is the best I can hope for. Intimations of failure are rushing in on me, Zada. Failed wife, failed mother, failed girlfriend/lover/partner/significant other.'

'I only caught a glimpse of your man. He seemed nice.'

'He is. But I treat him badly,'

'Why?'

'That's the question.'

There are a couple of wrought iron chairs further along the terrace and I move to sit down. Zada follows me. 'I was married for fifteen years to an overbearing man,' I say, 'and –'

Zada interrupts. 'I must say, I don't care much for him. A bit smarmy, the way he was all over Mummy. I don't think you should blame yourself for failure there.'

'Well, anyway, the only way not to get trampled on was to fight about everything. And it became a habit. And now I can't stop doing it, even with David.'

She laughs. 'Of course you can! You've analysed the problem – now fix it. You're a clever woman – don't tell me you can't do that.'

'Annie's not happy,' I say. 'And she says it doesn't matter.'

'It's funny to hear you call her *Annie*. I can't think of her as *Annie*.'

'Another mistake of mine.'

'Well, I'm not really the person to talk to about her. We have a complicated relationship. I stole Adam from her and now she seems to have got my Jon. So she ought to be happy is all I can say.'

'Will you be happy?'

'Oh yes. Babies will make me happy.' She stands up. 'Talking of which, Mrs Failure, Freda seems pretty keen on you. You haven't screwed that up yet.'

She pats me on the shoulder and trots back inside.

I watch Annie for a while, debating whether to go down and try to mend fences, but it's actually she who makes the first move. She comes slowly up the beach and sits down beside me.

'It was a bad time to hit you with that today,' she says without looking at me. 'After what happened to you. Sorry.'

I start to laugh. 'There would have been a good time?' I ask, and her face relaxes into a glimmer of an answering smile.

I don't go back for pudding and the warm embrace of Artos Petrosian. I haul myself upstairs and put myself to bed, stopping only to write a note for David and leave it in his toilet bag, where he will find it when he goes to clean his teeth.

20

DAY NINE

And in the upshot purposes mistook,
Fall'n on the inventors' heads. 5.2

I am so used to waking these mornings and finding David up and about and breakfast awaiting me, that I'm taken aback today to wake and find him still slumbering beside me. The electronic figures of the clock on the bedside table tell me it is 08.55. I shake him awake.

'The Wagners,' I say urgently as soon as he opens his eyes. 'Their plane's leaving at ten thirty. You have to catch him before he leaves the hotel.'

He lies there looking at me. 'What the hell are you talking about?'

'Didn't you say Ray doesn't admit to killing Conrad? Then I'm sure I'm right about what happened – I've known for days – but I've got no proof – everything's circumstantial. But I've got a question to ask Jacob Wagner and if I'm right about the answer then Anders Mortensen will have to see that my theory fits.'

'Gina, as far as he's concerned it's case closed. They've all got their passports back. They're going home. If you think someone else is –'

'Doesn't matter. Won't make any difference. But Ray didn't

do it and it could make a difference to him. He's a lunatic but he's got a right to justice like anyone else.'

He sits up. 'So what is it you want me to do?'

'Go down to breakfast. Find Jacob Wagner. Ask him this question.' I grab the complimentary hotel notepad and biro from beside the bed, and write down my question. I fold it over and write my answer on the other side. 'There you are, the question inside and my answer on the back.'

'Can I just ask,' he says, swinging his legs out of bed, 'why you can't put the question yourself?'

'Because Anders Mortensen will pay attention if you do it. And I think you'll have to do it as a policeman. It's such a weird question to be asking him now that there's no way of normalising it. I've thought about it but I can't see any way I could go up to him while he's eating his scrambled eggs and say, *Oh by the way I was just wondering...*'

He opens the sheet of paper and reads my question. 'I see what you mean,' he says, 'but it's hardly a police question either.'

'You'll manage,' I say. 'I have faith in you.'

After he has gone I check the bedside clock again – 09.15 – and I notice, lying beside it, my phone, wrapped in a plastic bag. David must have left it there last night. With it is my scrawled note from last night with a response from David – one word, *forgiven* – written underneath. OK, Zada? How am I doing?

I take a look at my phone and find I have a number of messages, mostly advertising things and all now redundant. Among my missed calls, however, are two from Mr Christodoulou. It really seems too late to follow up on them now but I'm still nagged by the oddity of his wanting to thank me. There is something undeniably ominous about that. I dial a different number.

228

'The Vice-Chancellor's office.' Janet sounds as brisk as ever, vacation or not.

'Janet? Gina Gray.'

I think I hear a muffled something or other before she says, 'Oh Gina. Hello. Having a good holiday?'

'Eventful. Look, Janet, what's going on with Anastasia Christodoulou? I've had a very weird conversation with her father but we got cut off and my phone's been – inaccessible and I haven't been able to phone him back.'

'You haven't read my email then?'

'Email? No. I've been reading my home emails but I haven't logged on to work emails.'

'Ah. Right,' she says ominously.

'So what does it say?'

'Ah. Well, the thing is, Gina, Anastasia's going to repeat the foundation year course.'

'She's what? But it was a decision of the examiners' board that there were no grounds for her being allowed to repeat the year. She failed everything as well as cheating.'

'The Vice-Chancellor felt that too much had been made of that aspect. He wasn't persuaded that she intended to cheat.'

'Wasn't persuaded? Who persuaded him otherwise?'

'Well he had a meeting with Mr Christodoulou and –'

'How much?' I ask.

'What?'

'How much was the bribe? What does the college get?'

'A generous donation to a conference centre,' she says.

'A conference centre? Where are they going to put it? There's not a square inch of the campus that hasn't been built on.'

'We've bought St Aidan's playing field. It's very convenient, just on the edge of the campus.'

'Good God! Are they still allowed to sell off school playing fields? Whatever happened to the Olympic legacy and the war on childhood obesity?'

She doesn't offer an answer.

'Put me through to him, Janet. I want to talk to him.'

'No.'

'What?'

'I can't.'

'Why? Where is he?'

'He's – here. But he won't talk to you.'

'What do you mean?'

'He told me he didn't want to talk to you.'

'What did he say?'

'Do you really want to know?'

'Yes.'

'He said, *And don't let that bloody woman anywhere near me. I don't want to see her and I don't want to have her shouting at me down the phone.*'

'Oh, did he? Well you tell him that he can't hide forever. I will get him and he's never going to know when it will be. Have you got that?'

'Yes.'

'Of all the –'

'Gina.'

'Yes?'

'I don't think it's fair, do you, because you can't shout at him to shout at me?'

'No. Sorry Janet. The man's a puny coward and it's not your fault. What exactly did Christodoulou get in exchange for his conference centre, do you know?'

'Well a second chance, obviously. I think there was an arrangement about accommodation, too. The girl wasn't happy with hers last year, if you remember.'

'I remember.'

'And permission to park on campus. And –'

'And?'

'And she requested not to be taught by you.'

'Halleluya! Not all bad news then.'

'What I don't understand is Greece is supposed to be bankrupt, isn't it? How come he has this sort of money to throw around?'

'I think you'll find that Greece is bankrupt precisely because people like Christodoulou build conference centres in far away places rather than paying their income tax.'

'Right. Well, enjoy the rest of your holiday, Gina.'

'I will. And, Janet, spit in his coffee for me, will you?'

I am still recovering from this conversation when David returns but the expression on his face brings me back to the matters of the moment.

'Did you find him?'

'Yes.'

'And?'

'And yes, you were right about the answer. And I'm beginning to see where it leads you.'

'Good.' I'm out of bed and on my way to the bathroom. 'Then come with me to Anders Mortensen and help me make my case.'

'Am I allowed breakfast first? It's a good spread down there?'

Replete with fruit, cheese, ham, a variety of breads, yoghourt, croissants eaten with rather strange jam and pints of coffee, we get in the car and head for the police station. David is by now up to speed on my theory and has phoned Anders Mortensen to tell him we're coming.

Mortensen looks less than delighted to see us, however, and I can understand why. It has been a troublesome and tiresome case; he got the wrong man and now he's got the right one and he would like to leave it at that. He was quite friendly after I was rescued yesterday, because I was a victim

231

of sorts, but he resents my amateur meddling and he would like me to go home. I try to be as brisk as possible.

'I don't believe that Ray Porter killed Conrad,' I say, as soon as we're settled in his office, 'and I don't think you'll ever pin it on him. I have two starting points; one is that no-one saw anyone except Conrad near the car at the time when the brakes must have been cut; the other is that his father believed that Conrad was going to be playing the part of Hamlet. David checked that with him this morning.'

Mortensen takes off his glasses and rubs his eyes wearily. 'One of the most difficult aspects of this case,' he says, 'is the significance that everyone gives to the performance of this play – a play acted by students for what – three or four evenings?'

'Well, you do have to accept that, I'm afraid. For some of them it was just a jaunt, but for some – Adam and Conrad especially – it meant everything. They saw it as the start of their careers.'

'OK. So what follows from this?'

'Conrad was desperate to play Hamlet. I've seen emails he sent to the director, begging for the part, and then when that didn't work he tried blackmail, but that was no good either because Karin wouldn't play. And then, just when he had to accept that he wasn't going to get the part, he got a text from his father saying he was coming to see the show. I saw the text and I saw how Conrad reacted when the text arrived. He threw his phone out into the garden.'

'Where you picked it up, I suppose?'

'Yes. And I thought his father was being sarcastic. It said, *Send dates and times. Will stop off on way home from Edinburgh. Can't miss you in such a great role.* You can't by any stretch call Rosencrantz a great role. Claudius, perhaps, or even Laertes or Horatio at a pinch, but not Rosencrantz. He's a kind of joke. Always yoked to Guildenstern – nobody can tell them apart.

They're bywords for nonentities. Jacob Wagner must have thought Conrad was playing Hamlet, and the only reason why he would think that was because Conrad told him so.'

'Why would he do that?'

'Ah, this is where some amateur psychology comes in, I'm afraid. I think Conrad was desperate to impress his father. His parents divorced when he was very young, his father has married again several times and there are several more children. Conrad never saw much of him. He was sent off to school in England and sometimes didn't even go back to the US for the holidays. What boy with a powerful, rich, famous, absent father doesn't want to make his father notice him and be proud of him? Conrad was determined that he was going to be a great actor and make his father proud. And along came an opportunity – Hamlet at Elsinore. When you're here, you realise it's not such a big deal at all – just a bunch of students performing to tourists – but it seemed like a big deal to them. And I guess Conrad really felt that he *was* Hamlet, with his father's spirit looming over him. He was convinced he would get the part – even dyed his hair blond like Olivier in the film. Have you seen it? Well, never mind. Anyway, I guess he was so convinced that he told his father he was doing it. And it wouldn't have mattered. His father would never have known that he wasn't except that Conrad hadn't reckoned with the Edinburgh Film Festival. And actually it's quite surprising that Jacob Wagner was there – it's not Cannes – but he was, so he was just a hop away in his private plane, ready to see his boy being a star.'

I pause for breath; Mortensen is making notes. He looks up. 'I suppose you have a scenario for what happened next?'

'I do. Conrad was in a desperate situation – he was facing being completely humiliated – so he took desperate measures. If he could get rid of James, he could play the part. He regarded himself as the understudy – he told the director that

233

– and he was probably deluded enough to have learnt the lines. I should have seen that he was plotting something – we all should, really. He had been vile to James, chipping away at him, really undermining him at rehearsals, and then suddenly he was all friendly, suggesting, of all things, that James came and helped him work on the car he'd hired. We all felt it was odd. I'm sure James did too. He told Conrad he knew nothing about cars, but Conrad insisted, and I guess James was happy for any respite from the carping so he went along with it. So they spent the morning together, Conrad tinkering with the car and James sitting around passing the occasional spanner, I suppose – at least, that's what they were doing when we went to call them to lunch. And then – I guess you know what happened then. James must have told you.'

'His story was that Wagner suddenly got angry about the way he was treating Sophie Forrester. Wagner, it seems, had agreed to drive her to a clinic that afternoon in København, for a termination of her pregnancy, but he told Asquith that he was the one who should do it.'

'And he stormed off and told him to get on with it.'

'Exactly.'

'Did James say why he didn't do that? Apart from the fact that he was supposed to be rehearsing that afternoon?'

'He said that his relationship with Sophie was no longer of such a kind that it would be appropriate for him to take her, and also that he doesn't have a driving licence.'

'Hah!' I can't help laughing, though really this is a miserably stupid business. 'Well, Conrad never thought of that.'

'So he expected that Asquith would drive the car and be killed or injured.' He shook his head. 'What did he think about Sophie, I wonder.'

'Leaning over backwards to be charitable, I'd say that he didn't really expect that James would take her to the clinic.

Conrad loved cars. He couldn't imagine, I suppose, how anyone could be handed the keys to a beautiful car and not want to drive it right away. Maybe he thought James would just get in the car and drive it around. And if he was just driving in the town he wouldn't be going that fast and he'd be more likely to be injured than killed.'

'That is a remarkably charitable view, I would say.'

'So would I,' I admit. 'It was a stupid, reckless, selfish, wicked thing to do and it seems like an act of Providence that he was the one to get killed. *'Hoist with his own petard'.'*

'What is that?'

'It's what happens to Rosencrantz and Guildenstern. Hamlet's uncle sends them with Hamlet to England, with an order to the English king to kill him. Only Hamlet finds the letter to the king and changes the order so that it's for R and G to be killed. Hamlet says it's like the *'enginer'* being *'hoist with his own petard'*. A petard is a bomb. We're not talking suicide bombers here, of course, but bombers accidentally blowing themselves up, like IRA bombers used to sometimes.'

And that seems to be the end of that. Mortensen thanks me and sees us to the door, and we walk away. 'He'll still try to pin it on Ray, won't he?' I ask David. 'He'll never be able to prove Conrad did it and convicting Ray will be better for his clear-up rate.'

'You may be right,' he says. 'Shall we go and have some lunch and not talk about it?'

So we do. We sit outside in the sun and eat seafood with mayonnaise, and I get quite drunk on two glasses of cold white wine and introduce the knotty subject of finding a name for our relationship. 'Zada last night referred to you as *your man*,' I say. 'I quite like that. It's simple and true.'

'Doesn't it make me sound like the butler?'

'Not if I say it right.'

'I don't think I can call you *my woman*.'

'Of course you can't. It sounds as though you drag me around by the hair.'

'So that doesn't work then, does it?'

'No. Gender asymmetry in titles and descriptors is very interesting. I'll tell you about it some time.'

'I'm sure you will.'

'As a matter of interest, how *do* you refer to me usually?'

'Well, if I refer to you at all, I just say *Gina*. If I'm talking to someone who hasn't met you, I think I say *this woman I know*.'

'How poetic. *Know* in the biblical sense, I presume.'

'I don't specify.'

I look at him sitting there trying not to laugh and it occurs to me that I really do love him. 'I know,' I say, 'what I'm going to call you.'

'Yes?'

'*My beloved. Let me introduce my beloved. I'm seeing my beloved this weekend. Is it all right if I bring my beloved with me?* What do you think?'

'I don't think I could reciprocate. I couldn't carry it off.'

'No. I shall have to go on being *this woman I know*. But I could carry it off, don't you think?'

'I'm sure you could,' he says.

EPILOGUE

Lord, we know what we are but we know not what we may be. 4.5

Annie and I patch things up, as we generally do, and over the next few months she keeps me apprised of developments in the lives of the people with whom we shared those ten strange days. The events themselves become dreamlike and no-one, she says, ever talks about them. I keep my fingers crossed for her and Jon, and work very hard at not thinking he is too good for her. David returns from his secondment in Brighton but we don't move in together. I refuse to move into his soulless box of a house, *convenient for railway station and access to M25*, and he refuses to move into my house because he says he would feel like a replacement for the cat (who, aged twenty, mewed her last while I was away, to the distress of the neighbour who was feeding her). I say I don't know what he means by this and he says I am being deliberately obtuse and so we get nowhere and continue to rattle to and fro between the two in an inconvenient way and frequently have to retrieve stuff we need for work that has ended up in the wrong house. Ellie is expecting a baby just before Christmas and Freda is ecstatic at the prospect of being a big sister. She has some experience of babies, however, and says she will come to stay at my house if the baby is too noisy.

At work, the Vice-Chancellor has actually run away from me twice: once when I came into the senior common room, where he was drinking coffee and he got up to leave so fast that he knocked his cup over, and once when he saw me approaching across the campus and ducked behind a building to escape. The file on Anastasia has little in it this year, so I imagine she will make it through. The site of the conference centre is protected from public view but the noise engendered dominates our working days.

As for the others, the first news comes only a couple of weeks after our return and is to be found on the front pages of most of the papers. I read about it in *The Guardian*, which tells the story straight and without speculation, but then I'm in a position to do my own speculating, aren't I?

RESIGNATION DISTURBS HARMONY

Sir Bruce Asquith, founder of the Harmony Party, has shocked friends and supporters by announcing that he is stepping down from leadership of the party. Even more surprising was the announcement that his twenty-two-year-old son, James, will take over as the party's leader. James Asquith has a first class Oxford degree in Arabic and Islamic Studies but has no political experience. It is understood that he has abandoned plans to work for a doctorate and will devote himself full time to Harmony.

Speaking at a fund-raising dinner last night, Sir Bruce said. 'It has been quite an exhausting business getting the party up and running and I feel now that I owe it to my wife and younger children to spend more time with them. James is extremely able, has a deep understanding of Islamic culture and has had the experience of living in the Middle East when he was of an impressionable age. I have every faith in his leadership of the party, and I am sure that Sophie will be a great support to him.

James Asquith will marry his girlfriend, Sophie Forrester,

'in the next few weeks', it was announced. The couple met as students at Oxford and have known each other for two years. Miss Forrester suffered head injuries when she was attacked in Denmark three weeks ago while taking part in a university production of *Hamlet*, but is said to have made a good recovery. Conrad Wagner, son of the film mogul, JC Wagner, was taking part in this same 'jinxed' production when he was killed in a car accident.

Speaking to reporters with her fiancé yesterday, Miss Forrester said, 'Having nearly lost me, I think James wanted to make sure he didn't lose me again. I know James and his family very well by now and we have no secrets from one another. James can depend on me to support him.'

The picture that accompanies the story is of James and his father standing rather stiffly together. Sir Bruce is wearing a professional smile but James is looking as if he might rather be somewhere else. He's going to have to work on that. I notice, when I'm in the supermarket, that most of the other papers go for a more romantic angle, with headlines like *Perfect Harmony* and pictures of the happy couple. They nearly all have the same picture – James and Sophie leaving last night's dinner. Sophie is wearing a silky turban of some sort – presumably because her head wound played havoc with her hair, but it also suggests a nod to the hijab. She has James's arm in a fearsome grip and a very determined expression on her face.

In September, Anders Mortensen lets David know that Ray has been convicted of attempted murder and assault. He was not prosecuted for Conrad's murder. There is a likelihood that he will serve part of his sentence at least in the UK. The news I get from Annie is altogether more momentous and entertaining. First, in October, she sends me a copy of *Hello!* This features a double page spread about *Brainy Beauty Zada*, who is to wed dot com billionaire Duncan Robertson next month. Robertson, I read, at twenty-nine, has already made one dot com fortune and has sold the business to start another one. He is known to shun the limelight and to live *modestly*, whatever that means in *Hello!* terms.

I have never handled a copy of *Hello!* before and I'm not prepared for the way it socks you on the jaw. There is Zada, airbrushed smile a-dazzle and glossy locks a-tumble, her breasts barely encased in silver and a scarlet-tipped finger wilting under the weight of a vast emerald. Taking a deep breath, I address myself to the column subtitled, *I have a thing for shy Scotsmen*.

'I love it that Duncan is shy,' says Zada, speaking at her millionaire father's London home, 'and I have a bit of a thing about Scotsmen. As soon as I met Duncan, I knew he was the one, but I knew I was the one who would have to make the running. I was quite shameless, really. I invited him to come on a family cruise on Daddy's yacht. We got to know each other and here we are, a whirlpool romance, you might say. We found that we both want the same things – lots of children most of all.' She leans forward and bats those long, dark lashes. 'I'll let you into a secret,' she says. 'I love babies so much I'm getting one started already.' She smiles happily. 'My father will be furious that I've told you,' she says.

Asked about Robertson's reputation as a workaholic, she says, 'Oh he is, completely. But that's all right. He can bring in the money and I'll spend it. One thing I did tell him was that I can't live in the wilds of Scotland. He doesn't like London but I need to be able to see my family, so we've compromised with Sussex – a lovely farmhouse with lots of land, quite near where the McCartneys brought their children up, and they did all right, didn't they?'

I send Zada an email to wish her well. *Be happy*, I write, and she replies *Trying to be good. Hope happiness is earned that way. Have given up the ciggies, so that's a start…*

Not long afterwards, I get another unexpected and unexplored magazine from Annie. This time it's a movie magazine and on its front cover it carries a picture of a tanned and tidy Adam Barrie. *Tyro British Director goes to Hollywood* the caption reads, and inside is the story.

23-year-old Adam Barrie's only experience as a director is from directing students on stage, but he is set to try his hand as a director for Wagner films. A chance meeting such as student directors can only dream of has led to Barrie being invited to Hollywood, where JC Wagner is said to be keen to improve the cultural image of his movie empire. Barrie is to start work shortly on a new film adaptation of *The Scarlet Letter,* a dramatic tale of sexual repression and hypocrisy set in the 17th century.

Barrie, who was a close friend of Wagner's eldest son, killed in a car crash earlier this year, impressed Wagner with his coolness in a crisis. 'We could do with some of that stiff upper lip in Hollywood,' he is reported as saying. Barrie remains cool at the prospect of making his debut as a film director. 'I always intended to go into straight theatre,' he told arts correspondents at a press conference yesterday, 'but this is a great opportunity. There will be technical things for me to learn but if I have a special skill as a director, it's what I'm able to get out of my actors, and that remains the same whatever medium you're working in.'

Finally, in December, Annie sends a copy of *The Oxford Mail.* On the front page is a picture of some very cold people holding a vigil in Christ Church meadow.

OUTRAGE AT MEADOW THEATRE PLAN

A group of over 300 people held a twenty-four hour vigil on Wednesday in freezing temperatures to protest against plans to build a 600-seat theatre in Christ Church meadow. The theatre, intended exclusively for university and college productions, is the brainchild of film magnate, JC Wagner, who wishes to build the theatre as a memorial to his son, who was killed during an OUDS tour earlier this year. Negotiations are at a very early stage but protests are snowballing against the proposal to build on land that has been a playground for undergraduates for hundreds of years. There are fears that in cash-strapped times the university authorities could be tempted by the offer of a very large sum.

Wagner Pictures' press office issued the following statement yesterday: 'Mr Wagner respects the feelings of those who oppose the use of this land for a theatre but he believes that it will be a great amenity for the university, offering student actors the opportunity to learn their craft in a state-of-the-art theatre. He intends The Jacob and Conrad Wagner Theatre as a memorial to his son, who promised to be a fine actor and died before his talent could be realised. It is a tribute from a father to a much-loved son.'